THE
DISAPPEARANCE OF
ALISTAIR AINSWORTH

ALSO BY LEONARD GOLDBERG

THE
DISAPPEARANCE OF
ALISTAIR AINSWORTH

A Daughter of Sherlock Holmes Mystery

Leonard Goldberg

MINOTAUR BOOKS
NEW YORK

THE DISAPPEARANCE OF ALISTAIR AINSWORTH. Copyright © 2019 by Leonard Goldberg. All rights reserved. Printed in the United States of America. For information, address St. Martin's Press, 175 Fifth Avenue, New York, N.Y. 10010.

www.minotaurbooks.com

Designed by Omar Chapa

The Library of Congress Cataloging-in-Publication Data is available upon request.

ISBN 978-1-250-10108-2 (hardcover)
ISBN 978-1-250-10109-9 (e-book)

Our books may be purchased in bulk for promotional, educational, or business use. Please contact your local bookseller or the Macmillan Corporate and Premium Sales Department at 1-800-221-7945, extension 5442, or by email at MacmillanSpecialMarkets@macmillan.com.

First Edition: June 2019

10 9 8 7 6 5 4 3 2 1

In memory of The Dink,
forever in our hearts

Contents

Silence speaks when words cannot.

—ANONYMOUS

THE DISAPPEARANCE OF
ALISTAIR AINSWORTH

1

The Unannounced Visitor

November 1915

There are times when the forces of nature are so fierce they demand we seek immediate shelter and warmth. Such was the midwinter's night that found us ensconced in our rooms at 221b Baker Street. Outside, the wind howled in powerful gusts and the rain pelted our window so intensely it produced a sound reminiscent of fingers tapping on glass. My father and I sat around a cheery fire and tried to distract ourselves from the inclement weather by reviewing an old case of Sherlock Holmes's, which interestingly enough took place on a similar, dreadful night in London some twenty years ago.

"Holmes believed the wind and rain gave the criminal every advantage," my father remarked.

"It certainly made the investigator's task far more difficult," said I.

"Indeed it would, but in ways one might not anticipate."

"Such as?"

"'Beyond the obvious,' Holmes had replied when I asked

him the very same question. Then he said no more." My father pondered the enigmatic answer briefly before glancing over to my wife. "Would you care to decipher that rather cryptic response, Joanna?"

She was standing by the window and staring out intently at the thoroughfare below, for something had caught and held her attention.

"What is it you see?" my father asked.

"Cover," Joanna replied.

"From what, pray tell?"

"From every crime you wish to mention," Joanna said, turning to us. "Which is also the answer to your first question. The obvious reason my father believed such weather favored the perpetrator is straightforward. It removes or distorts virtually every clue and track left behind. Give it a moment's thought and you can readily list the ways foul weather can throw the detective off."

"A strong wind and rain would certainly wash away any bloodstains or signs of a struggle," I proposed.

"But there would be other, less obvious advantages as well," Joanna went on. "The storm, along with its lightning and thunder, would drown out cries for help or screams of terror. And a heavy mist and rain would blind any eyewitnesses. You must also keep in mind that a lengthy gale, such as the one we are facing, would delay the arrival of Scotland Yard and give the criminals abundant time to escape and conceal their tracks."

I involuntarily raised my hand as a new thought came to mind. "Thus far, our discussion has been focused on crimes that occurred outdoors. Would not the dreadful weather be of less hindrance when the evil act is committed indoors?"

"The advantages, although somewhat diminished, would still hold for the criminal," said Joanna. "A clumsy investigator, along with a throng of constables, might well track mud and water onto the crime scene, and in the process muck up or eliminate any number of clues. Moreover, the thick walls of an enclosure would further dampen cries for help or screams of terror, which clearly work to the perpetrator's benefit."

"And Scotland Yard's response would remain less than prompt," my father noted.

"All of which explain why foul-weather crimes for the most part go unsolved," Joanna concluded.

Her attention was suddenly drawn back to the window. She moved in so close her nose seemed to be touching the glass pane. "I say! It seems we have a visitor coming our way."

My father and I hurried over and peered down at the hansom that had stopped at our doorstep. A hatless man, small and thin in figure, dashed toward the entrance of 221b Baker Street.

"Who would dare go out in this ungodly weather?" I asked.

"Someone with a most urgent need," Joanna replied.

"Which obviously cannot—" My voice was rendered inaudible by a loud crack of lightning, followed by a clap of thunder and an even heavier downpour of rain. Baker Street became little more than a blur through our window.

Moments later there was a soft rap on our door and our landlady, Miss Hudson, looked in. "Dr. Watson," she said to my father, "a Dr. Verner is downstairs and wishes to see you on a most pressing matter."

"Please show him up."

As the door closed, Joanna asked, "Do you know this Dr. Verner?"

"I do indeed," my father replied. "He bought my practice in Kensington just prior to my retirement."

"Have you remained in contact with him?"

"I happen upon him now and then at medical conferences I still manage to attend," said my father. "As a matter of fact, I chatted with him only last month at a symposium on malaria, at which time he informed me how well the practice was progressing. He also mentioned how superbly his son was performing at Eton, which of course is the same school your Johnny attends."

"Are they friends?"

"I asked, but Verner was unsure."

Joanna waved away that point of the conversation. "It is highly unlikely that he is here to talk of Eton or his son."

My father nodded. "Obviously it must concern a most serious medical dilemma."

"Do you believe he is here to consult on a former patient of yours?" I inquired.

"That would be most unusual, particularly at this time of night and in this weather, unless the patient was in great distress. If that was the case, such a patient would best be served in a hospital, like St. Bart's, where Verner has admitting privileges."

"Perhaps he wishes you to join him there," Joanna suggested.

My father pointed to the telephone. "That would not require an out-of-the-way journey to Baker Street. Bear in mind that when a patient is in dire straits, the smallest amount of time can be of the greatest consequence."

We heard a second rap on our door and Miss Hudson showed in the thin, rain-drenched visitor. Dr. Alexander Verner was even smaller than he appeared at a distance, with a height barely reaching five feet. His face had fine, gentle features, but there was distress in his eyes.

"Here," my father said, taking the doctor's soaked topcoat

and scarf. "Warm yourself by the fire while I hang up your garments."

As Verner sat in a cushioned chair, I noticed a tremor in his hands that could not have come from a chill, for our sitting room was nicely warmed by a three-log fire.

"How long was your walk?" Joanna asked.

Verner looked at her quizzically. "From my hansom to your doorstep?"

"No, no. From the lengthy walk you took prior to entering your hansom."

"How could you possibly know this?"

"From your soaked outer garments and shoes, the latter of which produce a watery squish with each step you take and leave behind a wet footprint on the floor of our parlor. Your shoes could not be so affected by the short journey from your hansom to our doorstep. They have obviously been exposed to a long walk elsewhere through the rain, for the mud and grass clinging to their soles and heels are not to be found on the cobblestone streets of London. So I can deduce you were very recently about in the countryside or in some locale that was similar to it."

Verner's face brightened for a moment. "You must be the daughter of Sherlock Holmes I have read of and so admired."

"I am indeed."

Verner turned to me and said, "And your resemblance to your father tells me you are the son of the good Dr. Watson."

"Correct, sir," I said.

"If you wish, my husband and I can adjourn to our room and give you and Dr. Watson total privacy," Joanna offered.

"Oh, please stay," Verner implored. "For I am certain it will require all of your minds and wits to make sense of the harrowing adventure I have just experienced."

"Harrowing, you say!" my father exclaimed as he drew up a chair.

"I do not exaggerate, my dear Watson. When I give you the particulars, you will understand how unnerving my journey was and continues to be. It all began with a late-afternoon caller to my practice who had a most unexpected request. He introduced himself as the representative of a distinguished personage who had a seizure disorder and was now suffering with abdominal pain. The visitor had learned of my knowledge in gastrointestinal disorders and implored me to come with him and see the patient. I of course agreed and closed my practice for the day, believing there was nothing peculiar about the caller or his request. But this changed the moment I stepped into the carriage awaiting us. Its windows were covered with thick cloth that allowed in only streaks of the late-afternoon light, which was quite dim because of the approaching storm. It was therefore impossible to see out and determine our direction. The visitor explained that it was necessary to keep the whereabouts of the ill patient a secret because neither his identity nor location were to be disclosed under any circumstances. Such measures, I was told, were required for high-profile, distinguished individuals for whom public disclosure of illness could have unwanted consequences. This suggested to me that the patient to be seen was either royalty or a governmental official of considerable standing. Despite these assurances I remained uneasy, for there was something foreboding about the caller. He projected an air of cruelty that indicated he was not a man to be trifled with."

Verner paused, as if to gather his thoughts. But the expression on his face turned more ominous. "I assumed the patient resided close by, but this was not the case. Our journey lasted at least thirty minutes, but it was not straightforward by any means. I had the distinct impression that at times we were traveling about in circles, followed by a series of sharp turns. It was impossible to tell where we were or our direction."

Joanna interrupted. "Were you moving over cobblestones or a paved road?"

"Both. While riding over cobblestones, the wheels produced noise that muffled the sounds outside our carriage. When we rode over smooth, paved streets, I occasionally heard motorcars passing by or the screech of brakes being applied."

"Were the brakes loud, such as those made by a bus or similar large transport vehicles?"

"I could not tell, for the rain was beginning to fall heavily and it muted other sounds. Is that important?"

"It could be, for we are dealing in darkness here and any glimmer of light might be most helpful."

"I did see streaks of light intermittently at the edge of the cloth curtains covering the carriage windows."

"For the entire journey?"

"For the first half or so."

"Which indicates you were on a major thoroughfare."

"But then it became quite dark."

"Which tells us you had most likely entered a residential neighborhood."

"And so we had," Verner concurred. "When the carriage came to a final stop, we were in a neighborhood that was quiet, with large, two-story houses belonging to the upper middle class. I should mention it was very dark indeed because the path leading up to the house was lined with trees and covered with shadows. I was hurried into a foyer that contained a small table with unopened mail stacked upon it. Unfortunately I was not near enough to read an address. As soon as my hat and coat were removed, I was led into a large, sparsely furnished bedroom. There was a single bed upon which rested a heavy-set man, with a protuberant abdomen and the look of distress on his face. At this point I was told that the patient was a mute and could communicate only in sign language, with which I am unfamiliar. Thus, the patient had to write down his symptoms using chalk and a small blackboard."

"Did he have a good command of the English language?" Joanna asked.

"Quite."

"Did he write like an Englishman would or was there evidence of foreign influence?"

"Definitely an Englishman."

"Pray continue."

"And so my examination began. He complained of abdominal pain of a day's duration, with some nausea and lack of appetite. I next went to palpating his abdomen and it was at this point I felt something was amiss. He had motioned to the umbilical area as being the area of greatest pain, and when I pressed upon it he moaned loudly."

"Nothing unusual there," my father remarked.

"What was unusual," Verner continued on, "was that he made no hand sign to express his pain. I have seen a number of mutes in my practice over the years, and when you press on a tender spot they automatically make a hand sign, indicating pain and telling you to stop. And they do not groan, but cry out with a high-pitched utterance. The patient did neither and I began to wonder if his complaints were those of a feigned illness.

"Now, I realize my conclusion thus far is based on subjective findings, but what I am about to disclose is not. When I asked the patient to point to the exact location of greatest pain, he took my hand and placed it to the right of the umbilicus. Then I inquired if the pain radiated away from that site and he slowly moved my hand to the left and surreptitiously spelled out the word *HELP*, which was written in letters."

"Are you absolutely certain of this?" Joanna asked at once.

"At first I was not, but then I asked the patient to again demonstrate how the pain radiated. Once more he carefully guided my hand and wrote the word *HELP*. I next adjusted the position of my body so the other man in the room could not visualize my hand, and I spelled out the word *NAME* on the patient's abdomen. He responded with the letters *TU* and was adding a third but did not continue, for the other man moved in for a closer look. Thus, no further messages could be transmitted between us."

"Could you make any meaning of the interrupted third letter?"

"It seemed to be a straight vertical line, with a curvature at its top, but it was indecipherable."

Joanna furrowed her brow in thought and began to softly utter a string of letters to herself. She would nod at one, then shake her head at another.

"Any ideas, Joanna?" I asked.

"Too many," she replied. "A straight vertical line with the beginning of a curve at its top could be a *b, d, p,* or *r*. And we do not know if it is a complete three-letter word or simply the start of a longer one. The possibilities are too numerous."

"My thoughts exactly," Verner said.

Joanna waved away the problem for the moment. "I take it the other man in the room watched your every move from then on."

"Like a hawk. Something I had done had obviously aroused his suspicions."

"Perhaps it was your prolonged examination of the patient's abdomen," my father surmised. "Or your movement to obscure the man's view of your hands."

"It could have been either or both," Verner said. "In any

event, I completed my examination and pronounced the diagnosis to be acute inflammation of the gallbladder that demanded immediate hospitalization. The other man stated this was not possible, for it would surely expose the patient's identity. Thus, all treatment would have to be done at home. I explained the risks if we followed that course of action, but it seemed to make no impression. Thus I had no choice but to prescribe laudanum for pain and asked to be notified if the patient's symptoms worsened."

My father asked, "Did you mention the possibility of peritonitis, which could be a death knell in this instance?"

Verner nodded. "I did, but to no avail. It was made quite clear that hospitalization was out of the question. Despite my dire warning, I was ushered out of the house and into the carriage with all of its windows still covered. I was instructed not to mention my visit or the patient to anyone, for to do so could result in incalculable harm. I was further told that if I did not follow these instructions, the consequences could be very unpleasant for all concerned. As I noted earlier, his voice was cold and menacing, and left no doubt whatsoever to whom the threat was directed. Trust me when I say I could not wait to separate myself from that man and his carriage. We proceeded to ride in silence over cobblestone and paved roads, with no sounds to be heard or sights to be seen. After nearly twenty minutes the carriage stopped and I was let out without a single word, although I was paid two pounds for my services. So here I was in the midst of a storm, with the cold wind howling and a pounding rain soaking me to the marrow. I walked a good mile before I came to Hampstead Station where I was able to hire a hansom that brought me to 221b Baker Street. I know my story sounds strange and most peculiar and at times farfetched, but I swear to you it is true in every regard. And although no crime can be proven here,

I fear a man's life may be in danger." Verner took a long, worrisome breath before adding, "Perhaps I should have gone to Scotland Yard."

Joanna flicked her wrist at the notion. "They would have paid little attention to your story. They would have demanded evidence that a crime had been committed or was in progress, and you had none."

"But the poor mate was crying out for help," I argued.

"Which breaks no law," Joanna countered. "Also, remember that the patient suffered from a seizure disorder. Had he experienced a recent attack, he may have been disoriented and unaware of the people around him. When introduced to the newly arrived Verner, he felt he could trust the kind doctor and thus issued a plea for help."

My father nodded in agreement. "When Joanna was a practicing nurse, she no doubt saw this strange transformation after a seizure. I too have seen the postictal phase of an attack last for half an hour or more, with disorientation a prominent feature."

"And this would be particularly pronounced in a dark room with no sound," Joanna added.

Verner stared at Joanna at length. "Are you telling me that no crime has been committed here?"

"No, Dr. Verner," Joanna said, reaching for a cigarette and carefully lighting it. "I am telling you why Scotland Yard would give little attention to your story. I, on the other hand, find your adventure to be of considerable interest. But I require more details if we are to put this puzzle together. Let us begin with the prisoner. Can you describe him for us?"

"I must tell you that the bedroom was not well lighted, and his bed was against a far wall where the lighting was dimmest. Thus it was not possible to delineate all his features. Nevertheless, I could ascertain he was a short, heavyset man, in his middle years, with unkempt hair and an unshaven face. The odor of his body indicated he had not bathed for a number of days."

"Were there any distinguishing features, such as scars, blemishes, or evidence of foul play?"

"None that could be seen."

"What of the bedroom he occupied? How was it furnished?"

"It was quite sparse, with only a bed and several wooden chairs."

"Did it contain mirrors or paintings on the wall?"

"None."

"A dresser?"

"No."

"Curtains?"

"Tightly drawn."

Joanna stood and began pacing the floor, leaving a trail of cigarette smoke behind. "Was the patient dressed in night-clothes?"

"He was not," Verner answered. "His shoes were removed, but he continued to wear trousers and shirt."

"Tell us of their quality."

"The trousers were well tailored and made of tightly woven wool. His shirt was opened so I could examine the patient's abdomen. It too was well made and had the feel of fine Egyptian cotton."

Joanna spun around. "Was there a monogram on the shirt?"

"None that could be seen."

"Most unfortunate," Joanna said, muttering to herself, as she went back to pacing. "When the mute patient answered your questions on the blackboard, are you quite certain he wrote as an Englishman would?"

"Very much so," Verner replied. "On my inquiring if he had gastric distress, he reported he had a *touch* of nausea. Not a little or small amount, but a *touch*, much like an Englishman would say."

"Well put," Joanna said, apparently pleased with the information. "Now be good enough to describe in detail the man who came to your office and guided you back to the patient."

"He was tall and broad shouldered, with a ramrod-straight posture, reminiscent of a military officer. His hair was blond and cut short, although I saw only its fringes because he wore a derby."

"And the color of his eyes?"

"Blue and cold as ice."

"Were there any distinguishing features about his face?"

"None that stood—" Verner stopped in mid-sentence and pointed to his cheek. "He had a noticeable tic about his left eye. The spasms around his orbit occurred with some frequency and involved both the face and eyelid."

"Was there any evidence of trauma around the affected eye?"

"None that I could see, which suggested it was a true nervous system disorder."

Joanna nodded at Verner's assessment and hummed softly to herself, indicating she was storing the presence of the facial tic in her memory bank. "Very good," she continued on. "Now please tell us about the man's voice."

"It was cold and menacing, and left no doubt that—"

"No, no," Joanna interrupted. "I am not interested in the emotions it elicited, but in its origin. Did the man speak English like it was his mother tongue?"

Verner gave the matter thought before answering. "His grammar was quite good, but at times he spoke as if he had learned the language in school."

"Let us have an example."

"When I completed my examination and was about to leave the bedroom, he said, 'Now we return to our carriage.' An Englishman would have never put it that way."

"Indeed," Joanna said, as a hint of a smile came to her face. "While you were in the house, did you come across any others, man or woman?"

"There was one other man whom I neither saw nor heard."

"Then how did you learn of his presence?"

"There was a bit of noise in an adjoining room that upset the man who brought me to the house. The man opened a side door and yelled out something that ended with the word *FENSTER*. It may well have been a person's name, of that I cannot be sure. Then I heard the sound of a drawer closing before the door was shut. Thus, I assumed there was another man present and that he had been given a command of some sort."

"I believe your assumptions are for the most part correct."

"And my assumption that the poor man is a prisoner being held against his will?"

"That too is correct."

"Then how will you proceed?"

"By making the necessary inquiries," Joanna said, and walked over to the rack that held Verner's topcoat and scarf. "And now the hour is late and you should be on your way. I take it your hansom awaits you?"

"It does," Verner said, being helped into his outer garments. "Is there any further assistance I can lend in this matter?"

"Not at the moment."

"What if the man returns for me to again examine the patient? I would have no choice but to accompany him back to the house that holds the prisoner. Indeed, I might be forced to do so."

Joanna considered the doctor's dilemma at length before asking, "Do you have chloroform in your office?"

"A goodly supply."

"Then somehow manage to spill some of it on your shoes prior to leaving with him."

"That is a rather odd request."

"Your life may depend on it."

Verner's eyes flew open. "Why would they do me harm?"

"Because you are the only link to the patient's true identity, and they will go to any lengths to ensure he remains nameless."

2

The Advertisement

As was my custom, I awoke early the next morning but found Joanna's side of the bed vacant. After dressing quickly, I entered our parlor and was greeted by a dense haze of cigarette smoke, through which Joanna was pacing back and forth. She rarely smoked except when involved in a difficult case, at which time she could easily consume two packs of cigarettes daily. And like her esteemed father before her, she could go sleepless for days until the problem was solved or she determined more data was needed before a solution could be reached. My father, attired in a maroon smoking jacket, was seated in a cushioned chair and puffing on his favorite cherrywood pipe, all the while watching Joanna pace.

"It appears my wife has a three-pipe problem before her," I remarked, referring to Sherlock Holmes's description of a perplexing case that required at least three pipes to bring to a successful conclusion.

"So it would appear," my father agreed. "Yet at the rate she is smoking, I fear the underlying reason for Verner's harrowing adventure continues to escape her."

"To the contrary, my dear Watson. The purpose is well in hand," Joanna said. "It is the solution that remains problematic."

"Please inform us of its purpose," I requested.

Our conversation was interrupted by a gentle rap on the door. Miss Hudson stepped in and was immediately aghast at the cloud of smoke that enveloped her. She hurried over to the window and opened it for fresh air to flow in.

"How can you possibly remain in this room under such foul conditions?" Miss Hudson asked.

"Because, Miss Hudson, the conditions lend themselves to solving a most urgent problem," Joanna replied.

Miss Hudson uttered a hopeless sigh and handed my father several morning newspapers. "Would now be a convenient time for breakfast, Dr. Watson?"

"If you would be so kind," my father said.

Upon Miss Hudson's departure, Joanna dashed over to close the window. "She means well, but is unaware of the high-stakes game that confronts us. You see, the captive that Verner described to us will shortly end up dead unless we intervene."

"What is this dreadful assumption based on?" I asked.

"Everything we have been told," Joanna replied. "The entire story of the mute patient is a total fabrication. First, we are required to believe that the patient is a distinguished personage in whom disclosure of illness would cause public alarm. This would indicate the individual is well-known royalty or a high-ranking official in the British government who would be easily recognized. All of which is absolute nonsense. Officials at the highest level, as well as the royalty, have their own personal physicians who are always at their immediate disposal. Furthermore we are asked to believe this well-known, distinguished individual is a mute. Is there a member of the royal family who is so afflicted? Can you envision any politician, whose career depends on his ability to speak and convince, being unable to do so? And if by chance there was such a rare individual, he would be widely publicized and instantly recognized by Dr. Verner. Thus, we can conclude this person is neither royalty nor a politician at the highest level nor a mute. He was presented as a mute and made to write his words to ensure he could not reveal his identity or circumstances."

"And Verner was under the impression that the patient was feigning his illness," my father added.

"Precisely," Joanna went on. "The prisoner feigned an illness so that his captors would have no recourse other than to call in a physician. This of course could provide him with an opportunity to inform the doctor of his situation. It may have represented his only chance of escape."

"The prisoner seems to be quite clever," I remarked.

"Even more clever than you believe," Joanna said. "His brain thinks several moves ahead, much like a chess master outmaneuvering his opponent. He could have chosen a variety of illnesses that required the presence of a doctor, yet he selected abdominal pain. Why? Because he knew the doctor would ask him the exact location of the pain and, since he could not speak, he could guide the doctor's hand to the right side of the abdomen. From there, he might be able to surreptitiously spell out his cry for help. So, taking into account the cut of his clothes, we have a very astute, upper-class Englishman who is being held captive."

"To what end?" I asked at once.

"For classified information, I would think."

My father and I exchanged puzzled glances before I asked, "Upon which evidence do you base this?"

"The identity of his captors," Joanna replied. "You see, he

is being held by Germans, which makes me believe they are holding him for information he has and they desperately want."

"How can you possibly know that the man's captors are German?"

"By their use of the word *FENSTER*, which Verner thought was the name of a man who was being called upon," Joanna answered. "Recall that Verner heard a sentence with the word *FENSTER* in it, and this was followed by the sound of a drawer being closed. He overheard correctly, but drew the wrong conclusion. *FENSTER* in German means window, and the man was ordering another to close a window. That was the sound Verner misinterpreted as being a drawer being shut."

My father bolted upright suddenly. "Are you saying the Englishman was taken captive by German agents?"

"Since we are currently at war with Germany, that would be a logical assumption," Joanna said. "But everything revolves around the man whose name begins with the letters *TU*. Until we know his identity, I fear we remain in the dark."

"With the prisoner's life at stake."

"That too."

"Scotland Yard must be notified," my father urged.

"So they shall be shortly," Joanna said, crushing out her cigarette in an overflowing ashtray. "But for now, Watson, I will leave you to your newspapers while I change into clothes more suitable for one of Miss Hudson's sumptuous breakfasts. I suggest you begin with the *Daily Telegraph,* which tends to report the more current London news."

"Is there anything in particular that I should search for?"

"Look for unusual happenings in the upper-class neighborhoods of Belgravia, Mayfair, and the like."

"Do you believe our man is an aristocrat?"

"Perhaps. Or with his sharp mind, he might have associates

in these neighborhoods and his absence would be noted and reported."

My father scanned the *Daily Telegraph* while I busied myself with the *Standard*. We saw nothing of interest on their fronts but, as we turned to the inner pages, my father abruptly jerked his head forward. He read hurriedly, moving his lips but making no sound until he cried out, "I think we have our man!"

Joanna rushed out of our bedroom and, sitting on the arm of his chair, peered over my father's shoulder as he read from the notice.

"Anyone supplying information on the whereabouts of Alistair Ainsworth, who also responds to the name Tubby, will be rewarded. Because of injury, he may not be aware of his identity. To gain the above reward, please reply to X2810."

Joanna jumped to her feet and asked my father, "Do you have Verner's phone number?"

My father reached for the nearby phone and quickly dialed the doctor's number by memory. Holding the phone close to his ear, he waited only a moment before dialing the number once more. "The line is busy," he announced.

Joanna raced for the bedroom as she called over her shoulder, "We must hurry!"

"To Scotland Yard?" my father asked.

Joanna shook her head. "To Verner's office, for his life is now in real and immediate danger."

"But he did not write the notice," I argued mildly. "He had no knowledge of the prisoner's name."

"It does not matter whether he wrote it or not, for the Germans will believe he did and thus want him silenced permanently," Joanna elucidated. "It is the time sequence that is so important here. Alistair Ainsworth has been missing, for days on end, as evidenced by his unkempt appearance, which Verner duly noted. Yet concern for his disappearance suddenly shows up in print only now, shortly after Verner's visit. The Germans may have no proof that Verner had the notice published, but they will suspect he did and take no chances."

We grabbed our coats and hats and dashed down the stairs, passing a startled Miss Hudson carrying up our breakfast tray.

"Will you be returning shortly?" she called out.

We did not bother to answer, for our minds were totally occupied with the terrible fate awaiting Alexander Verner.

3

Dr. Verner's Office

We did not make good time, for traffic was heavy and sections of the streets remained flooded with last evening's torrential downpour. Nevertheless, Joanna used my father's walking stick to repeatedly rap on the roof of our carriage, urging the driver to go faster and faster.

"Perhaps the Germans did not read the morning newspaper," I hoped.

"I can assure you they have," Joanna said. "They will scour over every page, searching for information about the missing man and whether there is any mention of an ongoing investigation. You see, the Germans are aware they have a valued prize on their hands and will wish to know if there are any clues indicating the authorities are closing in on them."

"But it is unlikely such information would find its way into the newspapers," I argued.

"To the contrary, Scotland Yard takes great delight in publicizing their pursuits and accomplishments, real or imagined. They do this to project an image of sharpness that is all too often lacking."

My father nodded at Joanna's assessment. "Holmes would tell you that, with few exceptions, they are a collection of bunglers who depend on informants to solve most of their cases. It is not that they don't have brains; it is that they refuse to use them."

"Then our last, best hope is that Verner read the morning papers and, realizing the danger, has fled," I said.

"That is wishful thinking," said Joanna. "Had Verner read the notice, he would have certainly called to inform us of the new information and to seek further instructions."

My father sighed dispiritedly. "Everything seems to be going against poor Verner."

"Let us pray we are not too late," said Joanna.

But it appeared we were. Stationed at the doorstep to Verner's practice were two police constables. Because of our past association with Scotland Yard, we were recognized and allowed immediate entrance. Expecting the worst, we hurried into Verner's surgery but found only Inspector Lestrade standing amidst evidence that indicated a struggle had taken place. A metal stool and instrument table were overturned, with scalpels and forceps strewn about the floor. Off to the side was a medicine cabinet, with its glass door shattered and blood smeared across its handle. The strong odor of chloroform filled the air.

Our presence seemed to catch Lestrade by surprise. He tipped his hat to us and, skipping the usual amenities, asked, "Are you friends with Dr. Verner?"

"He is a former colleague who bought my practice some years ago," my father replied.

"I take it this is not a social call."

"It is not."

"May I then inquire as to the purpose of your visit this morning?"

"We hoped to prevent harm from coming to Verner."

"And pray tell, how did you know this harm might occur?"

"Because my daughter-in-law predicted it."

Lestrade gave us a long quizzical look. "How did she arrive at this conclusion?"

"From a meeting we had with Verner late last night."

"Here?"

"In our rooms at 221b Baker Street."

"Might I know the reason for this late-night meeting?"

"Perhaps the most unusual tale you will ever hear," my father responded. "Please allow my daughter-in-law to describe the frightful journey Verner was compelled to take."

"Compelled, you say?" Lestrade asked at once.

"*Persuaded* may be a better word," Joanna said, and began a detailed narrative, often using Verner's own words to describe the major features.

Lestrade listened intently, but his interest was obviously piqued by the mention of a carriage, with its windows covered, that traveled a most circuitous route. He tapped a finger against his chin before asking, "The doctor had no idea of his destination?"

"None whatsoever," Joanna replied. "He was told the patient was a personage of high standing whose identity and location were not to be disclosed under any circumstances."

"Strange," Lestrade commented.

"Stranger yet was the fact that the patient was supposedly a mute who could only converse with chalk and blackboard, since Verner was not familiar with sign language. I will not go into detail at this point, but suffice it to say Verner was under the distinct impression that the patient was feigning his symptoms of abdominal discomfort."

"Why would the patient conjure up such an illness?"

"As a clever way to communicate. When asked where his

pain was most severe, the patient took Verner's hand and pressed it to his abdomen. When asked if the pain moved about, the patient surreptitiously guided the doctor's hand and spelled out the word *HELP* on his abdomen."

Lestrade's eyes widened. "Was Dr. Verner convinced of this?"

"Beyond any doubt, for Verner repeated the question and once more the patient wrote the word *HELP*. In that a secret method of communication was now established, Verner inquired as to the patient's name. The supposed mute was only able to spell the letters *TU* before he was compelled to stop because his captor had become suspicious and moved in for a closer look. Verner quick-wittedly made the diagnosis of acute inflammation of the gallbladder and advised immediate hospitalization in an effort to remove the patient from his captivity. But the captors refused to follow the advice and only asked for pain medication before sending Verner on his way."

Lestrade shook his head in wonderment. "In all my years I have never heard such a tale."

"Nor I," Joanna said. "And now allow me to explain why we feel Dr. Verner is in such danger. After departing the patient's house, he was driven some twenty minutes away and unceremoniously let out in the midst of a storm, with a most menacing warning not to mention the patient or his illness to anyone. He was told the consequences of such action would be very unpleasant for all involved. We of course advised Verner to follow those instructions while we devised a plan of action."

"I take it he did not and this is the reason for your alarm."

"Oh, but he did. Unfortunately his captors thought otherwise. You see, in the morning newspaper, there was a notice offering a reward for information on the whereabouts of Alistair Ainsworth who also responds to the name Tubby.

Thus it seems clear that our supposedly mute patient was attempting to spell out his nickname."

Lestrade's jaw dropped. In an instant he dashed to the door of the surgery and closed it securely. When he rejoined us, he spoke in a voice so low it resembled a whisper. "Have you spoken to anyone of this?"

"Only you," Joanna replied.

"See that it stays that way," Lestrade said. "For you have entered dangerous waters."

"Please be so kind as to—"

Lestrade held up his hand. "At this point, you must allow me to ask the questions, with you supplying the most detailed of answers. It is the location of the house the doctor visited that is of obvious importance. Although the windows of his carriage were covered, did he give you any information on the neighborhood they eventually reached?"

"Only that it was residential and of the upper class. It was quite dark, but he could discern the house was two storied and well built."

"And its interior?"

"Unremarkable, except there were indications the home was rented."

"Why rented?"

"A number of features, which included a lack of furniture and no mirrors or paintings on the walls. In addition, there was unopened mail stacked up on a table in the foyer. Obviously the captors had little interest in the mail. Long-term occupants would, short-term renters would not."

"Did Dr. Verner give a description of these captors?"

Joanna thought for a moment before saying, "He came in contact with only one. The man was tall and broad shouldered, with close-cut blond hair and a noticeable facial tic."

"His accent?" Lestrade asked pointedly.

"Neutral, but he was in all likelihood a German."

"Based on his physical characteristics?"

"Based on his use of the word *FENSTER*," Joanna said, and explained its German meaning and the context in which the term *window* was used. "There is no doubt that German was his native tongue."

An expression of deep concern came to Lestrade's face and this was attested to by the gravity of his next words. "We must locate this house at all costs. There is not a moment to lose."

"Unfortunately we have so little to go on," my father said unhappily. "There are dozens of upper-class residential neighborhoods in London, all of which have well-built houses too numerous to count."

"But the house was in all likelihood leased," Lestrade noted. "Perhaps we could narrow down our search somewhat by inquiring about recent rentals from leasing agents."

"That would take far too long," Joanna pointed out. "Moreover, we do not know if the house was in fact let by an agent and, if it was, how long ago the transaction took place."

"The owner could have simply posted a to-let advertisement in various bulletins or newspapers," I added.

Lestrade sighed resignedly. "I am open to any other courses of action we might pursue."

"There is one that may prove worthwhile," Joanna said, and motioned to a small broken bottle on the floor next to the bloodstained cabinet. "You will note the strong odor of chloroform that emanates from that broken vial. A fierce struggle took place here during which the cabinet door was smashed and a small bottle of chloroform fell to the tile floor and shattered. Dr. Verner and his captors may have stepped upon the damp areas of chloroform and thus they carry its scent on the soles and heels of their shoes."

"So?" Lestrade asked impatiently.

"It can be followed."

"By whom, may I ask?"

"By a hound named Toby Two who has the keenest nose in all London."

"Where do we find this hound?"

"At number three Pinchin Lane in the lower quarter of Lambeth," Joanna replied by memory. "Tell the kennel owner that only Toby Two will do and that the request is made by Dr. Watson, the longtime associate of Sherlock Holmes."

"Are you convinced the dog can perform such a feat?"

Joanna nodded firmly. "She once tracked the faint odor of French perfume from Victoria Station to the northern reaches of Edgware Road without missing a beat."

Lestrade raced for the door. "I must call Lieutenant Dunn and request that he join us at once."

"From Naval Intelligence?" I asked. "Is he the same officer who was a member of our team that solved the case of *A Study in Treason*?"

"The very same."

"So we are dealing here with espionage."

"I can say no more," Lestrade said. "Now I must ask that you remain in this room and speak to no one until Lieutenant Dunn arrives. A constable will be posted at the door to make certain no unauthorized person can enter this surgery."

"Please instruct the lieutenant to make haste, for we are faced with a most urgent matter," Joanna implored. "Dr. Verner's life is very much at stake here."

"As is the fate of all England," Lestrade said darkly, and closed the door behind him.

4

The Chase

Lieutenant Dunn arrived before Toby Two. On entering, he gave us a perfunctory nod, then led the way into a vacant, windowless office where, upon closing the door, he briefed us on the Official Secrets Act, to which we were about to be sworn. As he uttered the solemn oath that bound us to keep secret all matters revealed and committed to us, the gravity of the situation grew even greater. Lestrade's warning that "the fate of all England" may be at stake continued to ring in our ears.

"Now let us begin," Dunn said in an emotionless voice. "I would like you to again recount the entire story told to you by Dr. Verner. Give me only facts and avoid assumptions."

"Any assumptions I render will be based on fact and should not be so readily discarded," Joanna countered. "With so little to guide us, both could prove to be quite useful."

"Agreed, but you must distinguish between the two," Dunn said. "Please start with the moment Dr. Verner arrived at your rooms on Baker Street."

Joanna repeated the strange tale, providing the same details given to Inspector Lestrade. The only additions were the reasons why Verner believed the patient was not mute, but was instructed by his captors to act as if he were. "I assumed Verner was correct in believing Alistair Ainsworth was not mute."

Dunn did not reply to the assumption. "Was he restrained?"

"Not that Verner mentioned."

"Or evidence of torture?"

"Again none was mentioned, but I feel certain that, if any were present, Verner would have been impressed and brought them to our attention."

"Torture is not uncommon in these situations," Dunn remarked. He was a tall man, well built, with a resolute expression and deep-set, piercing eyes. "The Germans are quite expert at inflicting pain when it serves their purpose."

"It may have been used here, but the evidence was hidden from sight," Joanna replied. "When Vernon performed his examination, Ainsworth was fully clothed, with only his shirt opened to allow for inspection of the abdomen. Thus, torture applied to the captive's back and extremities would go unnoticed."

"Your point is well taken," Dunn said, with the briefest of nods, then tapped a finger against his chin while muttering something indecipherable under his breath. "Well, at the least he remains alive, which indicates they have not yet broken him."

"Perhaps they won't," Lestrade said, injecting a note of optimism.

"Every man has his breaking point," Dunn said stonily. "Even the toughest of them. And once broken, they spill everything."

"Exactly what is it that Mr. Ainsworth will be spilling?" Joanna asked. "And why is it so valuable to the Germans?"

Dunn's face closed. "You and your associates are on a need-to-know basis. The questions you ask are well beyond your purview."

"Do you wish our assistance?" Joanna asked.

"Indeed we do."

"Then you must remove our blindfolds, for if we remain in the dark, no solution will be reached."

"I can only state that Mr. Ainsworth was involved at the highest level of national security."

We returned to the examining room and carefully avoided stepping on the scattered glass and instruments strewn on the floor near the medicine cabinet. Joanna stressed the need to avoid anything that carried the aroma of chloroform, which was the scent to be followed.

"It will require the keenest of noses to track that evanescent odor across London," said Dunn.

"One is on the way," Joanna assured.

"Can the hound do it from a moving carriage?"

"That is where she performs best."

"So you have been told?"

"So I have witnessed."

The door to the examining room opened and Toby Two romped in, sliding across the slippery tile floor. She came to a stop at Joanna's feet and looked up, as if awaiting instructions. The hound appeared to ignore everyone else in the room.

Joanna reached down to scratch the dog's head, then grasped her leash before addressing the group. "Toby Two, Watson, my husband, and I will be in the lead carriage. Inspector Lestrade and Lieutenant Dunn should follow in a second carriage, accompanied by two constables. I would advise you have your weapons at the ready."

"How will you determine we are on the correct track?" Dunn asked.

"By observing Toby Two's tail," Joanna replied.

She went to the medicine cabinet to obtain an empty glass vial with a screw top. After opening it, she secured a small piece of glass from the shattered chloroform bottle and placed it into the vial before resealing it tightly.

"If we travel by motorcar, it will save a great deal of time," Dunn suggested.

"It might also confuse Toby Two," Joanna said. "Motor fumes carrying the strong smell of burned petrol will accumulate within the car and could throw Toby Two off her mark."

We hurried to our carriage and headed away from the heavily populated, commercial district of Kensington. Joanna waited until we were two blocks west of Verner's practice before opening the glass vial and placing it under Toby Two's nose. She waited only a few seconds for the hound to familiarize herself with the odor of chloroform, then resealed it and gave out instructions, "Go, girl! Go!"

In an instant Toby Two had her head out the carriage window, yelping happily, with her tail wagging at a rapid pace. There could be no doubt we were on track, which stirred excitement among us all. But the most vexing questions remained foremost in our minds. Who was Alistair Ainsworth and what was his governmental function that was so vital to England?

"Could Ainsworth be a spy?" I wondered aloud.

"That is unlikely," Joanna replied. "British spies for the most part operate in foreign countries, not in London."

"Perhaps he is a high-ranking officer in the Admiralty," my father suggested.

"Who was out of uniform when captured?" Joanna countered. "You may recall that Alistair Ainsworth was dressed in civilian attire when he was examined by Verner."

After a prolonged pause, I offered another possibility. "Perhaps he was a diplomat or courier of some sort."

Joanna flicked her wrist. "Guesses! All guesses, none of which advances our cause. All we can say with certainty is that Alistair Ainsworth was privy to very sensitive information that the Germans desperately wish to lay their hands on."

Suddenly Toby Two became overly excited. She yelped and, with her paws on the bottom of the window, extended her head out into the morning air. The strength of the scent had obviously intensified. All eyes went to the neighborhood we were passing through. It was not residential, but rather a street lined with fashionable stores and quaint shops. Toby Two was now leaning so far out the window I feared she would fall onto the cobblestones below. I grabbed her leash and tried to pull her back, but with little success.

Joanna rapped forcefully on the roof of our carriage and shouted up to the driver, "Stop immediately!"

Our carriage came to an abrupt halt and we hurriedly alighted onto a slate-covered footpath. Joanna took hold of the leash as Toby Two barked joyfully and led the way into a well-appointed tobacco shop. Behind a splendid display of cigars was a portly man, with thinning, dark hair and a well-trimmed goatee. He quickly straightened his posture at our entrance, his gaze going to the two uniformed constables now posted at the door.

"May I be of service?" he asked nervously.

"You are the owner, I presume?" Joanna said, bypassing the introductions.

"I am indeed."

"When did your shop open?"

"Just over an hour ago."

"How many customers have stepped through your door since opening?"

"Two."

"Describe them."

"The first was Mr. James, an elderly gentleman who favors Dutch Masters—"

"And the other?" Joanna interrupted.

"A large, broad-shouldered man who purchased a package of Pall Mall cigarettes."

"Was this his first visit to your shop?"

"To the best of my recollection."

"Could he have phoned in for a delivery?"

The owner shook his head. "We only deliver to known customers with accounts."

"Did he linger while in your fine shop?"

"No, madam. He seemed a bit hurried."

"And one final question," Joanna requested. "Did this particular customer have any unusual features about his face? A scar or blemish perhaps?"

The owner gave the matter thought before he nodded slowly. "He had a nervous tic that seemed to come and go."

"Thank you for your assistance," Joanna said and, pulling on Toby Two's leash, dashed out of the shop.

"We have our man!" Lestrade cried out.

"We also have a very ominous sign," Joanna said darkly.

Our carriages continued on their way, with all eyes now on the residential area we were entering. It appeared every house was white in color, at least two stories high, and shaded by tall trees. A passing dog on a leash barked at our carriage, but Toby Two ignored it, her nose ever to the wind. As we approached the corner, Toby Two let out the loudest of howls and pointed at a two-story, white house well back from the street. Her tail was now fixed and straight as an arrow.

"Here!" Joanna bellowed out.

The carriages screeched to a halt and all occupants bolted out, except for Toby Two who was tied to a seat and left behind. Lestrade and Dunn raced across the lawn, weapons drawn and at the ready. Every window in the house was closed, with their drapes tightly drawn.

Lestrade signaled the constables to cover the rear of the house, then pounded on the front door and called out, "We are here from Scotland Yard! You are to open the door immediately!"

A full thirty seconds passed without response. Our ears were tuned in to any sound emanating from within this stately house, but all remained silent. A constable's whistle sounded, indicating they were in place at the rear of the house.

Lestrade banged on the door once more and issued a final warning. "You have one minute before we resort to forced entry!"

Dunn waited only ten seconds to kick the front door off its hinges. He and Lestrade rushed in, but no shots were fired and we heard no sounds of a struggle. The two constables raced around from the rear of the house and entered the foyer at full speed. We could see them sprinting up a flight of stairs. The silence returned and continued until Lestrade appeared at the entrance and waved us in.

"The Germans have fled," he said gloomily.

"And Verner?" Joanna asked.

"Dead."

We hurried through the foyer and passed a small table covered with unopened mail. On entering a large bedroom that held an unmade bed, we were taken aback by the gruesome sight of Alexander Verner. He was seated in a wooden chair, with his wrists and ankles restrained by thick rope. But it was his facial expression that was so disturbing. It showed absolute terror. There was no sign of Alistair Ainsworth.

"They tortured the poor doctor," Dunn reported grimly. "They burned his palms and soles, which are the most sensitive parts of the body."

"Using lighted cigarettes, I presume," Joanna said.

"That appears to be the case," Dunn agreed. "But how could you discern that from across the room?"

"Because the German agent bought a single packet of Pall Mall cigarettes on his way back to the house," Joanna explained. "Here they were, racing against time in a mad dash to determine how much the doctor had divulged, yet they stopped for cigarettes. It was an utter waste of time, which they had little of."

"Perhaps he was strongly addicted to tobacco," Lestrade advanced. "The nicotine drive can be quite overpowering, as Dr. Watson can attest to."

"The evidence is twofold against a strong addiction," Joanna said, glancing down at the burn marks. "First, despite living close by, he had visited the tobacco shop only once. And secondly, a man heavily addicted to cigarettes would have bought several packets, not simply one. Thus I concluded the agent must have had another use for lighted cigarettes, such as torture."

"And Verner made no mention of a strong odor of tobacco smoke during his description of the house, which would have been present if any of the occupants were heavily addicted," my father noted.

"All well and good," Dunn said impatiently. "But unfortunately, this does not bring us any closer to Ainsworth's captors."

"Perhaps there is evidence on Verner that will tell us more," Joanna said as she briefly examined the doctor's outer garments. "Were his pockets searched?"

Dunn pointed to the belongings on the bed. There was a gold timepiece, a leather billfold containing seven pounds, a mechanical pen, and a set of keys. "They left nothing of value to us behind."

"Or so it would seem," Joanna said. "But we should allow my husband, who is an experienced pathologist, to examine the corpse and make certain there are no hidden clues."

Lestrade gestured his approval.

The smell of burned flesh, with which I was familiar, told me what to expect. On Verner's palms and soles were small, deep, blackened circles, some crusted over, others not. The burns penetrated well beneath the dermis of the skin and must have caused unbearable pain. There was dried blood on the right palm as well as rope indentations on both wrists, which were produced by Verner as he tried desperately to free himself. But his neck and eyes held the most unexpected findings.

"There is even more cruelty here that goes beyond words," I commented.

"How so?" Joanna asked.

"They not only restrained his neck, they throttled the poor man when they were done with him," I replied, and pointed to the rope around the victim's throat. "The rope marks are deep enough to compress Verner's trachea and thus prevent him from crying out while being tortured. But in addition, there are small hemorrhages, called petechiae, in his conjunctivae, which are clear evidence of strangulation. The forces closing off a person's airway also impede the return of blood from the head, which increases the venous pressure in the eyes and causes the small blood vessels within to rupture. I am confident a postmortem examination will reveal a fractured hyoid bone as well, and that is conclusive evidence he was strangled. Verner was no doubt aware this was happening and that accounts for the look of absolute terror on his face. He knew his end was near."

"Bloody Huns!" my father cried out, his face now red with rage. "Is there no end to their savagery?"

"Not in war," Dunn replied.

"But to do this to such a fine and gentle man who did only good while on this earth," my father said, taking a deep breath to control his anger. "There was no need for such cruelty."

Joanna leaned in for a closer inspection, seemingly unaffected by the viciousness of the crime. "Is the rope they used in any way remarkable?"

"I am afraid not," I replied. "It is made of common hemp and can be purchased at numerous stores throughout London."

Joanna sniffed the air. "The odor of chloroform still emanates from his shoes."

"I am surprised the Germans did not detect it."

"I'm certain they did, which gave them yet another reason to kill Verner." Joanna turned to Lestrade and Dunn and asked, "Was there any evidence upstairs that indicated the Germans' next move?"

"Nothing," Lestrade answered. "All of the rooms were bare, with no articles or written documents other than old newspapers."

"How old?" Joanna asked at once.

"Some dated back ten days."

"During which time they no doubt planned the details of the kidnapping. Which tells us this was no spur-of-the-moment event, but one that was carefully devised. They laid their trap and had this house waiting well in advance." Joanna thought for a moment, then returned to Lestrade. "Are you certain there were no receipts or delivery packages? After all, they were here for at least ten days and must have required food and drink and other essentials."

"Other than an unmade bed, there was nothing to indicate the house was lived in."

"What of the unopened mail in the foyer?"

"All notices and advertisements addressed to Occupant."

"These are very experienced agents," Joanna remarked.

"The Germans have obviously sent their best on this mission, which highlights its importance. They swept the entire house clean in a most professional manner."

"Surely they could not have been that perfect," said I. "Not in a house this large."

"Do not underestimate German obsessiveness when it comes to order," Joanna reminded. "Nonetheless, with their hurried departure, they may well have overlooked some small, secluded item."

"That very thought crossed my mind," said Lestrade. "For that reason, I have instructed the constables to perform yet another foot-by-foot search of each and every room."

"Any clue would be most welcome at this point," I remarked,

"Perhaps the nearby neighbors should be questioned," my father suggested.

"And so they shall," Dunn said. "But I have my doubts they will be of help. Keep in mind that foreign agents are for the most part very skilled at concealing themselves. They also know how to instantly disappear into thin air."

"So it would seem we have reached yet another dead end," Lestrade said dismally. "And all the while, Mr. Ainsworth's chances of survival are slipping away before our very eyes."

"And they will slip away altogether unless we quickly intervene," Joanna warned. "Once the Germans have the information they wish, Alistair Ainsworth is a dead man."

Our conversation was abruptly interrupted by a constable who dashed into the bedroom at full speed. He held up a dripping-wet wallet and announced, "Sir, we discovered this in the water tank of a nearby lavatory."

"Was it floating or had it sunk?" Joanna asked quickly.

"Floating, ma'am," the constable replied.

"Excellent," Joanna said, more to herself than to the others.

Lestrade took the wallet and, after dismissing the constable, asked, "Why is it so important that the wallet remained
afloat?"

"Because it tells us the wallet was recently placed in the
tank," Joanna elucidated. "Had it been deposited some time
ago, it would have become waterlogged and sunk."

"Why is that of significance?"

"Because the scrupulously neat Germans most assuredly
did not deposit it there," Joanna replied. "Thus, in all likelihood, the wallet belonged to Alistair Ainsworth, and since it
recently found its way into the water tank, we can deduce he
placed it there and was leaving us a trail to follow."

"Perhaps he was simply leaving us a sign to indicate he had
indeed been here," Lestrade proposed.

Outside, there was a loud roar of thunder followed by a
sudden, heavy downpour. The rain appeared to beat against
the window, much as it had done the night before.

"Bad," Joanna said, staring at the streaked windowpane.

"The rain?" I asked.

Joanna nodded. "It will wash away any trace of chloroform that might have rubbed off on the German agents and
their carriage."

"Rubbed off, you say?" Lestrade asked as he carefully
opened the soaked wallet.

Joanna nodded again. "Verner's shoes would have left
behind the evaporating scent of chloroform on the floor of the
carriage, and vapors of that aroma may have seeped into the
agents' shoes as well. Unfortunately now, with the rain pounding down, that scent will either disappear or become so faint
that even Toby Two will be unable to track it."

"So we have obviously lost that advantage," Lestrade
groused.

"I am afraid so, but we will give Toby Two an opportunity to pick up the scent, remote as it may be." Joanna moved in nearer to Lestrade who was emptying the contents of the wet wallet. There were two five-pound notes, several identification cards, and a soggy photograph of a middle-aged woman. He held the photo up to the light for a better view.

"Do you recognize her?" Joanna asked.

"She is Ainsworth's invalid sister who must be looked after," Lestrade replied. "They are very close."

"Have you questioned her?"

"At length and on two occasions. She only knew that he did not return home from his office and has been missing since. He had not called or made any contact with her, which was most unusual. Thus, she obviously feared for his safety."

"I presume it was she who posted the notification in the newspaper?"

"She did so without consulting us first," Lestrade grumbled.

"Which may have cost Verner his life," my father said.

"And might have encouraged the Germans to move along more quickly, for they will wonder whether Verner shared this information with the authorities," Joanna noted. "All of which places Ainsworth's life in even greater peril."

Lestrade nodded gloomily at the assessment.

"May I?" Joanna reached for the photograph and examined it carefully, then extracted a magnifying glass from her purse and focused in on something of obvious interest. "Her hands," she said to my father. "Look at her hands, Watson, and tell me what you see."

My father studied the photograph intently as he moved the magnifying glass back and forth in a slow, deliberate fashion. "Her fingers are deformed from a severe form of inflammatory rheumatism."

"Would it be generalized?"

"In all likelihood."

"I take it she would require assistance in her basic daily activities?"

"Beyond any question."

Joanna turned her attention to Dunn. "Did you question her as well, Lieutenant?"

"I did," Dunn replied.

"Were there others attending her?"

Dunn shook his head. "The housekeeper and cook were in the kitchen at the time. They too were interrogated, but could offer nothing that was helpful."

"So no one else was present?"

"No one."

Joanna gave Dunn a lengthy look, then reached in her purse for a cigarette and lighted it, all the while keeping her eyes fixed on the lieutenant. "There are too many missing pieces here."

"You have the information we have," Dunn said.

"To the contrary," Joanna countered. "I know little about Alistair Ainsworth and you know all."

Dunn stared at her in silence.

Joanna began pacing the floor, puffing absently on her Turkish cigarette. Back and forth she went, intermittently mumbling to herself or shaking her head at some notion that did not fit. A stream of blue smoke seemed to follow her across the room. Abruptly Joanna crushed out her cigarette in an ashtray and turned to Dunn. "I require detailed information on Ainsworth's secretive position."

"I can only tell you that his duties involve national security at the highest level," Dunn said carefully.

"That will not do," Joanna pressed.

"I regret I cannot divulge more."

"Without the information I requested, you make it impossible for me to reach a resolution. You are asking me to make bricks, yet you are unwilling to afford me the clay necessary to do so, which renders the task hopeless. I fear it would only be a waste of our time and yours for my colleagues and me to participate further in this investigation. And at this point, time is something we have precious little of. Surely you must realize that Alistair Ainsworth's life hangs in the balance and that chances of a rescue fade away with each passing hour." Joanna waited for a reply, but when none was forthcoming, she turned to my father and said, "Perhaps we should have Watson call the First Sea Lord and ask that he intervene."

"The First Sea Lord is not so easily reached," Dunn challenged.

"He is when you are a personal friend."

An uneasy silence hung in the air as Joanna and the lieutenant locked eyes, neither giving ground. Seconds slowly ticked by in the stillness.

"I believe I have his number," my father said, reaching into his coat pocket for a card that Sir Harold Whitlock had given him last year while visiting us at 221b Baker Street on a sensitive matter. "It is a direct line, as I recall."

"Allow me a moment," Dunn urged, and hurried over to a telephone on a desk in the far corner. We were to later learn that the Germans had insisted the homeowner's phone remain in place as part of the rental agreement, and had paid a handsome fee for this service. Dunn dialed a number, then turned his back to us and spoke in a low, indistinguishable voice. Apparently he was seeking permission from those in high position. But the request was no simple matter, for he was forced to wait several minutes before an answer was given. Finally Dunn replaced the receiver and turned to us.

"Keep in mind you are sworn to the Official Secrets Act," Dunn reminded.

"We are aware," Joanna said.

Dunn went to the door and ensured that it was tightly closed, then came back to us. Despite the total privacy, he spoke in a low voice. "What I am about to disclose to you is so sensitive it is known by only five people in the entire British Empire. These include the Prime Minister, the First Sea Lord, the director of Naval Intelligence, the assistant director, and myself. Not a word of what you hear is to be breathed outside this room. Am I clearly understood?"

The three of us nodded in unison.

"Alistair Ainsworth is the highest-ranking member in a clandestine, top-secret cryptanalysis unit. His primary function is to make certain all of our naval codes are fail-safe and cannot be deciphered by the enemy. Thus, coded messages of the greatest priority pass before his eyes on a daily basis. He and his colleagues study the code and once broken they then instruct us on how best to alter it to one that is indecipherable."

"I take it they have a high rate of success," Joanna ventured.

"Remarkably so. They seem to do it with such ease that we often ask them to assist in deciphering some of our enemy's most convoluted coded messages. And Ainsworth is the most talented of the lot." Dunn paused to take a long, heavy breath. "If he worked for the Germans, I fear we would have lost this war long ago. And now he may be doing exactly that."

Joanna asked, "You mentioned he worked within a group. How many are there?"

"Four, among which are some of the most unusual characters you will ever encounter. You see, they are creative thinkers, with remarkable intellects, whose greatest joy in life is unraveling complex riddles. They are nonmilitary personnel, with a variety of backgrounds; they include linguists, chess masters, and crossword experts. They can solve a difficult crossword puzzle in minutes, and untangle an anagram as soon as the letters are written down. Play charades with them and they not only produce the correct answer, but five others that are equally as good. They are multilingual and can speak German, French, and Spanish in the same paragraph. Yet they have no overwhelming ambition in life and are at their happiest when faced with a seemingly unsolvable problem. These features make them the perfect fit for our cryptanalysis unit. They break codes in an indirect and creative fashion, using reasoning that is not obvious and has no relation to step-by-step logic. Needless to say, their value is so great it cannot be measured."

"Ainsworth will no doubt be missed," my father said. "But you still have three members of this group to continue their important work."

"I am afraid our problem goes much deeper than that," Dunn explained. "You must keep in mind that German intelligence has no doubt intercepted most of the messages we have sent and, although undeciphered, have them on file. If Ainsworth is broken, they will read those coded messages as easily as they read their newspapers, and have access to the most vital information including our war plans, naval strategies, and clandestine operations. It would give Germany an advantage from which we might never recover."

"You are facing yet another dilemma that is equally serious," Joanna warned. "There is a spy in your midst. Someone had to know of Ainsworth's position and that someone pointed him out to the Germans."

"We are quite aware of that," Dunn said. "I can assure you that individual is not the Prime Minister, the First Sea Lord, the director of Intelligence, or the assistant director. That leaves Ainsworth, whom we can exclude, and his three colleagues whom we cannot."

"But if one of the three is involved, why bother to have Ainsworth kidnapped?" Joanna asked. "The Germans have their man planted in the group and capable of feeding them information on a continuing basis. Why would they even hint that they have a reliable, well-concealed operative in the unit?"

"Exactly, madam," said Dunn. "So you can see our quandary. We are faced with the crime of espionage and have no credible suspects."

"Every one of those mentioned is a suspect until proven otherwise," Joanna insisted.

"But certainly not the Prime Minister or First Sea Lord or—"

"They all have secretaries and undersecretaries close at hand," Joanna interrupted. "All that is required to set the wheels of espionage in motion is a simple eavesdrop or careless utterance or discarded document that should have been destroyed but wasn't. One misstep by those privy to this cryptanalysis unit and your wall of absolute security disappears."

"I remain convinced that those at the highest echelon are not involved," Dunn persisted. "It must be one of the three in the unit."

"Well then, you should pursue your avenue of investigation while we pursue ours."

"Which is?"

"Oh, there is no need to go into that now. It is best you take your route and we ours. Along the way we can compare findings, which may very well complement each other."

On that note we returned to our carriage where Toby Two, although happy to see us, showed no interest in tracking further. As Joanna had predicted, the heavy rain that was now coming to an end had blotted out any further traces of a chloroform trail.

"Where to now?" I asked.

"The single source most likely to lead us to Alistair Ainsworth."

Joanna held up an identification card taken from Alistair Ainsworth's wallet. Although the card was soaked, Ainsworth's home address remained clearly visible.

5

The Sister

As our carriage traveled south to Knightsbridge, Joanna peered out at the fashionable stores on Brompton Road and appeared to be preoccupied with her own thoughts. Her silence was unusual in that she believed nothing cleared up a puzzling case like stating it to another person. On occasion she would even wake me and my father in the middle of the night to serve as sounding boards for her conclusions. Thus, her lack of words during our journey made me wonder if Joanna already had a solution at hand. We rode on for several more blocks before she nodded to herself and turned her attention to us.

"At times," Joanna noted, "there is nothing more deceptive than an obvious fact."

"I recall Sherlock Holmes making a similar statement," my father said.

"And for good reason," Joanna continued on. "When a fact is taken for granted, it often loses its importance. Such as the instance of the wallet in the water tank."

I shrugged. "It is obvious that Alistair Ainsworth left it behind to alert us to his presence in the house."

"So it would appear on the surface."

"Do you believe Ainsworth had another purpose in mind?"

"Beyond any doubt. You see, he was convinced we would find the house where he was held captive."

"How could he possibly know that?"

"His major clue was the odor of chloroform Verner carried with him," Joanna elucidated. "When Verner was brought into the house, he was in all likelihood tortured in front of Ainsworth in an effort to frighten the intelligence agent and thus break him. Ainsworth detected the scent of chloroform on Verner's clothes and knew it had been placed there to serve as a trail to be followed."

"He could not have been aware of that," I argued. "Verner was a doctor and might have accidentally spilled a bit of chloroform on himself while opening a bottle of the anesthetic."

"No, no, John," Joanna said, shaking her head at me. "You are thinking like Lestrade and Dunn. Rather, you should place yourself in the position of Alistair Ainsworth who is a master when it comes to creating and solving puzzles. Let us go through the deductions, step by step, just as Ainsworth would have. First, Verner was taken captive early in the morning, prior to opening his practice. So the question must be asked— what was he doing with a bottle of chloroform at that moment, much less somehow managing to douse himself with it? Secondly, if that occurred, Verner had more than enough time to change clothes and remove the unpleasant odor from his examining room. Thus, with these points in mind, Ainsworth would have correctly deduced that Verner spilled chloroform on himself for the sole purpose of leaving a trail, just as I had instructed the doctor earlier. All of these facts, when taken together, allow for only one conclusion. Ainsworth knew the authorities would not be far behind."

"And closing in," my father added. "For there was the very real possibility that Verner had alerted Scotland Yard about the house and its captive."

"That too," Joanna said with a firm nod. "The German agents, who we know are very skilled, would have surely detected the odor of chloroform on Verner. Which of course was another reason for them to kill him. The last thing they wanted was to leave a strong scent for us to follow."

I said quickly, "But if Ainsworth was aware the authorities would arrive shortly to rescue him, why did he bother to leave his wallet in the water tank?"

"Because if the attempt was delayed or failed, he wanted to inform us how to go about finding him," Joanna replied.

My father gave her a puzzled look. "I am not sure I follow here. The wallet only contained two five-pound notes, several identification cards, and a picture of his frail sister."

"It was the sister's picture that was so revealing," Joanna told us. "He obviously loves her and cares for her very much, and that is why he carries her picture. We know she is crippled with severe rheumatism and is for the most part confined to her home. Thus, it is fair to assume that Alistair Ainsworth shares the stories of his life in London with her. It would be her major contact with the outside world."

"But Ainsworth's work with Naval Intelligence is so secret, he would never speak of this with her," I said.

"It is not his work, but his life away from the agency that is so vital here," Joanna explained. "Remember, Alistair Ainsworth was not taken prisoner in his workplace, but somewhere outside the agency, preferably in a secluded location where no one could see the capture or hear his cry for help."

"A wooded area? A forest perhaps?" my father suggested.

"Not necessarily," Joanna said. "There are more than a few

tucked-away places in London where capture could have oc-curred."

"Such as?"

"A pub on a dark street late at night, a female companion who lives on the outskirts of the city, and so on. The list is quite long."

"How do we go about narrowing it down?"

"Like most of us, Alistair Ainsworth is a creature of habit, and that will dictate his whereabouts. Thus, our best course of action is to learn of his daily habits and follow them."

"Which of course his invalid sister could provide."

"Spot on, Watson, for it is with her that he shares the de-tails of his life away from home."

"And you believe this will lead us to Ainsworth's captors?"

Joanna nodded as we turned onto a street lined with stately, handsome homes. "Think of it as the first piece of the puz-zle. Solve it and the other pieces will begin to fall into place."

Our carriage drew up to the curb in front of a two-story, sandstone house on Cadogan Square. It had an imposing ma-hogany door, with brass fittings that shone in the late-morning light. Another carriage was waiting outside.

"We must be delicate with our questioning," Joanna cau-tioned. "Make no comments or inquiries that might dispar-age the man, for his sister will be very protective of him."

"But surely we will have to ask about possible vices," I said.

"If the subject arises, pry gently."

As we alighted from our carriage, the drapes covering a first-floor window opened briefly, then closed. I thought I saw a fleeting shadow behind them, but could not be sure. It re-quired a full minute before our rap on the mahogany door was answered.

"May I help you?" asked a rotund housekeeper with her gray hair held tightly in place by a bun.

"We are here to see Miss Ainsworth," Joanna replied.

"She is not receiving visitors today, madam."

"Oh, I am certain she will see us," Joanna said. "Tell her that the daughter of Sherlock Holmes wishes to speak with her."

"Y-yes, ma'am," the housekeeper stammered, obviously in awe of Joanna and her lineage. "Please come in and wait while I announce your presence."

The name of Sherlock Holmes was still like magic in all of London and this aura carried over to Joanna, in large measure because of the stories I chronicled about her remarkable crime-solving skills. Indeed, her public esteem was now approaching the same level as that of her father before her. Yet Joanna for the most part appeared unimpressed by her fame. To her, it was just a by-product of her deductive abilities.

We stepped into an eye-catching foyer that spoke of both wealth and taste. It was done in white marble, with a fresco of angelic figures painted on the ceiling that were reminiscent of those in Michelangelo's Sistine Chapel. The air around us was still and very, very warm and held the aroma of burned wood.

Joanna whispered, "I take it those with chronic illnesses are quite sensitive to the cold."

My father nodded. "Particularly those with painful rheumatism."

"If the conversation turns to her rheumatic condition, I should like you to do the questioning."

"Are there areas I should avoid?"

"Use your own discretion."

The housekeeper returned and, with a half bow, led us into a large drawing room. The temperature of the air was now even higher, due in part to a large fireplace with its logs burning brightly. The furniture was French antique, the walls adorned with Italian tapestries and paintings of aristocratic personages. Near the fireplace sat a tiny, frail woman in a cushioned wheelchair. Despite the deformities of her hands, she was well groomed, with her hair neatly cut and dyed and her makeup carefully applied. By contrast, next to her was a tall, large-boned woman, with a most attractive face and long, brown hair that cascaded down to her shoulders.

"Thank you for seeing us on such short notice," Joanna began after introducing us and stating the purpose of our visit.

"It is I who should thank you," Emma Ainsworth replied. "I believe you know my dear friend Lady Jane Hamilton."

"Indeed I do, for my late husband, John Blalock, was best man at her wedding," Joanna said, and turned to the visitor. "It is always good to see you, Jane, but of course not under these dreadful circumstances."

"I too wish it was otherwise," said Lady Jane. "We so hope you can solve this terrible mystery and help locate our Tubby."

"I shall do my best."

"If you wish, I can leave and give you complete privacy," Lady Jane offered.

"Please stay, for you may be able to provide information that could assist our search."

After we were all seated, Joanna asked, "May I inquire as to how your brother acquired the nickname Tubby?"

A faint smile came to Emma Ainsworth's face. "As a child my brother loved to play with his toy boats while bathing in a tub. Our parents had to literally pull him from the water, against his pleas and demands to remain. He would cry out, 'The battle is not done!'"

"The battle?" Joanna queried.

Emma nodded. "Yes, the battle. You see, Tubby did not

simply play with the ships, as one might expect. He would set up harbors and fortifications, then move the fleet around so he could devise various strategies for naval warfare. He could recite the tonnage and speeds of the ships, from destroyers to battleships, and how well they could maneuver and what their strengths and weaknesses were. My brother has always been remarkably bright, and this was evident even as a child."

"I suspect it was this obvious intellect that led to his current position in the government," Joanna pried gently.

Emma shrugged. "He never spoke of it, except to say it was part of the war effort."

Lady Jane volunteered, "He once confided that his assignment was top secret, but would say no more. He would not speak of where he worked and with whom."

"As would be expected," Joanna said, and leaned in closer to the fire to warm her hands before turning to Emma Ainsworth. "On the day of your brother's disappearance, please recall every step that you knew he took."

"It was his habit to awaken early, usually at six, dress and have breakfast by seven, then read the newspaper prior to departing. He did precisely this on the last day I saw him. He called at three to inform me not to wait for dinner, for he would be dining out with a friend."

"Did he mention which friend?" Joanna asked.

"He did not, although I assumed it would be Roger Marlowe, who is a lifelong chum and works alongside Tubby at the government office."

"Could you give me a bit more information on Roger Marlowe?" Joanna requested.

"It might be best to let Jane answer," Emma replied. "She and Roger and Tubby grew up together, and she was once engaged to Roger."

"Briefly engaged," Lady Jane said with no bitterness. "But

in response to your question, Tubby and Roger are much the same. Both are exceptionally bright, both educated at Eton, then Cambridge where they received honors degrees in archaeology. Shortly thereafter they traveled to Germany to study ancient Greek at the University of Heidelberg. They were both very keen on interpreting some recently discovered papyrus sheets that dated back thousands of years."

"What year were they at Heidelberg?" Joanna asked at once.

"Just before the turn of the century," Lady Jane recalled.

"Eighteen ninety-seven, to be exact," Emma answered.

"Did they stay on longer?" Joanna asked.

"Oh yes, but in a roundabout way," Emma replied. "They mastered ancient Greek in short order and went on numerous archaeological expeditions that were sponsored by the university. I believe those were the best years of Tubby's life, but they were interrupted when I came down with severe rheumatism and he had to return home to look after me. I always felt very guilty about that."

"He was simply doing what would be expected of a good brother," my father commented.

"True," Emma said. "But that did not lessen my guilt. To be near me, Tubby took a position at Imperial College where he remained until being called into government service."

"Did Roger Marlowe return as well?" Joanna asked.

Emma shook her head, which brought about neck pain and caused her to wince. "Not for several years. He continued to excel at Heidelberg and became so fluent in German that he was given the opportunity to join their faculty. But he chose to return to Cambridge where he delved into mathematics. It was during this time that Roger's family suffered painful financial reverses that forced him to return to London where a more gainful position awaited him."

"His mathematical equations were so astute that several

were adopted by the London School of Economics," Lady Jane noted. "He was eventually offered a professorship there, but it held little interest for him."

Joanna's brow went up. "But surely such an advancement would have been far more remunerative and aided his family who was in need at the time."

"It would have kept them afloat, but little more," Lady Jane said. "However, with the sale of country land, the family straightened out their affairs, but never to the level they once enjoyed."

"So you have kept up with Roger over the years," Joanna concluded.

"We would run into each other on occasion," Lady Jane said evasively.

"At Cambridge?"

"At social gatherings here in London," Lady Jane replied. "He left Cambridge for his current position several years ago."

"I take it that Alistair and Roger Marlowe have remained close friends," Joanna said.

"The best of friends," Emma emphasized. "In addition to their remarkable intellects, they share a good many other qualities. Both are what one would call delightful rogues. They enjoy life to the fullest in every way."

"Such as?" Joanna probed.

"They enjoy their drink and can often be found at the Admiralty where they are well-known."

Joanna's brow went up again, but this time it stayed up. "The Admiralty? Are you referring to His Majesty's Navy?"

A brief smile crossed Emma's face. "It is a pub located near Trafalgar Square. They frequent the Admiralty prior to gaming at various casinos."

"Do they gamble often?"

"Quite."

"Is there a single casino they favor?"

"Laurent's is the one Tubby usually speaks of."

"Do you know if they bet heavily?"

I could readily see the reasoning behind Joanna's line of questioning. Betting large sums could lead to large debts that could lead to blackmail.

Emma gave the matter thought. "I do not believe they bet heavily, but they do win with great frequency. You see, both Tubby and Roger are wonderful at mathematics and have thought up a method for counting cards in play and predicting those that remain in the deck."

"The casinos must be aware of this."

Emma nodded. "So much so that Tubby and Roger have reached an agreement with the casino, in which they are allowed to play but must limit their winnings to twenty pounds or less. Again you can see that it is not the money but the challenge of defeating a skilled opponent that is so important to my brother."

"But their constant winning must have drawn the attention of other gamblers," Joanna said. "I would expect the casinos to somehow limit your brother's access to the gaming tables."

"Oh, I can assure you they try. Since the owners cannot lawfully deny my brother and Roger entrance to their establishment, they have devised a method to keep them away from the tables. As soon as the casino operators see the faces of Tubby and Roger, they signal for employees who are mingling about to quickly take all the open seats at the table. Thus, none are available for the new arrivals. I forget the names by which these employees are called, but Tubby assures me they are present and perform their tasks on a moment's notice."

"They are referred to as *bonnets*," Joanna informed.

"Yes! Exactly! How did you come by this information?"

"I read it in a magazine," Joanna said. "Their usual role is to play at the table and bet heavily, using the casino's money. They either win or lose large sums and act out their feigned emotions while doing so. These acts are said to draw crowds to the table and encourage others to bet."

"That is word for word what Tubby once told me," Emma said, and gave Joanna an admiring look. "It is extraordinary that you would know this."

Joanna waved away the compliment and asked directly, "Does your brother drink a great deal at home or at the Admiralty?"

Emma shook her head, but this time slowly and carefully. "He never imbibes more than a glass or two of Scotch, and I have never seen him intoxicated."

"Does he have any vices you disapprove of?"

"Only his occasional visits to the opium dens," Emma said frankly.

"How often were these visits?"

"Quite infrequent, I believe," Emma answered. "It only came up because I once noticed the peculiar aroma of burned maple on his jacket. He explained it was the smell of opium that resulted from a visit to the opium den. He apologized for the aroma, and since I never encountered it again, I assumed he did not revisit the opium den."

"A reasonable assumption," Joanna said, and leaned back in her chair. I could sense there was another question she wished to ask about the use of opium, but decided against it. "Tell me, Miss Ainsworth, has your brother in the past ever spent the night away?"

"Only on the rarest of occasions. When he does, he always calls to inform me and make certain the housekeeper will stay the night to look after my needs."

"And to make certain you take your medicines," my father added.

"Indeed, Dr. Watson," Emma said, and held up her gnarled fingers. "Even with medication, these poor fingers can barely grasp the aspirin tablets I require on a continuing basis."

"I know they give you some comfort."

"They ease the pain, but unfortunately do little to prevent the unsightly deformities." Emma attempted to make a pinching motion with her fingers, but was unable to do so. "I can no longer hold a chess piece, not even a king or queen, and am thus prevented from playing my favorite game with my brother, who is a chess master. I am convinced it is the heaviest toll this awful disease has taken from me."

"Are you as talented at chess as your brother?" Joanna asked.

"Oh, heavens no! As a matter of fact, Tubby would have been promoted to grandmaster if he so desired," Emma replied. "A number of England's grandmasters will attest to Tubby's remarkable ability at chess. They will tell you that my brother does not concern himself with titles, but only with the challenge of the game."

"Has he actually defeated grandmasters?"

"I believe so from the reports of others, but Tubby would never make mention of it," Emma said, then sighed regretfully and gazed down at her deformed fingers. "I only wish these hands would allow me to play once again with my dear brother."

"There are now several glovelike devices that could help you in that regard," my father suggested.

"I was unaware," Emma said, and seemed to perk up at the helpful advice. "I shall inform Tubby when he—" She stopped in mid-sentence and sadly corrected herself. "If he returns home."

Joanna rose and said, "You have provided information that may well be of assistance."

"So you believe there is hope yet?" Emma asked.

"Only a glimmer," Joanna replied honestly. "But rest assured we shall do our best to bring your brother home safely."

We walked out into a gray, gloomy day and spoke no further until we were seated in our carriage. Joanna stared out at the dense fog that was gathering around us, as if the answer to our problem might lie within.

"I fail to see the glimmer of hope you mentioned," my father said.

"Do not focus on the end, but concern yourself with the beginning," Joanna told him. "There are links here, each of which has to be carefully examined and placed in its appropriate position."

"Like pieces of a game puzzle?"

"Precisely. You see, an observer who has thoroughly understood one link in a series of events should be able to connect all the others, before and after."

"But which is the one link that will lead to the others?"

"That is what we must determine."

Our carriage rode away just as another sudden downpour began. The dour weather so matched my mood that I could not help but comment, "I am afraid time is very much against us. We have so little to go on and soon Ainsworth will be broken, and all will be lost."

"And once they break him, he is a dead man," my father said.

"Do not be so certain of that," Joanna advised.

"Surely once they have the codes in their possession, they will have no further use for him."

"Oh, I suspect that might not be the case."

"Based on what?"

"The fact that Alistair Ainsworth is a chess master and the Germans are not."

6

The Trail

We dined early at 221b Baker Street because Joanna had a surprise journey in store for us later that evening. After a superb dinner of roast beef and Yorkshire pudding, my father and I settled in front of a glowing fire while Joanna paced back and forth across the parlor, oblivious to my presence. The speed of her pacing seemed to correlate with the rate of her deductions, as she nodded at one conclusion and grumbled at another. She continued on for several minutes before reaching for another Turkish cigarette. But then she changed her mind and abruptly turned to us.

"There are three major links that point to the disappearance of Alistair Ainsworth," Joanna proclaimed. "These are . . . the Admiralty pub, Laurent's casino, and an opium den. Which do you consider the most promising?"

My father and I exchanged puzzled looks before I said, "But you stated earlier that Ainsworth was taken prisoner in a secluded location. None of the sites you mentioned measure up. In fact, they are often crowded with people who know one another."

"That is so during the early hours of the evening, but the crowds thin later on. At that time the streets will be deserted, with only a straggler or two about. It is then that the moment is ideal for kidnapping."

"I favor a casino, for they stay open until the wee hours of the morning," my father proposed.

"They do indeed," Joanna agreed. "But keep in mind the players in these gambling halls are for the most part well-to-do and would have their carriages waiting at the doorstep."

"But the same would hold true for the Admiralty pub and most certainly for the opium dens, for the latter are located in the very worst section of London," I argued. "Ainsworth's carriage would be within shouting distance."

"True," Joanna said. "So we can conclude that the location does not seem to favor one establishment over the other. Nevertheless, I favor the pub or the opium den, for after drinks or drugs one's defenses would be impaired and thus make the taking easier."

"But that alone would not exclude the casino," I countered.

"Of course not, and that is why we must visit all three tonight."

I gave the plan thought and a difficulty came immediately to mind. "We know the location of the Admiralty pub and Laurent's casino, but finding the opium den Ainsworth visited is another matter. There are dozens of those establishments in East London, some of which are hidden from sight."

"There is a way to narrow down the number," Joanna said, unconcerned.

My father asked, "Would it not be easier to simply call Roger Marlowe, with whom Ainsworth presumably spent the evening, and inquire about the places they visited?"

"You are assuming Roger Marlowe is not involved in the kidnapping," Joanna said.

"But he works for the intelligence unit," my father asserted. "I am certain he was carefully vetted before being allowed in. In addition, he and Ainsworth are the closest of friends."

"That does not exclude him," Joanna said. "Recall that Marlowe spent years at the University of Heidelberg and was so well thought of he was offered a faculty position. Moreover, he speaks the language fluently and no doubt still has friends and contacts there."

"Are you contending that he may have an allegiance to Germany?" my father cried out.

"I am saying that everyone is a suspect until proven otherwise," Joanna said. "With of course the exception of Emma Ainsworth."

"And Lady Jane Hamilton," I opined.

"Do not be so quick there," Joanna cautioned. "There is a history behind this woman that you may not be aware of."

My father and I leaned forward to catch every word.

"Some is gossip, some is fact," Joanna said carefully.

"How are we to distinguish between the two?" I asked.

"In this case it is the opinion of most that the truth outweighed the rumor," Joanna said, then continued on with the story. "It was widely believed that Lady Jane had an affair with a handsome German diplomat some years ago while her husband was at sea in command of one of His Majesty's warships. The affair ended with the return of her husband and the transfer of her lover to another part of the Continent."

"Are you saying the affair continues?" I asked in a low voice.

"I am saying no one knows," Joanna replied. "But the connection was there and may still exist."

"And there was her involvement with Roger Marlowe who may have also come under German influence," I noted.

"*Was* involved, you say?" Joanna asked in a questioning tone. "What makes you believe it has ended?"

"She stated their engagement was brief," I recalled.

"That does not exclude a secret, ongoing romance," Joanna said. "A married woman who has strayed once may well do so again, particularly with a former lover."

"For which we have no proof," I remarked.

"But the suspicion remains," Joanna said. "And it thus should be kept in mind."

"Which brings yet another unknown piece to the puzzle," I grumbled. "We seem to be going off on tangents."

"I too am not certain these confusing details bring us any closer to Alistair Ainsworth," my father agreed. "If anything, they seem to be clouding the picture even more."

"To the contrary, Watson," Joanna said. "I believe a solution will shortly be at hand."

"And how do you propose coming to such a resolution?"

"By employing my father's deductive reasoning," Joanna replied. "I shall take note of all the details and circumstances relating to a single event—namely the disappearance of Alistair Ainsworth—and put them together in their proper order. Once this is done, we shall be able to explain how the event occurred."

"But where do we begin?"

"By discovering the major link that holds the key to our mystery," Joanna responded. "Everything revolves around the site where the kidnapping occurred. That is where the link lies."

"Pray tell, Joanna, why do you place such emphasis on the locale from which Ainsworth disappeared?"

"Because, if my assumptions are correct, it will lead us to the person who betrayed him."

Before leaving our rooms, Joanna called Inspector Lestrade and asked that he join us at Laurent's casino. The request was most unusual, for Joanna much preferred to follow her own line of investigation while Scotland Yard went about theirs. From experience she felt Lestrade, although tough and tenacious, could all too often be led astray and pursue avenues that were unproductive.

"Lestrade is so unimaginative," Joanna said as our carriage passed the Marble Arch and turned onto Park Lane. "He searches for hidden clues when the most important ones lie before his very eyes."

"Why then invite him to join us at Laurent's?" I asked.

"Keep in mind, John, that Lestrade has police powers and we do not," Joanna replied. "We could be denied entrance to the casino, but not with the inspector at our side. He can enter, investigate, and even obtain search warrants, all under the law. In addition, my questions will be answered more truthfully in Lestrade's presence, for not to do so could be considered obstruction of justice. Thus at times Lestrade can be a most helpful ally. The powers he has also explain why he is so intimately associated with Lieutenant Dunn's search for Alistair Ainsworth. Dunn's Naval Intelligence unit is a division of His Majesty's Secret Service, which has immense authority but no police powers. For this reason Dunn requires the inspector's presence."

"Do you believe Lestrade will bring Dunn along to the casino?" my father asked.

"I would think not," Joanna replied. "A uniformed naval officer would be of no help at this point and might well serve as an unwanted distraction."

Our carriage came to a stop at the elegant entrance to Laurent's casino, whereupon a uniformed doorman rushed up to open our door. As we stepped out, Inspector Lestrade hurried over to us.

He tipped his derby and, after the amenities, asked, "Is there reason to believe the casino is involved?"

"That is to be determined," Joanna said.

We entered a large front room that was brilliantly lighted. On one side stood a buffet covered with wine and liquors and behind that a smaller room given up to cold chicken, salads, and other dishes. Directly before us were long gaming tables covered with green cloth that were surrounded by players and governed by croupiers and dealers. Toward the rear were round card tables above which arose a cloud of tobacco smoke. The noise of loud conversations filled the air.

A short, rotund man wearing a well-fitted tuxedo rushed over to us. Behind the casino manager were two large, formidable men who blocked our view of the gaming room. They positioned themselves so that we could not see the throng of gamblers, nor could the gamblers see us. Their purpose, I assume, was to keep the well-known Inspector Lestrade out of sight, so as not to upset those at the tables. For obvious reasons, the presence of police was not welcomed at casinos.

"May I be of service, Inspector?" the casino manager asked.

"There are questions my associates believe you can answer," Lestrade replied. "Please do so and keep in mind this is an official investigation."

"Is this regarding activities of an employee within our casino?" the manager asked worriedly.

"It is regarding one of your players," Joanna said, stepping forward. "We are told he frequents your establishment. His name is Alistair Ainsworth."

"We are very much aware of Mr. Ainsworth, but have not seen him this week."

"Is that unusual?"

"Quite so, madam. We count on him visiting the casino every Monday night, for that is his custom."

"As is his custom of winning."

"He does well."

"Not to exceed twenty pounds."

"He has set limits," the manager said, now alerted that Joanna already knew a great deal about Alistair Ainsworth, for this information would only be shared by those closest to the gambler. "This is mutually agreed upon."

"But I suspect this agreement did not extend to his losses."

The casino manager nodded ever so briefly, as if not willing to acknowledge the fact.

"Was Mr. Ainsworth accompanied by others while gambling?"

"Sometimes he was alone, but on most occasions Mr. Marlowe sat across from him."

"Was the limit to include Mr. Marlowe's winnings as well?"

"It was and for good reason," the manager answered. "They had a method, we believe, in which they could mentally count cards and know which remained in the deck."

"Cheating, were they?" Lestrade interrupted.

"They claimed it was simply luck, but we thought otherwise," the manager said. "Is that the purpose of your visit tonight?"

Joanna ignored the question. "Was Mr. Ainsworth accompanied by anyone other than Mr. Marlowe?"

The manager thought for a moment. "On a number of occasions, a rather striking woman was with them."

"Describe her in detail," Joanna said at once.

"She was a large woman, not in girth, but about the up-per torso, with a most attractive face and long, brown hair that flowed down to her shoulders. It was her hair that immedi-ately grabbed one's attention."

Lady Jane Hamilton! My father and I exchanged knowing glances, for the manager had described the woman perfectly.

"Did she gamble?" Joanna asked.

"Never."

"Did they leave together?"

"Always, and usually quite late."

"To the best of your recollection, did Mr. Ainsworth as-sociate with any others in the casino?"

"Not that I was aware."

Joanna let the new information sink in, then looked over to my father and me. "Do either of you have questions?"

"Just one or two," my father said. "Tell me, manager, has anyone else inquired about Mr. Ainsworth?"

"Not to my knowledge," the manager answered promptly. "But if one did, it would prove fruitless. We scrupulously guard any and all information about our clientele."

"Did you ever see Mr. Ainsworth intoxicated?"

"Never."

My father gestured to me but I hesitated, for I had no fur-ther questions regarding Ainsworth. Yet Lady Jane Hamilton remained on my mind. "You mentioned a female companion a moment ago. Do you know her name?"

"I did not inquire."

"Did it appear there was a special relationship between the woman and either man?"

"None was apparent."

Joanna nodded at my question, obviously pleased I had asked it. Seeing we had no further inquiries, she thanked the manager for his time and led the way out into a clear, brisk evening. The traffic on Park Lane was heavy and loud, so there was little chance we would be overheard as we strolled toward our carriage.

"Not very informative," Lestrade pronounced.

"At least we can say with certainty that Ainsworth was not taken at the casino," Joanna noted.

"Which I would have thought unlikely, even before our visit," Lestrade said.

"True," Joanna said. "But now it is entirely out of the question, for Ainsworth was frequently accompanied by friends and that would have surely dissuaded the Germans."

Lestrade shrugged his shoulders, unimpressed with Joanna's conclusions. "In your phone call you mentioned a second place you wished to visit. Perhaps that will prove more rewarding."

"We shall see. Please be good enough to follow us to the Admiralty, a pub frequented by Alistair Ainsworth."

We remained silent as our carriage traveled down Park Lane and turned left at the statue of the Duke of Wellington. But our collective minds were centered on Lady Jane Hamilton. Why had she lied to us? Why had she told us she occasionally ran into Roger Marlowe while in fact she was a frequent companion at Laurent's casino? Was she still close and romantically involved with Marlowe, and was either or both still connected to the Germans? There was one certainty, however. Both knew of Alistair Ainsworth's habits and could have betrayed him to the enemy.

"Perhaps we should requestion Lady Jane," I suggested, breaking the silence.

"To what end?" Joanna asked. "She would simply say she had forgotten about the visits to the casino and considered them unimportant. She might insist they were spur-of-the-moment invitations."

"While we believe otherwise."

"But cannot prove."

I was surprised by Joanna's response. "Are you saying we should ignore it?"

"I am saying we should docket the information, for it may become important later on," Joanna advised. "We should do nothing to alienate or alarm Lady Jane, for I believe there is much more to her than meets the eye."

"Such as a romantic assignation with Roger Marlowe?"

"At this point that is a guess and guesses will not help our cause," Joanna said. "For the present, let us be aware that Lady Jane is being less than honest, and thus she is hiding something."

"But what?"

"A secret that she guards closely."

Our carriage continued on, and reached Piccadilly Circus with its fashionable shops and restaurants. Couples were leisurely strolling about on a pleasant evening, seemingly oblivious to the depressing news from the war front. The Second Champagne Offensive was not going well and our losses were said to be dreadful. It was fortunate indeed that the public was unaware of the disappearance of Alistair Ainsworth and the disaster that awaited England were he not rescued promptly. As Dunn had stated, every man had his breaking point and it was only a matter of time before Ainsworth reached his.

We came to a halt in front of the Admiralty, which was located on Trafalgar Square, just across from Lord Nelson's monument. Lestrade led our way into the large, well-appointed pub that had a long, polished bar with throngs of people crowded around it. A curved flight of stairs ascended gracefully to a noisy second tier. Lestrade was familiar with the Admiralty and explained that such crowds were not unusual at this hour, for it was a favorite of theatergoers and government officials who worked nearby. From my vantage point, all those in attendance appeared to be well dressed and upper middle class.

At the bar Lestrade showed his credentials to the barkeep and said, "We require information on one of your patrons. Any and all details may prove to be helpful, and thus nothing should be withheld."

The tone of Lestrade's voice placed the barkeep instantly on guard. "Is—is this individual said to be a regular here?"

"That is to be determined," Lestrade went on, without answering the question. "The gentleman we are interested in is Mr. Alistair Ainsworth."

"Oh, of course," the barkeep said, now at ease. "We see Mr. Ainsworth virtually every evening at six or so."

"Was he in attendance this past Monday evening?"

The barkeep thought back before answering with a firm nod. "He stopped in, with his colleague, Mr. Marlowe, at the usual time."

"How long did they stay?"

"No more than a half hour, during which they both enjoyed a glass of single-malt Scotch before going on their way."

"Did they chat with others?"

"Of that I can't be sure."

"Yet you seemed to remember their presence without hesitation."

"That is because they always order *Old Vatted Glenlivet*, a most expensive Scotch that very few can afford."

"Were there any foreigners about that evening?"

The barkeep shrugged. "Inspector, we see a good many tourists in our establishment."

"Any of German extraction?"

The barkeep's face hardened. "They would not dare."

Lestrade motioned to Joanna to indicate his line of questioning was finished.

"I assume that Mr. Ainsworth and Mr. Marlowe are employed nearby, like many of your patrons," Joanna began.

"Indeed they are, ma'am," the barkeep replied promptly. "They labor with the Admiralty Club."

"The Admiralty Club, you say!" Joanna exclaimed, feigning real interest. "Are they associated with His Majesty's Royal Navy?"

"Oh no, ma'am," the barkeep replied. "I believe they took that name because the rooms they occupy are located on the uppermost floor above us."

I smiled inwardly, admiring Joanna's clever interrogation technique. She was well aware of how the club had gained its name, but pretended ignorance to gauge the accuracy and depth of the barkeep's knowledge.

"Did you ever inquire about their work?" Joanna asked.

"I did, and they were quite eager to speak of it. They spend all their time devising word games and puzzles for newspapers and magazines. Since they were so finely dressed and drank the most expensive of Scotches, I could only assume they were well paid for their services."

"Are they the only members of the Admiralty Club?"

"I can't be sure of that, ma'am. You see, they do not go through the pub to reach the third floor. There are stairs at the rear of the building that allow them to enter."

"I take it you never hear voices through your ceiling."

The barkeep shook his head. "They are quiet as church mice."

"Do the pair ever stay late into the evening?"

"Never."

"Are they ever accompanied by a woman?"

"Not to my knowledge."

"I have one final question that I would like you to consider carefully," Joanna said. "Is it possible that Mr. Ainsworth, without your knowledge, returned later this past evening for a nightcap?"

The barkeep rubbed his forehead while he concentrated. "I think that is most unlikely. As I mentioned, the gentlemen insisted on *Old Vatted Glenlivet*. When I served them Monday evening, I noted the bottle was nearly depleted and had enough remaining for only two or so more drinks. Because of this, I placed an order for an additional bottle." He turned and reached for an elegantly crafted bottle on a shelf behind him, then held it up for us to see. "The amount remaining is the same as when I poured the pair their drinks earlier Monday evening."

"An astute observation," Joanna praised. "Thank you for your assistance."

Outside, a thick mist was forming and the air was once again filled with moisture. Joanna looked about before gazing up to the windows on the third floor. I followed her line of vision and saw that the rooms were dimly lighted. There were no shadows or figures moving about.

"I believe you have dug another dry well," Lestrade remarked.

"So it would seem," Joanna said.

"I trust there are no other stops required of me this evening."

"None that cannot wait."

"Well and good, then," Lestrade said and, tipping his derby, bade us a pleasant good-night.

We entered our carriage and remained silent until Lestrade was far out of earshot. Only then did Joanna rap on the ceiling and give the driver an East London address.

She sighed to herself and commented, "Lestrade detects the important clues, but in this instance fails to see their significance."

"Which clues in particular?" I asked.

"The ones that make it clear that Ainsworth was not taken captive in the early evening at the pub, which indicates the capture took place elsewhere."

"But there are no clues to indicate where."

"Those will not be handed down to you on a platter, John. They must be sought and placed in order to learn where Ainsworth and Marlowe traveled to after leaving the pub."

"How can one go about gaining that information?"

"By a number of avenues," Joanna said, as we left Trafalgar Square behind. "First, as you no doubt noticed, there is a line of taxis outside the pub that drop people off and take them away. It would not be difficult to question the drivers and learn if one picked up the pair and where they were let off."

"That seems a long shot," my father mused aloud.

"Well then, here is one that is not so long," Joanna went on. "It is now close to eight, yet the lights are still on in the rooms occupied by the Admiralty Club."

"So?" I questioned.

"Which indicates they work into the late hours. It would have taken only a moment to go to those rooms and ask the members if Ainsworth or Marlowe mentioned where they were headed that evening. It is the trail that is so important here and following it has allowed us to exclude the casino and pub as the site of Ainsworth's disappearance."

"If your assumption on the three possible locations is correct, then the opium den is our last and best hope."

"It is, and I believed that to be the case from the very start," Joanna said. "There would be no better place for kidnapping than an opium den that is dimly lighted and open until the late, late hours when the streets are empty and taxis in short supply. In addition, the victim would be groggy and under the influence of the drug, thus rendering him defenseless and easy to capture."

"But there are dozens of these dens in East London, many of which are well hidden."

"True," Joanna said. "But there is only one major player who will know all. His name is Ah Sing and he owns a string of opium dens, which are said to be among the more exclusive in that community. I have read that this particular Chinaman is reputed to know the secret of mixing the best of opium that affords the most pleasant of effects. Our Alistair Ainsworth is accustomed to only the highest quality, as witnessed by his selection of twenty-five-year-old *Old Vatted Glenlivet* at the Admiralty. I therefore believe it is fair to say he would frequent an opium den of the highest quality, such as Ah Sing's."

We rode on in silence until we reached the dark district of Limehouse in East London. Our carriage turned onto Narrow Street and continued on for another block before coming to a stop at a storefront that had Chinese characters written upon its window. Lurking about in a nearby alley I could see shadowy figures in the dimness. The entire setting was ominous, to say the least.

"Perhaps we should have brought Lestrade along, if only for protection," I thought aloud.

Joanna waved away the suggestion. "With the presence of police, everyone within the den would have instantly clammed up or taken cover and our journey would have been wasted."

I motioned with my head toward the alleyway. "Nevertheless, I sense real danger here."

"They are here to protect the clientele," Joanna said without concern. "Should anyone cause a disturbance, those in the shadows would see to it that person disappeared. You must remember that Ah Sing is a businessman, first and foremost, and he will not allow anything or anybody to interfere with his income."

"May I inquire how you came upon this knowledge?"

"I asked," Joanna said, and left it at that.

She rapped on the thick door, which opened immediately. A young, sharp-featured Chinese woman led us into a smoke-hazed den, where beds and mats took up most of the space. Upon them rested Englishmen, upper and lower class, all puffing on long pipes that were being held over lamps. The patrons were reclining in order to hold their lengthy opium pipes over oil lamps that heated the drug until it evaporated, thus allowing the smoker to inhale the vapor.

We were approached by a stout Chinaman in his middle years, wearing Oriental garb and slippers. His jacket was made of blue silk, as was his simple hat that covered all of his hair except for a tightly braided pigtail that extended halfway down his back.

"May I be of service?" he asked in perfect English.

"Are you Ah Sing?" Joanna returned the question.

"I am."

"Excellent. Do you have an office where we can speak?"

"This is my office."

"Then we shall conduct our business here," Joanna said, but moved the conversation nearer to the door, putting some distance between us and the opium smokers. "I have come for information that I believe you can provide. If you are unwilling to do so, I can return later with Inspector Lestrade of Scotland Yard."

Ah Sing seemed unmoved by the mention of Scotland Yard. "May I ask who you are?"

"I am the daughter of Sherlock Holmes."

A hint of a smile came to Ah Sing's inscrutable face. "Are you truly as keen and clever a detective as your father before you?"

"There are those who believe so, Mr. John Johnson," Joanna replied. "Or do you prefer to be called Ah Sing?"

"In here, the name Ah Sing suits me best."

For the hundredth time or more, I was amazed at the depth of Joanna's knowledge of such a wide variety of subjects—which included the mean streets of East London. She seemed to know so much about opium and opium dens, and even more about Ah Sing who had apparently taken on an English name.

"Well then, Ah Sing, tell us if you can recall a frequent visitor to your establishment whose name is Alistair Ainsworth."

Without hesitation, Ah Sing said, "He, along with his friend, preferred the mats in the corner."

"His friend's name?"

"Mr. Marlowe. He never gave us his first name."

"Were they frequent users?"

"They were not addicted, if that is your question. Their custom was to arrive just before nine every Monday night, smoke a pipeful or two and then be on their way."

"Always at that time?"

"Always," Ah Sing reaffirmed. "They insisted on having mats in the far corner, which I reserved for them at an additional fee, I should add."

"Am I to assume Mr. Ainsworth was here this past Monday night?"

"Correct. He arrived at nine and smoked two pipefuls."

"Did Mr. Marlowe do the same?"

Ah Sing considered the question briefly. "I believe he left early, after a single pipeful." He snapped his fingers to a small Chinese woman sitting at a nearby table and uttered a command in their language. In an instant she hurried over and handed him a thick notebook. Ah Sing quickly thumbed through its pages, which recorded the patron's name and amount of opium he used. "Yes. One pipeful for Mr. Marlowe, two for Mr. Ainsworth."

"Was that their usual consumption?"

"On most occasions they each smoked two, but as I said Mr. Marlowe left early, which accounts for his single pipeful."

"So I take it Mr. Ainsworth remained alone to enjoy his second purchase."

"But only briefly, for another customer appeared and took the mat Mr. Marlowe had vacated."

Joanna's brow went up. "Was this new arrival a friend?"

"I could not be certain, but they did talk at length."

"Had you seen this man before?" Joanna asked quickly.

"On occasion," Ah Sing answered. "But he was not a user of any significance. He never had more than one pipeful and rarely finished that."

"I would like you to describe this man in detail," Joanna urged.

Ah Sing thought back, as if trying to picture the man. "He was Caucasian and quite tall, with broad shoulders."

"His hair color?"

"I cannot recall."

"Did you yourself serve him?"

"I did."

"Can you remember any feature of his face that may have stood out? I am thinking in terms of blemishes or scars."

"He had none of those, although I did wonder if he had some ailment affecting his eye," Ah Sing replied. "He continued to blink, as if something was caught up in it."

The German agent with a facial tic! the three of us thought simultaneously. The description was a perfect match.

"Do you have a name recorded for this man?" Joanna asked without inflection.

Ah Sing shook his head. "There was no need, for his visits were so infrequent."

"Did the two of them leave together?"

"Of that I cannot be certain."

Joanna gazed over to my father. "Do you have any questions, Watson?"

"Ah, the inestimable associate of the late Sherlock Holmes," Ah Sing said, obviously pleased with my father's presence.

"I am indeed," my father said, with an acknowledging bow of his head.

"And beside you is your son who so resembles you and has taken over the role of chronicler of the daughter's detective skills."

"I take it you have read his accounts of our mysteries."

"As has every Londoner," Ah Sing said. "It would be my honor to answer any of your questions."

"I have only a few," my father began. "Did you speak with the man?"

"I did."

"Could you detect a foreign accent?"

"Not that I recall."

"From your description of the man, I would think he was a novice at opium smoking."

"Quite. Why a man would spend for a pipeful and use only half is beyond me."

"If there was a fight or struggle or cry for help, would your men stationed in the alley intervene?"

"Instantly," Ah Sing replied. "And the person causing such a disturbance would leave with a reminder never to return."

"Finally, was the duo of Mr. Ainsworth and Mr. Marlowe ever accompanied by a woman?"

"Never in my presence."

A group of Chinese sailors appeared at the door, obviously in a cheerful mood. Ah Sing waved to them and, turning back to us, asked to be excused.

"Of course," Joanna said. "And thank you for your assistance. You have been most helpful."

"So there will be no need for Inspector Lestrade to visit?"

"None whatsoever."

We walked out into a light drizzle and hurried to our carriage. Again I saw lurking shadows in the dark, nearby alley, but now they seemed comforting rather than menacing. And more importantly, it was clear that were Alistair Ainsworth to cry out for help, his attacker would have no doubt been brutally punished, for Ainsworth was obviously a favored patron at the opium den.

"You have concluded that Alistair Ainsworth could not have been taken captive here," Joanna said matter-of-factly.

"How do you manage to read my mind so?" I asked in bewilderment.

"You stared at the shadows in the alleyway and your expression, rather than tightening, became relaxed," Joanna elucidated. "Thus, you no longer see them as a threat, but as protectors who would instantly come to Ainsworth's aid if he cried for assistance. The Germans would have been aware of this as well and planned their attack to take place some distance away from Ah Sing's. With all these facts in mind, you reached the correct conclusion."

"Kudos to both of you," my father chimed in. "Although I must admit that I too was reaching the very same conclusion, based primarily on the shadowy figures lurking nearby."

Joanna nodded. "That was the defining feature."

"And you knew beforehand that the abduction of Alistair

Ainsworth would take place in the vicinity of the opium den," I continued on.

"It was the most likely scenario, but needed to be proven."

"So it seems that question has been answered with certainty," I said. "But does that bring us any closer to finding Alistair Ainsworth?"

"I believe so," Joanna replied. "For it now asks the most important question. Namely, how did the Germans know Ainsworth visited Ah Sing's with such regularity every Monday night at nine o'clock promptly?"

"Because the Germans had to have seen him in the opium den," I answered. "The agent's presence was observed by Ah Sing on several occasions."

"Do you believe the German agent, who was clearly unaccustomed to using opium, just happened to stop in to Ah Sing's and spot Ainsworth in a smoke-filled corner?"

"He had to be informed," I said at once.

"Of course he was. The agent was tipped off by someone who knew exactly every step of Ainsworth's routine."

"It had to be someone in the Admiralty Club," my father concluded.

"Such as Roger Marlowe who departed the den early that evening and left Ainsworth alone," I added.

"His departure was most convenient," Joanna noted.

"But Marlowe's early departure does not prove him guilty of treason," my father said.

"It does not prove him innocent either," said Joanna, and stared out into the rain now pounding down on the dark streets of East London. "We are moving into murky waters here."

"But surely the list of guilty candidates has been narrowed down," my father asserted.

"Do not be so certain of that, Watson," Joanna said as she leaned back and closed her eyes.

It was her way of ending a conversation. It was also her method of concentrating on every clue and detail of a difficult case, and arranging them in an order that led to resolution.

We continued on in silence, with the only sound being made by the wheels of our carriage clocking against the cobblestone road. But my mind remained fixed on who had betrayed Alistair Ainsworth. Certainly Roger Marlowe stood high on the list, with his *convenient* absence from Ah Sing's the night Ainsworth disappeared. Yet there were a number of unnamed suspects to be considered as well, such as anyone who had access to Ainsworth's file at the Admiralty's Office of Naval Intelligence. Or, as Joanna had suggested earlier, perhaps it was a careless word or a document that should have been destroyed but wasn't that led to Ainsworth's identity being uncovered. The possibilities seemed endless.

Turning onto Edgware Road I became acutely aware of the eerie blackness that surrounded us. There was hardly a light to be seen, for even the streetlights had been turned off. All of London was now under a blackout, so as not to guide Germany's zeppelin fleet to its bombing target. Blackouts were only instituted when there was a warning that the hydrogen-filled zeppelins were silently approaching, but these events were happening all too often, bringing terror to London and its nearby cities. In the distance I heard the muffled sound of exploding bombs and could only hope they would not draw closer.

Our carriage came to a stop outside our rooms at 221b Baker Street and we hurried up the stairs to dim the light that remained on in our parlor. At the door we heard the sound of a loudly ringing telephone and dashed in, the three of us wondering who would be calling at this late hour and for what reason. From our collective experience in medicine and crime, we knew such calls often brought the worst of news.

Joanna reached the phone first, with my father and I only a step behind, our ears pricked to catch every word.

"Yes?" Joanna answered, then, after a brief pause, responded, "Ah, Johnny! How are you, my dear son?"

She listened intently for a moment before the worry left her face. Only then did she place a hand over the receiver and whisper to us, "He is well."

My father and I nevertheless remained concerned, for the lad rarely called home and never after the ten o'clock hour. There had to be a problem of some magnitude. But what?

Pressing the phone to her ear, Joanna seemed to be concentrating on each word, yet her face remained expressionless. After a long interval, she spoke again. "How very kind of you . . . Of course. We shall meet you at Paddington Station tomorrow morning . . . Yes, yes. Until then, my dear son."

Placing the phone down, Joanna explained the nature of the call. "What a strange set of events Verner's death has brought into play."

"Pray tell, what?" I asked anxiously.

"It seems that Johnny and Verner's son, Thomas, are friends," Joanna replied. "Poor Thomas is grief-stricken by his father's passing, and the headmaster at Eton thought it best he be accompanied home by a friend. Our Johnny volunteered without hesitation."

"Good show!" my father pronounced proudly.

"As would be expected of the lad," I added. "But I am somewhat surprised they are such close friends, for the good Dr. Verner appeared to be well into his middle years and thus his son should be considerably older than Johnny."

"One might think so," said my father. "But Verner married

late in life to a lovely nurse from St. Bartholomew's Hospital, and his son's age is in all likelihood close to Johnny's."

Joanna asked, "Would I have been familiar with his wife during my stay at St. Bart's?"

"Perhaps," my father replied. "Her maiden name was Mary Todd, as I recall. She was a head nurse on the medical ward, while you spent your days in the surgery section. Still, your paths may have crossed."

"I do believe I remember her," Joanna said, thinking back in time. "She was somewhat delicate, with a kind face and prematurely graying hair."

"That is her."

"How sad for such a tragic circumstance to bring us together again."

"A tragic circumstance indeed," my father concurred. "But I must admit that I am relieved that the phone call did not tell of any misgivings for our Johnny."

"Of that, I am not certain," Joanna said.

"Why so? Was there something amiss in his tone of voice or in the words he spoke?"

"Nothing that one could detect."

"Then what is the basis for your worry?"

"Maternal instinct," Joanna said, and without further comment, she drew the curtains and retired for the night.

7

Paddington Station

An early morning rain was beginning to fall as our four-wheeler turned sharply off Edgware Road and onto Praed Street, where Paddington Station was located. We were making good time and well ahead of schedule when traffic came to an abrupt halt, for before us was a line of ambulances offloading patients into St. Mary's Hospital, which was situated next to the train station.

"Are these casualties from the war?" I inquired.

"I think not," my father replied. "Most likely they are the injured from last night's bombing raid that took its toll on Surrey." He pointed to an arriving vehicle that had the county's name printed on it before adding, "According to the morning newspapers, a nursing home suffered a direct hit, with dozens killed and wounded."

"Bombs have no conscience," said I.

"Nor do the pilots of the zeppelins," my father remarked.

Joanna asked, "Will St. Mary's be prepared to deal with so many badly wounded patients?"

"Not all will come here, for there is a mass casualty plan in place that distributes the patients to the major hospitals throughout the greater London area," my father responded. "But those who are admitted to St. Mary's will receive the best of care, for it has an excellent staff in both surgery and medicine."

"Did you have admitting privileges here?"

My father nodded. "I held that privilege for many years, as did Alexander Verner. As a matter of fact, it was there that I first met him and became aware of his remarkable diagnostic skills. He could solve the most difficult of cases, as the royal family can attest to."

"The royal family, you say?" Joanna asked, leaning forward with interest.

"Close to the king himself," my father replied. "A royal, who shall remain nameless, had a dreadful fever of unknown origin. Despite being seen by numerous specialists and undergoing countless tests, no one could come up with a diagnosis. Verner was called in and made the diagnosis of a hidden abscess that was treated surgically and cured. For his efforts, Verner was invited to tea at Buckingham Palace."

"That must have been the talk of the hospital," I ventured.

"It was, but not because Verner spoke of it, for he never did," my father reminisced warmly.

"Doctor-patient confidentiality, I would think," said Joanna.

"That and the fact that Alexander Verner was a most humble man who never considered himself extraordinary, although he obviously was."

Traffic began moving again and we quickly reached the front entrance to Paddington Station. Hurrying in, I was immediately impressed with the major upgrades the station had undergone, while preserving its basic architecture as much as possible. A number of additional platforms had been built and service kiosks installed, all housed beneath a glazed, curved ceiling that rose to a height of over a hundred feet. For reasons known only to God, the station had been spared damage from the multiple bombing raids. Glancing about, we had no difficulty locating the correct arrival platform, for my father recognized Alexander Verner's widow standing near a giant, elevated clock. She was a thin, small woman, in her middle years, with snow-white hair and dressed entirely in black. By her side on a short leash was a huge, brown mastiff that had a black snout and a gaping mouth. The massive hound sat on its haunches and carefully eyed anyone who approached.

"It is unfortunate the mastiff was not with Verner the morning the Germans barged into his office," I remarked in a low voice.

"Indeed," Joanna agreed.

No introductions were necessary, for Mary Verner seemed to remember us from our time together at St. Bartholomew's. Despite her very white hair, she had aged well, with her delicate features for the most part unchanged. But the signs of sorrow were obvious, as evidenced by her reddened eyes and the corners of her lips being slightly pulled down. It was with effort that she managed a weak smile.

"Allow me to offer our deepest sympathy on the passing of your husband," my father consoled. "He was such a fine doctor and an even finer gentleman."

"He thought the world of you as well, John," Mary responded in a soft voice. "He often told me that if he were to become ill, you would be the doctor he would choose."

"That is high praise indeed," my father said, with a half bow before turning to us. "I take it that you remember my son and his wife, Joanna, from your nursing days at St. Bart's."

"I do indeed," Mary replied. "I particularly recall Joanna

for her skills in the operating room. We were all quite envi-
ous of you back then."

"Thank you for such a kind remembrance," said Joanna.

"Not at all," Mary went on. "And now you have made
quite a name for yourself as a most capable private detective. I
was more than pleased to learn from Inspector Lestrade that
you are now involved in this detestable crime. I can only hope
you will bring those responsible to justice."

"I shall do my very best," Joanna promised as her brow
furrowed briefly. "May I ask why the inspector contacted
you?"

"It was I who contacted him," Mary replied. "I called
because I remembered something my husband had told me the
evening before his death. While relaxing from his ordeal over
brandy, he recalled hearing one of those dreadful people shout
the word *rot* from an upper floor. This occurred as my husband was departing from the patient's residence. He did not
know if the word had significance nor did I, but I thought it
best to bring it to the inspector's attention."

"Most wise," Joanna agreed. "But was it simply *rot* he overheard or was there a word before or after it?"

"Just *rot* as he recalled," Mary answered. "Is that important?"

"Perhaps," Joanna said. "We shall see."

Our conversation was interrupted by the approaching train
from Eton. We stepped back to allow Mary Verner room to
embrace her grieving son. It was the worst of all situations, I
thought, as I envisioned a grief-stricken son coming home to
a grief-stricken mother, with each trying to somehow comfort the other. A son returning from school was usually a most
joyous event. Today it would be sad beyond words.

Moments later the two lads disembarked and, after wav-
ing, hurried over to us. Thomas Verner was small and quite

thin, much like his father, except his hair was long and tousled, with a lock hanging over his forehead. By contrast, Johnny Blalock was tall for a boy of twelve, with a handsome, narrow face and a jutting jaw. Yet it was his eyes that caught your attention. They were half lidded and gave him a serious, studious look. For those familiar with a photograph of a young Sherlock Holmes, Johnny could have passed as Sherlock's twin.

Thomas raced to his mother and tightly embraced her, with tears now flowing freely across his cheeks. The boy continued to sob uncontrollably, pausing only to say, "Oh, Mother! Oh, Mother!"

We decided to take our leave, for there was little we could do to comfort the heartbroken family. But before our departure, Mary asked my father if he would be good enough to serve as a pallbearer at her husband's funeral. My father was greatly moved and responded that it would be his honor to do so.

It was only after passing through the station's front entrance that Johnny and his mother exchanged warm cheek kisses. Joanna then took a moment to straighten Johnny's tie that had gone a bit askew.

"Thank you, Mother."

"You are welcome," Joanna said. "Now tell us, how was your trip?"

"Dreadful," Johnny replied. "Poor Thomas was inconsolable."

"Which is understandable, for he has lost a dear father, much as you did," Joanna reminded him.

"The sadness and grief are to be expected, but I see no need for it to be publicly displayed."

"Some are not as strong and resolute as you are," my father remarked. "Nevertheless, it was fortunate he had a close friend to lean upon."

"We are not close, but simply acquaintances," Johnny said candidly. "Since no one else volunteered for the journey, I decided I should, for it was obvious that Thomas would have difficulty traveling alone."

"It was still good of you to do so," my father commended.

"Yes, it was," Johnny said and left it at that.

My father and I exchanged knowing glances, with both of us no doubt thinking the same thought. Not only was Johnny's appearance remarkably similar to Sherlock Holmes, so was his emotional control. Statement of fact and deductive reasoning took precedence over feelings, which were either pushed aside or absent.

As we took our seats in a waiting carriage, Johnny asked, "May I know the details of Dr. Verner's death?"

"He was tortured and murdered," replied Joanna.

"Tortured? How?"

"With a burning cigarette."

"Most painful," Johnny said, seemingly unmoved by the suffering Verner must have endured. "But why?"

"To obtain information."

"What sort?"

"That is undetermined."

"But what has been determined is a proper hanging for those responsible." My father bristled, his anger showing briefly.

Johnny noted my father's change in temper and remarked, "Thomas mentioned that you and Dr. Verner were colleagues."

"And good friends," my father said, then added firmly, "I will not rest until those responsible are apprehended and punished."

Johnny pondered the matter before asking, "Are there any clues as to who carried out such a heinous act?"

My father looked at Joanna who answered, "We believe foreign agents."

Johnny's half-lidded eyes abruptly widened. "Was Dr. Verner somehow involved with foreign agents?"

"So it would seem."

The information Joanna gave was now public knowledge, with all newspapers reporting the details of the crime, but without mention of Alistair Ainsworth or his abduction. My attention returned to Johnny who was gazing intently at his mother. It was as if he were trying to read her mind without success.

"Mother," he said finally, "I do believe you are withholding important clues."

"For now, I am afraid I must," Joanna said, then flicked her wrist to dismiss the subject. "So tell me, dear son, how go your studies at Eton?"

"Well enough, but I am bored."

"Your grades say otherwise."

Johnny shrugged indifferently. "But the subjects have little appeal. I am expected to memorize facts that have no bearing on the profession I have chosen to pursue. You see, Mother, I plan to follow in your footsteps and become a private detective. I truly believe that is my calling."

"That calling must await your completing your studies," said Joanna. "You will soon learn that the seemingly irrelevant facts you commit to memory now will become most useful in the future."

"Oh, I wish to continue my studies, but not at Eton."

"Where then?"

"At home, here in London at 221b Baker Street," Johnny continued on eagerly. "We shall choose the subjects that provide the information that is paramount in criminal investigation. We can hire a tutor to guide me, much as we did when living with Grandfather Blalock."

"A formal education is much preferred, for it will greatly increase the scope of your knowledge, far more than will

tutorial learning," Joanna explained patiently. "And life ex-
periences away from home will sharpen your instincts and in-
sights in ways that books cannot."

"You really should finish up your studies at Eton, for you
may decide on yet another profession later on," my father
chimed in.

"And an honors degree from Eton will pave the road to
success, no matter the field you choose to pursue," I added.

"My mind will not change," Johnny said stubbornly. "I
carry the genes of Sherlock Holmes and they will dictate what
I do in life."

Joanna sighed resignedly. "I take it you have given this decision considerable thought."

"I have, Mother."

"Then I will ask that you give the matter even more careful consideration, for such changes often do not work out
well."

"This will be for the better," Johnny persisted. "Of that,
I am certain."

"It may be so," Joanna agreed halfheartedly. "Only time
will tell."

Johnny brightened. "Does that mean I have your permission to withdraw from Eton?"

"It means the matter is not entirely settled," Joanna said
in a measured voice. She seemed to think further before asking, "When are you expected to return to Eton?"

"Within the week."

"That is time enough for you to reconsider, for I wish you
to do so," Joanna urged. "You will give the matter careful
thought, paying particular attention to the advantages and disadvantages of leaving a distinguished school like Eton, in favor
of a private, tutored education at home. At the end of the

week, you will let me know of your decision and the reasons behind it."

"You make it sound like a formal presentation."

"It is, for you must convince both yourself and your mother that such a move is to your advantage."

"I can do that."

"I suspect you can."

As our carriage continued on, Johnny sat back with a confident smile on his face. He was beyond a doubt certain he would prevail. I gazed over to Joanna, expecting her to be disheartened or, at a minimum, concerned over her son's plans, which were so clearly to his disadvantage. Instead, she gave me the subtlest of smiles that told me that young Johnny Blalock was destined to return to Eton and complete his studies there.

8

The Admiralty Club

Having left Johnny in our rooms to enjoy a well-deserved nap, we hurried to Trafalgar Square where a most important meeting awaited us. With Lieutenant Dunn's permission and under his supervision, we visited the Admiralty Club just as Big Ben struck the noon hour. The third floor was designed most peculiarly and was not what we expected. Illuminated by a skylight, it contained a large, circular center that opened to four separate offices, three of which were currently occupied by the three remaining members of the secret organization. Off to the side near the entrance was an armed guard wearing the uniform of His Majesty's Navy.

Joanna carefully studied him before turning to Dunn. "Is it not odd to have such an important unit housed above a pub? Surely a more secure location would be in order."

"It is odd indeed, but please keep in mind the type of individuals we are dealing with. They are free thinkers to the greatest extent and will not accept military discipline or regimentation of any sort. They do as they wish when they wish and will ignore any restrictions you place on them. So it was not surprising that they refused to be housed at the Admiralty in Whitehall where they would be forced to sign in and out and be subjected to repeated interruptions. They demanded a comfortable situation that was distant and separate from the Royal Navy. In their minds, these rooms provided the ideal location to perform their vital work."

"It sounds as if the Royal Navy bent to the group's every command."

"We had little choice. Under ordinary circumstances, they would have been conscripted and ordered to commence with their duties, but you can easily imagine where this would have taken us with this independent group. So we reached a compromise. The rooms above the Admiralty pub were selected, but only after the group's approval, of course. With reluctance, they accepted the presence of an armed guard at the door to deny entrance to unwanted visitors or intruders."

"Does the guard remain on duty into the night?"

Dunn shook his head. "He departs promptly at six, with me, after the messages and communiqués have been collected."

"I take it the armed guard is at your side when you arrive in the morning."

"He is. As a matter of fact, the attaché case holding the coded messages is never out of his sight."

"Be so good as to describe how the messages are gathered at Whitehall and then distributed to the individual members of the group."

"The coded messages are placed in an attaché case under the eyes of the assistant director of Naval Intelligence, then brought to these rooms at eight A.M. promptly. Here, the case is opened and the documents disseminated to the group by Alistair Ainsworth. Each document is numbered so they can be easily tracked if necessary. I return at six P.M. sharp and the decoded messages are placed in the attaché case, after which the case is locked. The lock is such that it cannot be opened except by special key that is only available at Whitehall."

"Are all documents retrieved?"

"Without fail. We carefully check the numbers on all of the coded messages and their translated counterparts, and only then are they placed in the attaché case and locked away."

"What of the scattered notes and reminders that the members may have jotted down?"

"All are collected."

"So none are allowed to leave these rooms?"

"That is an absolute restriction."

"Are the members searched as they depart for the evening?"

"They would not stand for that."

"Then you have an obvious breach in your security."

"It is possible," Dunn conceded. "But I doubt anyone could make much from their scribbled notes."

"That depends entirely on who is reading the scribble." Joanna gazed around the room once more until her eyes came to rest on the entry door. "I assume the door is securely locked after hours."

"When the last person leaves, the door is to be locked shut."

Joanna nodded, but the furrowing of her brow told us she was not satisfied with Dunn's answers. Something about the door caught her interest, for she continued to stare at it and the guard beside it.

"Are there other questions?" Dunn asked impatiently.

"None at the moment."

"Then let us proceed."

We began our questioning with Mrs. Mary Ellington who we were told had recently lost her son on a battlefield in Belgium. She was a small woman, slight of frame, with a kind face and gray-brown hair pulled back tightly into a bun. If she was intimidated by our presence, she showed no signs of it.

"I do hope Tubby is all right," Mary said, leaning back in a swivel chair, with her hands clasped together behind her head.

"As do we," Joanna said.

"But I fear the worst."

"Why?"

"Because Tubby is a man of strict habits," Mary replied. "Only the direst of circumstances would cause him to deviate."

"Did you know him well?"

"You make it sound as if he is already dead."

"Do you know him well?" Joanna corrected.

"Well enough, but only at work in these rooms," Mary replied. "Yet his routine is so precise and predictable, one could set a clock by his actions."

"Was this the case the Monday of his disappearance?"

"In every way. He arrived at eight sharp, stayed in his office until teatime at ten thirty, left for lunch at one, returned at two, used the loo at three, and worked until six on the dot, at which time he departed for the pub downstairs."

"Did you speak with him that day?"

"We chatted only briefly, for we tend to work alone in our offices, where we can produce the best results. On occasion, however, we do collaborate, particularly when we require another's skill set."

"Could you give us an example?"

Dunn quickly intervened. "I do not think we should go there."

"Oh, come now, Lieutenant," Mary said briskly. "Do you consider the daughter of Sherlock Holmes and the Watsons untrustworthy?"

Lieutenant Dunn stared at her, tight-lipped, but gave no response.

"My particular skill deals with codes that consist of numbers and symbols," Mary continued on. "If I come across anything that has overtones of German history or geography, I would consult with Roger Marlowe who is very familiar with that dreadful country. Tubby, on the other hand, is a wizard with word games, such as puzzles and anagrams."

"Both are also very good at mathematics as well, I was told."

"So am I," Mary interjected. "Which is attested to by my honors degree from Oxford. I consider mathematics my strong point."

Here was a woman not to be trifled with, I thought. She would easily be a match for either Ainsworth or Marlowe, and her forthright manner indicated she would not tolerate a pecking order in the group. At that moment, I noticed her black armband and recalled she had recently lost her son in the war.

"I know you are quite occupied with your work, so I shan't take up more of your time," Joanna said. "However, I do need to know if Alistair Ainsworth ever mentioned he was being followed."

"Never," Mary answered promptly. "And were that the case, it would have been brought to the attention of our intelligence liaison officer."

"Lieutenant Dunn?"

"Lieutenant Dunn."

"Did you see or chat with Ainsworth on the day of his disappearance?"

"I only saw him briefly and that was at a small, nearby café where I passed his table at lunch. He was seated with Roger Marlowe and a rather attractive woman who was introduced as Lady Jane something or other. From their seating arrangement, I would guess she was there with Roger rather than Tubby."

"Close, were they?"

"Quite."

"Thank you for your time and service to England," Joanna said, then added, "and we should like to offer our condolences on the loss of your son in defense of our country."

Mary Ellington nodded ever so solemnly. "He was such a good boy."

"I am certain he was."

We returned to the central area where we waited while Lieutenant Dunn took a phone call in Alistair Ainsworth's vacant office. The other doors were closed and we could hear no sounds coming from within.

"Mary Ellington seems to be holding up well from her loss," I commented.

"Some women are better than others at hiding broken hearts," Joanna said, then turned to Lieutenant Dunn as he returned. "Let us move on to the next member of the group."

"His name is Geoffrey Montclair, a genius at design engineering," said Dunn. "In addition, he has a photographic memory and can memorize a chapter from a book or a long conversation and repeat it verbatim a week later. You can see his value when dealing with a multitude of codes that may have similarities."

We entered Geoffrey Montclair's office and found him feeding and talking to a caged parakeet. The bird responded with a series of pleasant chirps.

"I do wish you would leave the parakeet at home," Dunn admonished.

"He becomes lonely," Montclair said, and ignored Dunn as he dusted off his hands and introduced himself. He was a tall, lean man, with rosy cheeks and curly blond hair. His graceful, exaggerated motions, together with his high-pitched voice, gave him a somewhat feminine flair. "It is so unlike Tubby to go missing."

"How well did you know him?" Joanna asked.

"We did not socialize together, but crossed paths often enough at chess matches."

"Were both of you masters?"

"Yes, although I considered my game superior to Tubby's."

"Did Ainsworth share this opinion?"

"Quite the opposite," Montclair said, with a smile. "We didn't take each other too seriously. It was all in good fun."

"When was the last chess tournament?"

"A month or so ago."

"I would assume that most of the players were Englishmen?"

"Oh, there were some from the Continent as well, primarily Poles and Russians."

"Was that the last time you saw Ainsworth outside the office?"

"It was."

"On the day of his disappearance, did you converse with him at all?"

The parakeet began tweeting loudly from its cage. It was not a single chirp, but seemed to go on and on. Montclair turned to the bird and hissed, "Hush! You silly bird!"

The bird obeyed and went about pruning its feathers quietly.

"Tubby and I spoke briefly." Montclair came back to Joanna's question. "He mentioned that he and Marlowe would be dining at Simpson's-in-the-Strand, which is a restaurant we both favor."

"I take it that was late in the afternoon."

Montclair nodded. "On his way out."

"Thank you for your time and assistance."

Once we were in the central area and the door to Montclair's office closed, Joanna turned to Dunn and asked, "How thoroughly was Geoffrey Montclair vetted?"

"Most thoroughly, top to bottom," Dunn said. "His record and résumé were spotless."

"Is he or was he ever married?"

"No," Dunn replied. "Nor was he known to be involved in any long-term relationships. His social life was investigated vigorously and there was nothing unusual discovered."

"I see," Joanna said, but the tone of her voice indicated she was not convinced. "Were there any particular women in his life?"

"Some years ago he was involved with a secretary at a prominent law firm."

"Was she looked into?"

"In detail," Dunn reported. "She spoke of him as being charming and witty, and liked by all."

"It sounds as if their relationship was never serious on a romantic scale."

"That was our impression as well, but I can see what your questions are leading to. And the answer is there was no evidence of sexual deviation."

"Yet for a man Montclair's age to have had only a single, lukewarm relationship over the years would surely strike one as being unusual."

Dunn shrugged indifferently. "Some men are simply put together that way."

"So I have been told," Joanna said as we strode toward Roger Marlowe's office.

But I could tell the matter of Montclair's sexuality was of real concern to her, for homosexuality could be used as a tool for blackmail. In several well-publicized cases, personages in high places were forced to resign and leave office because of their sexual orientation and the vulnerability that accompanied it. With this in mind, I concluded that while Dunn's investigation of Geoffrey Montclair may have ended, Joanna's most assuredly had not.

"Allow me to provide you with the details on Roger Marlowe whom you will interview next," Dunn said.

We listened with feigned interest to the lieutenant's description of Marlowe's background, which was not nearly as complete as the information we had received from Emma Ainsworth and Lady Jane Hamilton. Dunn appeared to believe that Roger Marlowe's time and contacts during his years at the University of Heidelberg were a major asset rather than a dangerous liability.

"I doubt that he will be able to add much to your investigation," Dunn stated, ending his summary.

"We shall see," Joanna said.

Following Dunn into an office larger than the others, we had to step around a chair that held a carelessly placed cashmere topcoat. I paid little attention to the ruffled coat whilst Joanna gave it a quick, yet studied glance. Standing behind an orderly desk was an imposing man wearing a dark, expensively tailored suit and red silk tie. Roger Marlowe was both dashing and handsome, with aristocratic features and dark hair that was beginning to gray at the temples. He was clearly forthright and accustomed to taking control of a given situation.

"Allow me to summarize," he said, obviously aware of who we were. "Tubby Ainsworth and I are lifelong friends. We grew up together, went to Eton, Cambridge, and Heidelberg as a pair, and stayed close after our return to England. We dated the same girls, fell in love with the same woman, and never married because the single life was so enjoyable. Our lives remain intertwined, for we delight in the best of food and drink, as well as in the thrill of gambling and the pleasure of an occasional pipeful of opium. We are more like brothers than friends, and I am with the Admiralty Club at his urging, although I must admit I find the challenge of codebreaking irresistible."

"Thank you for your concise summary," Joanna said. "It is most helpful, but it is the details of your last evening with Alistair Ainsworth that we need to hear. We know of your visit to the Admiralty pub where you ordered your usual *Old Vatted Glenlivet*, and of your final stop at Ah Sing's."

"You neglected our fine dinner at Simpson's."

"Only because it has no importance, unless you believe otherwise."

"I do not."

"Excellent. Then let us stay on course and learn the particulars of your early departure from Ah Sing's."

Marlowe reached for an engraved silver cigarette case and slowly extracted a cigarette, his eyes never leaving Joanna. One could almost sense the man's brain at work. "I see the circle you are drawing. We smoke a pipeful of opium and drift off into a haze-filled dream, at which point I depart, leaving Tubby alone and defenseless. Then he disappears, which happens to coincide with my disappearance."

"That is the sequence," Joanna agreed.

"But you have ignored the reason for my departure. I left early because of a blinding headache that the drug can sometimes induce. The doctors Watson can attest to this side effect."

My father and I nodded simultaneously, for although opium was a painkiller, it at times induced headaches similar to a migraine.

"Tubby wished to leave with me, but I insisted he stay and enjoy the remainder of the evening," Marlowe went on. "To ensure his safety, I arranged for a taxi to be at his disposal."

"Do you know if Ainsworth actually took the taxi?"

"I assume he did, for I paid the driver his fee well in advance."

Joanna dug into her purse for a Turkish cigarette and lighted it carefully, then blew smoke in the direction of Roger Marlowe. I had the distinct impression that a war of wits was about to begin.

"I can assure you I had no part in Tubby's disappearance," Marlowe said earnestly. "He is the dearest of friends and I now fear for his life."

"From whom?"

"Let us not waste time with the obvious."

"Which brings us to my next line of inquiry," Joanna said, taking another deep draw on her cigarette but keeping her focus directed at Marlowe. "I am referring to the individual who befriended Ainsworth after your departure."

Marlowe's eyes narrowed noticeably. "That would be most unlike Tubby. He did not stray outside his social circle, and went to great lengths to avoid others who frequented Ah Sing's."

"That being the reason he insisted on occupying mats in the far corner away from the other customers."

"Exactly. He and I paid an extra fee for that consideration."

"The man who appeared to befriend Ainsworth was said by Ah Sing to be large and broad shouldered."

"There are no doubt dozens who would fit that description."

"But this one had a distinctive facial tic."

Marlowe nodded at once. "I remember the fellow, but he was hardly a friend. We chatted with him briefly on occasion, and nothing more."

"Was he an Englishman?"

Marlowe shrugged. "I do not recall an accent, if that is what you are referring to."

"Did he give his name?"

"I have no such recollection. But you may wish to ask Ah Sing, for he keeps a careful record on all his clientele."

"So we shall," Joanna said, and crushed out her cigarette.

Marlowe was reaching for the ashtray when the phone on his desk rang. He quickly brought the receiver to his ear and said only, "Yes?" which was followed by a terse "Who?"

Marlowe listened intently as a most serious expression crossed his face. He handed the phone to Dunn, saying, "For your ears only."

We were ushered out to the central circular area and told to remain there, with instructions not to continue further interviews without Dunn being present. Once Marlowe closed the door to his office behind him, Joanna hurriedly turned to us.

"We must delve deeply into Marlowe's finances," she said in a whisper.

"Because of his excellent tastes?" I whispered back.

"Because his tastes are far too expensive for a man of his apparent income."

"Dinner at Simpson's and a nightly glass of *Old Vatted Glenlivet* would surely be within his means," my father said.

Joanna shook her head firmly. "Did you not notice his cashmere topcoat, with a label stating it was made by Gieves and Hawkes, the most expensive tailor on Savile Row? Were you not impressed by his bespoke suit and his sterling silver cigarette case that had its engravings filled with semiprecious stones? I can assure you these items greatly exceed his level of pay. There must be an outside source of income to account for these expenditures."

"Such as?"

"There is a foreign country that would pay handsomely for his knowledge," Joanna said.

The door to Marlowe's office opened and we were permitted to enter once again. If the two men standing beside the desk had encountered a reversal of some sort, they showed no evidence of it. Nevertheless, the tone of Dunn's voice indicated the amount of time allotted to us was now limited.

"You may continue with your questions," Dunn said tersely. "But please be concise."

"We shall be as concise as the answers we receive," Joanna retorted, then turned to Marlowe. "We were speaking of the man whom Ainsworth happened to meet at Ah Sing's. Did you by chance ever see this fellow at Laurent's casino?"

"Never."

"Might he have chatted briefly with Ainsworth or the lady who often accompanied you there?"

"That would have been most unlikely, for our attention was focused entirely on the cards that had been played. We would not have tolerated interruption from anyone."

"Including the rather attractive woman who was always at your shoulder?"

"Jane?" Marlowe said, with a forced laugh. "Her only concern was attempting to learn the method we employed to win so frequently."

"Did she?"

"We did not disclose our method to her, or to anyone else for that matter," Marlowe lied easily.

"Could you be so good as to tell us about this woman Jane?"

"Her full name is Lady Jane Hamilton, a good and close friend to both Tubby and me through the years. It was Tubby who was closest growing up, for they lived only houses apart."

"Did this association continue after she married?"

"With Tubby it did. For he shared with her a talent I do not possess. Tubby is a gourmet cook whose dishes and delicacies can rival any restaurant in London. He loves to prepare dishes for her and his invalid sister Emma, and does so at least once a week."

"I take it Lady Jane supplies the essentials since the sister cannot."

"She does indeed," Marlowe replied. "And she is very good at that, but does so under Tubby's supervision."

"She actually shops with him?"

"Hardly," Marlowe said, with another forced laugh. "She sends her grossly overweight cook to the Covent Garden market every Thursday where she meets with Tubby at the poulterer's stall. There, Tubby selects the finest goose, duck, or pheasant, which will serve as the entrée. My friend has amazing knowledge about these fowl and has no difficulty selecting the finest for the oven."

"I am surprised that Ainsworth takes such time away from his important work with the Admiralty Club."

Marlowe flicked his wrist at the perception. "He only goes on Thursday and meets with the cook promptly at noon in front of Hoover's stall. Tubby skips lunch that day, I might add, so the king still obtains a full day's work from him."

"This poulterer Hoover must be rather exceptional."

"He is among the best of the lot."

"My father-in-law is virtually addicted to the taste of fine pheasant," Joanna remarked. "But the birds our fine landlady has brought home lately are somewhat lacking in quality."

"Then Hoover is the poulterer you must see."

"H-O-O-V-E-R?"

"Yes. It is so spelled over his stall."

"Have you actually been there?"

Marlowe shook his head. "Tubby showed it to me in a photograph that was taken of him standing beside the poulterer."

"So I should have no difficulty finding the stall."

"None whatsoever."

Lieutenant Dunn was more than anxious to usher us out, but not before reminding us that we remained sworn under the Official Secrets Act. We carefully descended the wet stairs at the rear of the building, then circled back to Trafalgar Square, which was now heavily populated with tourists and pigeons waiting to be fed.

Using his umbrella, my father hailed an empty four-wheeler that promptly pulled up in front of us. As we climbed in, my father asked, "What say you, Joanna?"

"I say we go to Covent Garden on Thursday."

"To what end?"

"To see the poulterer Hoover."

"Why is he of such interest to you?"

"His name."

"What of it?"

"Hoover is the anglicized version of the German surname Huber."

9

Blood Smears

Our plans for the following day included a visit with Sir David Shaw, an old friend of my father's, who was currently a curator in charge of Mesopotamian script and languages at the British Museum. Johnny showed scant interest in such a trip, believing that museums were little more than storehouses for ancient relics and various remains from the long-ago past. But he became quite excited when he learned that Inspector Lestrade had called and asked us to return to the crime scene, for something curious had been discovered in the late Dr. Verner's office.

After calling Sir David to inform him that our arrival would be delayed, we hurried over to the Kensington address and found a constable standing guard at the front steps of the practice. With a knowing nod, the officer allowed us immediate entrance, although his eyes narrowed somewhat at the presence of young Johnny.

In a low voice, I asked Joanna, "Did Lestrade give any clues as to this new finding?"

"Only that it was noticed by a cleaning crew brought in

by Mrs. Verner to scrub the office," Joanna replied. "Apparently the practice will soon be placed on the market, and thus all traces of a murder must be removed."

"But, Mother," Johnny argued mildly, "the dreadful death of Dr. Verner will have been reported in all the newspapers, so all the public will surely be aware."

"Reading about a murder and viewing the evidence of one are two entirely different matters," Joanna explained, bringing a finger to her lips as we approached the office. "Now, Johnny, you must not ask questions or in any way involve yourself, for this is an official police investigation. And if the inspector asks you to leave, you must do so without delay, regardless of any keen interest you may have."

"I understand, Mother."

On entering the office one could still detect the faint aroma of chloroform in the air. It emanated from a towel beneath the bloodied cabinet, which had apparently become doused during the course of the crime. Even with the passage of time, some dampness remained and accounted for the characteristic odor.

"What is that smell?" Johnny asked, unable to control his curiosity.

"No questions," Joanna said, and gave her son a stern look. "But in this instance, I will permit it and answer your inquiry. It is the singular aroma of chloroform, which a student in an advanced chemistry class would instantly recognize."

My father and I exchanged subtle smiles, for Johnny was now being educated in more ways than one. Yes, I thought, the aroma of chloroform would certainly be experienced in a chemistry laboratory at Eton, but never during a tutor's lesson. I glanced over to Joanna's son to determine if the point had been made, but his expression remained unchanged.

Standing by the broken medicine cabinet, Inspector

Lestrade greeted us with a tip of his derby. "It was good of you to come so promptly," he said, with his eyes fixed on Johnny.

"Not at all," Joanna replied before introducing her son. "We were about to depart for the British Museum when your call came. I trust you will not be bothered by the presence of my son, but if so, I can have him wait in our carriage. I hope the latter will not be necessary, for the morning air is unseasonably cold."

"Under the vast majority of circumstances, this would not be allowed," Lestrade said. "However, since virtually all of the evidence has been removed, I see no harm in it, as long as the lad is not upset by the sight of dried blood. Of course details of the case must not be discussed in his presence, nor should he later speak of what he sees in this office, for it is best kept from the public eye."

"But, sir," Johnny interrupted politely, "it is already being spoken of by the cleaners who could barely wait to tell their friends and fellow laborers."

Lestrade was caught off guard by the lad's keen insight, but recovered rapidly. "Nevertheless, I prefer you make no mention of it."

"Then I shan't," Johnny promised, and quickly began glancing around the office. "Where is this dried blood you referred to?"

Joanna gave her son another sharp stare of displeasure.

"Sorry," Johnny murmured, his face coloring at the silent reprimand.

"Which you should be," said Joanna. "Now, Inspector, please proceed."

"The stain is on the cabinet itself, which was the last standing item the cleaners were to tidy up," Lestrade told us. "Here, I will show you."

As we walked over, my father stepped on a large shred of

brown glass that, despite his weight, remained intact. He used the toe of his shoe to move the shred aside.

"The cleaners were to do the floor as they departed," Lestrade explained.

Johnny stared down at the piece of glass and asked, "Why did it not splinter when stepped upon so firmly?"

Joanna sighed resignedly, understanding there was no way to suppress the lad's curiosity. She picked up the fragment and held it under Johnny's nose. "What do you detect?"

"The aroma of chloroform!"

"Precisely," said Joanna. "And in what type of bottle would you find chloroform?"

Johnny shrugged, saying, "I am unsure."

"Perhaps we should ask Watson, who has experienced chloroform in both a chemistry laboratory and in the practice of medicine."

"It is always contained in a thick, brown glass bottle that prevents the container from breaking were it to fall accidentally," my father elucidated.

"Then why did it shatter here?" Lestrade inquired.

"Because Verner meant it to," Joanna replied. "He must have thrown it to the floor with some force, so that its contents would spill out and leave a trail to follow."

"A most clever deduction," Lestrade said admiringly.

"Based on my wife's experience with chloroform as a surgical nurse," I surmised.

"Actually I first learned about its properties in a class at nursing school," Joanna said, in a comment clearly made for her son.

Lestrade brought our attention to the far side of the medicine cabinet. Written on its white wall was a streak of blood that was shaped like the letter *h*. There was a large, nondescript smudge of blood directly above it.

Joanna moved in with her magnifying glass and carefully examined the streak and the smudge. She performed this maneuver twice, paying particular scrutiny to the smudge, before turning to me and asking, "Did you notice any lacerations on Verner's hands when you examined them at the murder scene?"

I thought back and shook my head. "There were none. His hands were tightly bound to the arms of the chair, but I detected neither cuts nor gashes, which would have been quite evident."

"Did you examine both the palms as well as the dorsal surfaces of the hands?"

"Both were clear except for the cigarette burns and a broad bloodstain on the right palm."

"Then, in all likelihood, the blood belonged to the German," Joanna concluded.

"Does it matter whose blood it is?" Lestrade asked.

"A great deal," Joanna replied, and studied the stains yet again with her magnifying glass. "For it informs us what transpired during the struggle and who his captors were."

"Why, the Germans."

"Where is your proof?"

"There is circumstantial evidence."

"Not good enough."

Lestrade blinked repeatedly as he tried to come up with a more convincing answer.

"It is here in the stain, for everything points to Dr. Verner cutting his captor's hand and using the blood to write a message," Joanna elucidated.

Johnny stepped in closer to see what his mother saw, but the expression on his face told us he did not. Yet the lad's inquisitive mind and brightness were more than obvious, as was his maturity that was far beyond his twelve years. "Mother, could you please explain the bloodstain to me?"

"And to me," Lestrade added.

Joanna handed her son the magnifying glass and said, "Examine the smudge and look for a pattern within, then tell me what produced it."

Johnny studied the smudge at length before noting, "I see the impression of lines, many of which are slanted, although a few are vertical."

"What would make such an imprint?" Joanna asked.

"I am at a loss."

Joanna reached for a gooseneck lamp and turned it on prior to placing it by the bloodstains. "Now tell me what you see."

Johnny closely reexamined the smudge for a full half minute, then jerked his head up and exclaimed, "It is a palm print!"

"But whose?"

"It is impossible to tell."

"Gaze carefully at the top of the narrow streak and determine if there is yet another imprint."

After a quick study, Johnny cried out, "A fingerprint!"

"Excellent!" Joanna lauded. "So would it not be a reasonable assumption to say that the fingerprint and the palm print were made by the same individual?"

"Almost certainly."

"Thus, we appear to have an uncut hand making a bloodied palm print and, in all likelihood, a finger on this very hand dropping down to leave its print before forming the letter *h*."

Johnny looked at his mother quizzically. "I am having difficulty following your line of thought."

"All of the evidence points to the fact that the blood on the palm print and fingerprint did not come from Dr. Verner."

"So Dr. Verner did not make the prints."

"I did not say that," Joanna corrected. "I distinctly said that the blood on the prints did not come from him."

"But how then—"

"It is blood from a German," Joanna pronounced. "The sequence of events occurred in this order. Verner sees the Germans coming for him, so he dashes to the medicine cabinet for the bottle of chloroform. As he reaches in, the German grabs Verner's hand, but the doctor resists, and in the process manages to push the German's hand against the broken glass in the cabinet door."

"But Verner was a small man and could not have possibly overpowered the German," Lestrade argued.

"Small, but with a powerful grip," my father informed us. "Alfred Verner had incredibly strong arms that could restrain a highly agitated patient without great effort. I myself witnessed this feat at St. Mary's Hospital."

"Thank you for that helpful information, Watson," said Joanna. "So Verner's hidden power allows him to push the captor's hand into the broken glass, which causes a deep laceration that bled heavily. The blood soaks the surface of Verner's hand and eventually produced a bloodied palm print. Verner then uses the blood to leave us a message as to the identity of his abductors."

"How can you know this?" Lestrade asked.

"Because at the very top of the bloodied streak is a fingerprint, no doubt belonging to Verner, which will descend and form the letter *h,* for us to see."

"And what do you believe the *h* stands for?"

"*Hun,*" Joanna replied. "Verner was telling us he was taken prisoner by the Huns."

"As in Attila the Hun?" Johnny inquired.

Joanna nodded. "*Hun* is a derogatory term for the Germans, who are known for their viciousness in battle."

"Of course Verner could not have used the *G,* for the Germans would have noticed it and had it removed," Lestrade surmised.

"Nor could he have scripted a *D*, which his captors would have known stood for *Deutschland*, the German word for their fatherland."

"It does all seem to fit, yet you must admit your evidence remains circumstantial," Lestrade challenged.

"But can be proven beyond a doubt," Joanna countered. "Have a fingerprint taken from Verner's remains and matched against the bloodied print on the cabinet. I am certain the Fingerprint Branch of Scotland Yard would be up to the task."

"Indeed they would," Lestrade concurred, and quickly jotted down a note to himself. He paused for a moment as he tapped his finger against the notepad, obviously lost in thought. "I am still not convinced that a small man like Verner could struggle against a larger foe and inflict such damage, at least not with the evidence we have on hand."

"There is more," Joanna went on. "For embedded in the top of the bloodied smudge is a fragment of human tissue, which in all likelihood was gouged from the German's hand."

"Pray tell, how do you know it is human tissue?"

"Because it has several hairs protruding from it, and one of those hairs appears to be blond, which Verner was not," Joanna affirmed. "This tissue comes from a German, who now has a gouged-out wound on his hand that bled excessively."

Johnny asked, "Did he place a bandage over it, Mother?"

"He may have, but it was a very serious laceration that would continue to bleed."

Johnny considered the matter further before saying, "Perhaps he persuaded Dr. Verner to care for it."

Joanna's eyes suddenly widened as a smile came to her face. She reached over to affectionately ruffle her son's hair. "A most excellent thought, and one that had not crossed my mind."

"Is it helpful?"

"Very," Joanna said, and turned to the group. "With a

large, deep wound that continued to bleed, the German may well have required medical attention and would certainly not depend on Verner, who was to be tortured and killed as quickly as possible. He would have most likely gone to a clinic or private physician for treatment. You see, such a wound would undoubtedly require sutures. This being the case, he would not have sought treatment nearby, for they would have hurried to depart the area."

Lestrade nodded his agreement. "They were aware of the trail left by chloroform, which could be followed."

"They were not fools," Joanna went on. "So they would have visited a doctor or clinic away from the crime scene and nearer their next residence. With this in mind, a bulletin should be sent out to every physician in the metropolitan London area, seeking information on a Teutonic-appearing patient, perhaps with a facial tic, who was treated for a serious laceration of the hand."

"But the event would have occurred days ago," Lestrade countered. "The patient is in all likelihood long gone by now, and may have even relocated to yet another neighborhood."

"True," said Joanna. "But keep in mind, sutures had to be used to close the wound and must remain in place for at least a week to allow for complete healing. Once that has occurred, the sutures must be removed. And the physician who inserted the sutures will be the one to remove them."

"A bulletin will be sent out to *all* physicians in London as well as to those in its remote suburbs," Lestrade said, with a firm nod. Turning to Johnny, he added, "That was a fine observation on your part."

Johnny showed no response, other than to say, "It was obvious the wound would require care."

Again my father and I exchanged knowing glances. The lad was so much like his mother and grandfather before him, in that praise meant little, the significance of an observation everything.

"Mother, what determines how much time will be needed for a wound to heal?"

"It might be best for Dr. Watson to answer your question, for he has extensive knowledge on the subject, both in war and peace."

"Healing time is largely measured by the size and depth of the wound," my father informed. "A superficial laceration caused by a knife or razor would heal nicely in a week after suturing. By contrast, a jagged, wide wound caused by a shell fragment would require weeks. If it was too wide to suture together, it would heal from the bottom up by the process of granulation, which could take a month or more."

"Can you determine beforehand the time needed for a terrible wound to heal?" Johnny asked thoughtfully.

"Not precisely," my father replied. "That requires repeated examinations of the wound, which allows one to estimate the rate of healing."

"So, here it depends on the doctor's experience."

My father shook his head gently. "Here it depends on what one has learned in the classroom about the signs of healing, which can then be applied to the examiner's careful observations, which in turn will lead to an accurate assessment. You see, without facts, observations have little merit or even less depth."

Johnny nodded ever so slightly, then mused to himself, "Facts together with observation is the key."

"Facts together with observation is the key," my father reiterated.

Another lesson learned, I thought, watching the subtlest of smiles cross Joanna's face.

As we headed for the door, Johnny stopped to stomp down

on a large piece of brown glass from the chloroform bottle. He then leaned over to pick up and study the piece, which had remained intact. Satisfied, he tossed the shard aside. Like the best of investigators, he was unwilling to accept the observations of others, but would depend only on those he himself made.

10

The British Museum

We hurried into the British Museum, for we were already twenty minutes late for our meeting with Sir David Shaw. As was frequently the case, the first floor was crowded with tourists, many of whom seemed to congregate around the Rosetta Stone, which was considered a most prized possession of the museum.

"Why do people find that large stone so interesting, Mother?" Johnny asked.

"Because the writings on it provided the key to unlocking the mystery of Egyptian hieroglyphs," Joanna replied.

"Why was that so important?"

"For many reasons, but mainly because it was a script that mystified the world for thousands of years," Joanna explained. "It also told the history of ancient Egypt in great detail."

"Did they not have books back then?"

"Apparently not."

"So these peculiar figures carved into stone were like a secret language?"

"One might very well say that," said Joanna, as we strode by the Rosetta Stone. "But you should save your questions for Sir David Shaw who is a true expert on the subject."

"How do you come to know him?"

"Through Dr. Watson, for they are friends dating back to the Second Afghan War."

Johnny quickly turned to my father, his curiosity aroused. "I had no idea you fought in that war."

"It was a very long time ago," my father said, downplaying his soldiering days.

"Were you wounded?"

My father nodded. "A jezail bullet found its mark in my shoulder."

"How long did it take to heal?"

"Over a month, for although the wound was sutured, its edges did not hold well."

"Thus, it had to heal from the bottom up."

"So it did in large measure."

"I believe you called the process granulation."

"That is the correct term."

How remarkable, I thought. The lad had a mind like a steel trap, for once a fact entered it, it did not escape.

"And now," called out a guide leading a group of tourists, "we shall visit the Elgin Marbles."

The announcement was greeted with loud and obvious approval. En masse the group moved away from the Rosetta Stone, but Johnny kept his eyes on them as they walked on.

Joanna smiled at her son. "And now you no doubt wish to know what these Elgin Marbles are."

"I do indeed, for they seemed to generate a lot of interest."

"I am afraid my knowledge on this matter is somewhat limited," said Joanna. "I was told these huge slabs of marble, with their intricate carvings, were taken from the Acropolis in Greece by Lord Elgin during the last century, and eventually found their way into the British Museum."

"Were they stolen?" Johnny asked, searching for a possible crime.

"That is another question we might ask Sir David," Joanna replied. "Or perhaps we should purchase a monograph on the subject that will provide even more detailed information."

"I favor the monograph, which I can discuss with the tutor we shall choose."

We took the stairs to a quiet, upper floor, with my father and Johnny leading the way. The corridor itself was vacant, but we could hear muted conversations coming from behind closed doors. A stale, musty odor filled the air.

"Pray tell, Joanna, what brings us to see Sir David?" my father asked quietly.

"He is a multilingual codebreaker, is he not?" Joanna replied.

"Of the first order."

"Then we shall present him with the German word *rot,*" Joanna went on. "You may recall that the good Dr. Verner heard that word being shouted from the house where the prisoner was held."

"It was from the second story."

"Precisely," said Joanna. "What do you make of it?"

My father shrugged. "I am afraid French is my only foreign language."

Joanna turned to her son. "And what about you, Johnny?"

"We are just beginning the class in German at Eton and have not yet come to *rot.*"

"It means red."

Johnny gave the matter thought. "I trust the word has some significance here."

"It does indeed."

"Well, I am certain my tutor here in London will inform me of the German term for red and its variations."

"I am certain he would," Joanna said. "But he would teach you grammatical German, which will give you a fine vocabulary, but will not give you the fluency you require as an investigator," Joanna cautioned. "To that end, Eton will serve your purpose far better. In your classes and clubs you will have no choice but to speak German, and thus learn all of its subtleties and nuances. If you are not entirely fluent in a language, it will be of little help in your investigation, for you will only be aware of the obvious. You do wish to be a cut above the others, do you not?"

"I do, Mother."

"Then carefully consider my words."

"Nuances and subtleties," Johnny uttered to himself.

Upon turning a sharp corner, my hand touched Joanna's and I allowed my cheek to brush up against her hair. We exchanged secret smiles as a warm, wonderful feeling flowed through both of us. My mind went back to our first journey together at the British Museum when our hands had touched and brought about the very same captivating sensation. Then as now, I was certain I would never grow accustomed to the wondrous affection that such simple contact brought with it. For the hundredth time I was reminded how fortunate I was to have married the most stunningly unique woman I had ever encountered.

Approaching Sir David's office, Joanna reached into her purse for a folded slip of paper and gave it to Johnny, with the following instructions. "You are to open it once we leave the museum."

"Is it a puzzle?" Johnny asked.

"More like a solution," Joanna replied.

Sir David Shaw met us at the door to his office, and I was again struck by how odd the man looked. He was tall and stoop shouldered, with reddish-gray hair and a hawklike nose upon which rested the thickest spectacles I had ever seen. But behind those heavy lenses was a brilliant mind, the owner of which had been knighted by Queen Victoria for his wartime skills in deciphering top secret, coded messages, some of which were so sensitive they would never be allowed to see the light of day.

"Ah, Watson!" Sir David greeted, and cordially extended his hand to my father. "What a pleasure to see you again."

"The pleasure is mine," said my father, with a most vigorous handshake. "I believe you recall my son and his wife, Joanna, from our earlier visit."

"I do indeed."

"And with them is Joanna's son, Johnny, who has a number of questions for you."

Sir David gave the lad a half bow. "Are these questions of yours difficult to answer?"

"So it would seem, sir."

"Good," Sir David approved. "For those are the only questions worth asking." He gestured to the chairs in front of his cluttered desk and waited for us to be seated before sitting and continuing on. "Now, my good fellow, tell me of your questions. Do they have a unifying topic?"

"They concern the Egyptian hieroglyphs, sir."

"Ah, the mystery of all mysteries," Sir David cooed, obviously warming to the subject. "Let us begin with the Rosetta Stone. Are you aware of its significance?"

"Only that it is said to be the key."

"Oh yes! But a marvelous key to a script so complex it baffled us for thousands of years." Sir David reached for a clay tablet that had hieroglyphs written upon it and handed it to Johnny for examination. "Tell us what you can make out."

Johnny studied the tablet at length before noting, "I see rows of small figures that have no meaning."

"Ah, but to the Egyptian scribes who devised the script they had every meaning," Sir David said. "Believe it or not, the hieroglyph system contains over seven hundred basic symbols, pictures, and signs that represent objects, activities, sounds, and ideas. All of it was indecipherable until Napoleon's soldiers discovered the Rosetta Stone in the Egyptian desert. The stone had three distinct scripts carved into it. The upper text was Egyptian hieroglyphs, the middle written in demotic Egyptian, and the lower in ancient Greek. Because all three read essentially the same, it unlocked the mystery of the Egyptian hieroglyphs. The tablet you are holding contains one of the simpler hieroglyphs."

Johnny restudied the tablet at length in an attempt to decipher the hieroglyphs. "I clearly see a drawing of a bird in profile."

"Which translates to weak or small," Sir David said.

"And a feather."

"That signifies justice or balance."

"What of the reclining lion?"

"It designates a temple or tomb."

"Then I note a circle with a dot in its center."

"Which indicates the sun or strong light."

Johnny furrowed his brow in concentration before a faint smile crossed his face. "The circle with the dot precedes the reclining lion and that tells us the sun was shining on a temple."

"A born cryptographer!" Sir David praised.

"But I chose the simplest of the hieroglyphs to interpret," Johnny said candidly.

"An important first step nonetheless."

"Do you function as a tutor in hieroglyphic script?"

"I cannot spare the time, but there is an informal class that meets here at eleven each morning, if you are interested."

"I most certainly am, sir," Johnny said eagerly, and turned to Joanna who nodded her approval.

"But will this not interfere with your formal education?" Sir David queried.

Johnny hesitated before answering. "Well, sir, I am currently enrolled at Eton—"

"Excellent!" Sir David broke in. "There is a Museum of Antiquities at Eton that has a superb Egyptian section, the director of which is a personal friend. I shall arrange for you to continue your study of hieroglyphics under his tutelage." After jotting down a note to himself, he looked to Joanna and said, "Now let us turn to the puzzle you wish to bring to my attention."

Johnny quickly raised his hand. "Sir, may I be permitted one last question?"

"Of course," Sir David replied patiently.

"Could there be a hidden code within the hieroglyphs that we have yet to decipher?"

"It is a possibility."

"But what do you believe?"

"I am very careful in my beliefs, for in my world things are often not what they appear to be."

"So too is it in the world of crime, which brings us to the purpose of our visit," said Joanna. "Watson mentioned that you were fluent in many languages, including German."

"Seven to be exact. English, French, German, Spanish, Arabic, Dari, and Pashto."

"It is German I am most interested in," Joanna went on.

"Because of the sensitivity of the case, I can give you only limited background information."

Sir David tilted back in his chair, but his eyes never left Joanna. "The words *German* and *sensitivity* are usually not found in adjoining sentences at this moment in history—unless of course one is speaking of espionage or war plans."

Joanna ignored the conclusion and continued on. "An Englishman was abducted by people unknown. Someone overheard the word *rot* being shouted from the second floor of the house in which the Englishman was being held captive. What do you make of it?"

"What do you?"

"*Rot* is the German word for red."

"Yes."

"But is there more to it?"

"Perhaps," Sir David said. "But I require more information. To begin with, was the word cried out *rot* or *rotes*?"

"*Rot* as far as we know."

"Good. For *rotes* is the adjective form of *rot,* so in all likelihood we are dealing with the noun—*rot* or red. This would tend to exclude the possibility that the crier was referring to an object, such as *rotes Hausen* or red house."

Johnny raised his hand. "Could it not be a red bandage covering a cut, Mother?"

I could not help but be astonished at the lad's quick mind. He was connecting a red bandage to the deep gash in the German agent's hand. He was unaware that the shout of *rot* had occurred prior to the struggle in Verner's office.

"I am afraid that would still involve the use of the adjective *rotes,*" Sir David said. "A red bandage would be *ein rotes Verband.*"

"More importantly, the Germans would never use that

term for a bloody bandage," Joanna informed. "They would say *blutig Verband.*"

Sir David nodded. "I see you too are well versed in German."

"I have some grasp of the language," Joanna told him. "I accompanied my late husband, John Blalock, on a sabbatical to Berlin where he learned new techniques for tendon and ligament repair. For six months I worked beside him as a surgical nurse."

"Where you no doubt saw more than your share of *blutig Verbanden,*" Sir David said.

"I did indeed."

"This must have occurred when relations between the two countries were far more cordial."

"A lifetime ago," Joanna said with a hint of melancholy, then flicked her wrist to dismiss the subject. "But let us redirect our attention back to the word *rot,* which we believe was not used to denote an object. So it must be a person."

"Most likely," Sir David agreed. "But what kind of person? A red can refer to a communist or socialist, which of course is the antithesis of the German mind-set. Or could red be part of an address where a given man lives?"

"There is a Red Lion Street in Holborn," my father recalled. "And a Red Lion Square."

"I would still favor it being the name of a person," Sir David said. "But to my knowledge, there is no German name such as Red."

"A nickname, perhaps," I suggested.

"Very unlikely in German," Sir David answered at once. "First, in contrast to England, nicknames are seldom used in public for adults. They are primarily employed as terms of endearments. Secondly, five to ten percent of the German population, depending on the region, is redheaded, so the name Red would not be very distinguishing."

"Are you excluding *Rot* as a name?" Joanna asked.

"I am excluding it as a nickname," Sir David corrected. "You must allow me to put all of your clues together in a neat little package. You initially told me we are dealing with an individual shouting out the word *rot*, which indicates that person possesses a German vocabulary. You also informed me that this matter is very sensitive and cannot be spoken of in detail, and that indicates this German should not be in England. And since we are at war with Germany, I think it fair to conclude this German is here secretly and is up to no good. It all smells of espionage, and I therefore believe *rot* in fact refers to *Rot*, the code name of an agent."

"You have been very helpful," Joanna said as she pushed her chair back. "I trust you will not speak further of this matter."

"Most assuredly." Sir David rose and said a final word to Johnny. "We shall see you tomorrow morning."

"Indeed you shall, sir."

Hurrying down the corridor, we remained silent, for there were others strolling about. We passed a group of chattering children in their school uniforms on the stairs, then went by a throng of tourists clustered around the Rosetta Stone. Only once we were outside did we speak of our meeting with Sir David.

"It would appear we have a nest of Huns amongst us," my father grumbled. "Heaven knows how many."

"Four at a minimum," Joanna estimated, then counted them off on her fingers. "Number one has a facial tic. Number two is the agent who closed the window in the adjoining room, and number three is the just-mentioned Rot."

"Who is number four?" I asked.

"The driver of the carriage who delivered Verner to the house," Joanna replied. "They would not dare assign that role to an outsider."

"Your knowledge of German has served you well yet again," my father remarked. "Nevertheless, even with your fluency in the language, we required Sir David's assistance to come up with the notion that Rot was in fact the name of one of their agents. But then again, he was knighted for seeing things others did not."

"But Mother helped him along," Johnny asserted.

Joanna turned to her son and gave him a warm smile. "You may now read the slip of paper I gave you."

As Johnny unfolded the slip, my father and I glanced over his shoulder at Joanna's writing. It read:

CODE NAME FOR GERMAN SPY

Johnny nodded slowly to himself. "One has to be aware of the nuances of the language."

"Quite so," Joanna agreed. "But it is always wise to seek a second opinion from a renowned expert, eh, Watson?"

"It is the smart move and an important one, for now we can place a name on a member of the spy ring," my father replied. "Perhaps Scotland Yard or Naval Intelligence can put a face to the name."

"If so, they may have the names and descriptions of Rot's usual associates," I added.

"You both are making a number of assumptions that for the most part are highly unlikely," Joanna said. "What are the chances our agencies would have photographs of Rot or know of his associates?" She paused a moment before answering her question. "Very small indeed."

"But surely there is no harm in asking," I ventured.

"Oh, but there is," Joanna cautioned. "Keep in mind we have a traitor amongst us, and one loose tongue will alert Rot we are aware of his presence, which would send him into deeper cover or cause him to flee England altogether. And that, dear John, is what we must avoid, for it will remove any advantage we now have."

"But how then are we to delve into the identity of Rot and his associates?" my father asked.

"There are a number of avenues, including a phone call to Sir Harold Whitlock, the First Sea Lord, who knows us well," Joanna responded. "He could surely make a quiet inquiry into the matter."

"Lestrade and Dunn will be most unhappy with your decision."

"I am not concerned with their happiness, but only with the rescue of Alistair Ainsworth," said Joanna, as she gestured to a nearby carriage. "And if we ruffle some feathers along the way, so be it."

11

Covent Garden

Joanna awoke the next morning with a dreadful cold, yet still managed to see Johnny off for his hieroglyphics class at the museum. Coughing and hoarse, she had no choice but to remain home in bed. But she stressed the importance of investigating Hoover the poulterer, and bade us to take her place at the Covent Garden market.

"You must be very careful," Joanna implored, with a raspy voice. "Do not speak condescendingly to Hoover, but rather engage him, like someone interested in sharing information about geese. He will know vastly more than you, but you will have enough knowledge to indicate you are not novices on the topic and only wish to learn more from an experienced hand. He will then speak freely and take delight in conversing with gentlemen of your obvious standing."

"But neither of us has the knowledge you speak of," my father said.

"You will shortly," Joanna said, and paused to loudly sniff and swallow. "Follow my instructions and this will play out the way we wish it to. First, do not make idle conversation when you approach the poulterer's stall. Go directly to a goose and examine the bird with your hands. Smell it and comment on the aroma in one fashion or the other. An unpleasant odor tells you of poor quality, you see. Pick the bird up and determine if the skin is smooth and free of bruises or blemishes, for these are always absent in the best of geese. When you finally decide on which to purchase, make certain it is plump and well formed, since this will cook best. Make a point to ask if the goose you select is country or city bred."

"Does this matter a great deal?" I interrupted.

"It does to those who know their way around geese," Joanna replied. "Those raised in the country feed only on grass, which gives their meat a richer, tastier flavor. In addition, the country bred are reputed to be quite tender, and for all these reasons are far more desirable."

"What about size?" my father asked. "Should we select a larger bird?"

"You must be careful here," Joanna cautioned. "Have the poulterer weigh the bird, for you must stay below ten pounds. Those that are larger often yield the tougher meat."

My father and I had to smile at one another, both of us dazzled by Joanna's command of such a peculiar subject. We were aware she could talk exceedingly well on a broad variety of topics, but usually chose not to show her brilliance unless it could be readily applied to a criminal investigation. Yet how she became so informed about geese was a wonderment. In our year of marriage I'd never seen her once go near Miss Hudson's kitchen or inquire about recipes or makings of a dish.

"How did you come by all this information on geese?" I asked. "And please do not tell us you simply read about it."

"I had no such books to consult," Joanna said.

"Then how?"

"By asking Miss Hudson the name of her poulterer and

spending an hour with him yesterday afternoon. He was most helpful." Joanna arose from her chair by the fireplace as she suppressed a weak cough. "Now you should be on your way, for we are only an hour from noon at which time Lady Jane's cook will arrive at Hoover's stall. You must remain unnoticed, but close enough to observe the interchange between the cook and the poulterer. Only approach Hoover's stall when it is clear of customers."

"It is difficult to believe a simple poulterer is involved," my father said. "What purpose could he possibly serve?"

"Keep in mind the Germans never forget the Fatherland," Joanna replied. "It runs in their blood."

"I am still not following you."

"He could be a go-between," Joanna explained. "The traitor and his German masters will stay as far apart as possible to avoid raising suspicion. Nevertheless, they must have a method to communicate and exchange messages. If Lady Jane is the guilty party, what better liaison than an inconspicuous poulterer who is available every day and on a moment's notice."

"The messages might even be concealed within a plump goose," I ventured.

"Which could be purchased on site and delivered to a given address," my father added.

"Precisely," Joanna said. "That is why I inquired whether there was evidence of food being delivered to the empty house the Germans once occupied. If wrappings containing goose feathers had been found, it would have represented a most compelling clue. But unfortunately, that was not the case." She coughed weakly again and cursed at her illness. "In any event you must shortly be on your way. I suggest you take a very slow stroll over to Covent Garden, which is just over a mile south. By my estimation you should arrive shortly before noon. Remember to stand well back from the stall and watch the cook's hands as well as those of the poulterer. Stroll over to the stall only after the purchase is made and the cook departed."

"Should we mention Alistair Ainsworth to the poulterer?" I asked.

"Yes, but only casually and in the course of your conversation," Joanna replied. "For example, if Hoover were to inquire how you came upon his stall, say that you were referred by Alistair Ainsworth and watch for the poulterer's reaction. See if his face loses color or his mannerisms become abrupt. But appear not to notice."

"Your keen eye would be most helpful here," my father said.

"But alas, my keen eye will have to remain in bed with my miserable cold," Joanna said, and headed for her bedroom. "Now be on your way."

We took my wife's advice and set out on a slow stroll to Covent Garden, timing our walk so we would arrive at the appropriate time. All the while we wondered if Lady Jane Hamilton, her cook, and the poulterer could all be intertwined in a most traitorous affair. It seemed so unlikely that Lady Jane, a woman of such high standing, would be involved in this sordid matter, and even less likely that a simple poulterer would be by her side. But, as my father reminded, we should never underestimate Joanna's keen instincts. She often saw what others failed to see.

As we approached Covent Garden, one could not help but be impressed by the size of the marketplace and the huge crowds mingling through it. Carts and wagons and lorries rumbled into three acres of profusion, bringing with them the produce of nearby farms that were in such abundance they dazzled the eye. It was a world of vegetables and fruits in all their splendor, which included oranges, tangerines, festoons of grapes, Canadian apples, and grapefruit from Cuba. And to this assemblage, add the colors of masses of glorious flowers. Making our way through the crowd we came upon a line of stalls, some large, others small and barely a yard wide. One of the more prominent ones had a sign that read Hoover & Son, Poulterers.

At the stall's counter was the heaviest woman I had ever encountered. At five feet in height, she weighed in excess of two hundred pounds, with rolls of fat stretching her garments to the breaking point. But she seemed nimble enough as she began her examination of a snow-white goose. Lifting the bird's wings, she gave the underneath skin a most careful study. Satisfied, she next went to the goose's head and neck. All the while the poulterer remained well back from the counter, his hands clasped together upon his apron.

"I believe she is unaccompanied," I said from the side of my mouth.

"Which is to be expected," my father said. "If Lady Jane is implicated, she would wish to keep her distance from the poulterer."

I gestured with my head toward the stall. "Ah! She has made her purchase. See how well the goose is being wrapped."

"I noticed nothing untoward with the poulterer's or cook's hands," my father remarked.

"Nor did I."

We concentrated further on the happenings at the poulterer's stall, but our line of vision was abruptly interrupted by a rather tall flower girl, with long blond hair that was covered with a tattered bonnet. She was more woman than girl, with a sad face and a smudge of dirt on her chin. Her sadness seemed to be exaggerated by her spectacles, which had a cracked lens. The white blouse and floral skirt she wore were so threadbare that light could go through them.

"Please, guv'nor, please buy me flowers," she begged, holding up a packed basket. Her Cockney accent was so deep it was difficult to understand. "Two bundles a penny, primroses!"

"Be on your way," my father ordered, making a sweeping motion with his hand. "We have important business here."

The flower girl stood her ground, undeterred. "Sweet violets, penny for the whole bunch!"

"Later perhaps," my father offered. "You must move on at once!"

The flower girl hung her head in defeat and, approaching the next prospective customer, called out, "Buy me violets, oh do, please!"

We returned our gaze to the poulterer's stall and watched the massively overweight cook waddle away, with the wrapped goose under her arm. She apparently was well-known in the market, for she waved to more than a few and stopped to chat with a man of middle years, who was likewise considerably overweight.

"The cook is distracted, so let us commence," my father said. "I shall do the talking, but feel free to enter the conversation at any time. And remember, be pleasant and be interested."

The poulterer saw us approaching and, sizing up our fine attire, hurriedly swept the counter clean of goose feathers and other debris. Involuntarily he rubbed his hands over his soiled apron, then straightened his tie.

"May I be of service, gentlemen?" the poulterer offered.

"We are searching for a fine goose as a present to a friend," my father replied.

"Then you have come to the right place."

My father reached for a large goose at the end of the counter and mimicked the cook's method of examination.

With a careful eye, he studied the bird's entire skin, beak to tail, then raised its wings for a close inspection of what lay beneath. Turning the bird, my father pointed to a small bruise on the lower belly.

"This will not do," he said with the tone of authority.

"A minor blemish," the poulterer attempted to excuse.

"But our friend is quite special, and so must our gift goose be," my father insisted.

"Then I shall show you my very finest," the poulterer said, and reached for a large bird whose neck hung over a side counter. "You will not find a blemish or bruise on this one, mark my words."

As my father began another examination, I gazed about at the assortment of people passing by. They were laborers and merchants, along with the rich and penniless, and a scattering of individuals from foreign lands, with their distinctive features and attire. It was a splendid cross-section of modern-day London. In my peripheral vision, I saw the obese cook some ten yards away, now engaged in a lively conversation with the flower girl we had encountered earlier. They seemed to be having a cheerful, animated talk. The cook appeared oblivious to our presence.

"Country bird, was it?" my father inquired.

"Every day of its life," the poulterer replied. "It fed only on sweet grass and never saw a speck of grain."

"Which renders the meat tender and gives it a much richer taste."

"Indeed it does, sir," the poulterer said. "Which of course makes it a shilling or two dearer than those that are city bred."

My father flicked his wrist dismissively at the added expense. "How much does this bird weigh?"

"Eight pounds and an ounce over."

"Which assures its tenderness."

The poulterer nodded in a most pleasing manner. "You know your way around geese, sir."

"As does my friend Mr. Alistair Ainsworth, who referred us here."

"Ah, Mr. Ainsworth!" The poulterer's face lighted up. "Now there is a gentleman who is an expert on geese, by anyone's measure. But I see in the newspapers that he has gone missing."

"So it would appear."

"Let us pray no harm has come to him."

"We shall."

"And now, sir, if I may, could I ask for your name? I should very much like to list you among my special customers."

"Of course." My father obliged and handed the poulterer his personal card.

We purchased the goose and set off for Baker Street, with the wrapped bird tucked securely under my arm. Along the way we stopped at a small café for tea, over which we discussed our adventure in the Covent Garden market. The café was crowded, with noisy conversations filling the air, but we still kept our voices low so as not to be overheard.

"That was a fine performance, Father," I praised.

"I did a bit of acting at Cambridge," he commented, with some pride.

"It certainly came in quite handy today."

"As it did in the past with Sherlock," my father reminisced, and took a deep sip of Earl Grey tea. "But I'm afraid my acting served no purpose, for nothing of value was uncovered at the poulterer's stall. There was no evidence of an exchange of messages between the poulterer and the cook."

"None whatsoever," I agreed. "I kept my eyes on their hands throughout their meeting and saw nothing out of the ordinary."

"And my mention of Alistair Ainsworth elicited a most pleased reaction," my father noted. "I had the impression the poulterer genuinely missed seeing him alongside the cook."

"As did I. Thus, it would appear we have not advanced our cause one iota."

"Nor shall we, it would seem, as long as Joanna is confined to her bed."

We enjoyed a second cup of tea, during which we recounted every detail of our visit to Covent Garden, but could discover nothing that would have been of interest to Joanna. Nevertheless we both had the uneasy feeling that we had overlooked something Joanna would have seen and docketed. She had often remarked that it was the trivial that at times led to the significant. Yet using the best of our minds, we could not come up with even a minor happening worthy of note.

A half hour later we arrived at 221b Baker Street and were met at the door by Miss Hudson. With her keen olfactory sense she sniffed at the wrapped package I held, and a look of displeasure crossed her face.

"I smell goose," she pronounced.

"It is," I said.

"Has something been amiss with the goose dishes I have prepared?"

"They have been outstanding, and that is why my father and I journeyed to Covent Garden to find the perfect goose as a present to you."

"In gratitude for your most excellent food," my father added. "Which we always look forward to."

Miss Hudson blushed and brought a hand up to cover it. "Why, thank you! That is ever so thoughtful."

"Not at all."

"Would you like it for dinner tonight?"

"Under ordinary circumstances we would be delighted,

but unfortunately Joanna has come down with a rather nasty cold and would have little appetite for a tasty goose."

"Poor thing," Miss Hudson remarked. "She sounded awful when I saw her by the stairs as she was seeing her son off. I offered her tea and honey, which I thought might soothe her throat."

"Did she partake?" I asked.

Miss Hudson shook her head. "She only wished to climb back into bed and not be disturbed."

We adjourned to our rooms and, after lighting a cheery fire, sat in front of it to enjoy our pipefuls. Outside, the sky was rapidly darkening, bringing with it the promise of yet more rain. With the wind beginning to gust, we felt great comfort being in the pleasant warmth of our drawing room. Our quiet peace, however, was soon interrupted by a rap on the door. It was Miss Hudson and we feared something was amiss with the goose.

"I am sorry to bother you, Dr. Watson, but there is a flower girl downstairs who insists on seeing you," she announced. "The girl claims you dropped something at Covent Garden market and wishes to return it."

My father and I rapidly checked our pockets and found nothing missing. Wallets, timepieces, keys, and coinage were accounted for. "Did she mention what item we had lost?"

"She did not," Miss Hudson replied. "But she demanded to return it in person, for a reward I would guess."

"Please show her up," my father said, rechecking his pockets as the door closed.

"I wonder how the flower girl learned of our address," I queried.

"Probably from the card I gave the poulterer," my father said.

Moments later the flower girl entered our drawing room

and did a brief curtsy. Her white blouse was now damp from the rain that was beginning to fall. She had both hands around her basket of flowers.

"I'll wager a shilling you'll buy me flowers now," she said.

"What exactly have you found?" I asked.

"Information that could prove most useful," Joanna said, removing her bonnet, blond wig, and broken spectacles.

To say that my father and I were stunned by the sudden transformation would be an understatement. Her disguise was so ingenious that there was not a single inkling to indicate Joanna Blalock Watson was beneath it. Even the sharp-eyed Miss Hudson who viewed all visitors with suspicion had been fooled.

"I have many questions," my father said finally. "But first off, how did you manage this clever charade with such a terrible cold?"

"Because there was no cold," Joanna answered. "All that is required to imitate one is a sniff of black pepper. Inhale a healthy dose and you will repeatedly sneeze as your nose runs rampant. Another dose will irritate your throat and produce a raspy voice and cough."

"But why?" I asked. "Why not include us in your carefully constructed masquerade?"

"For several very good reasons. First, I had to make certain my disguise and accent were spot on and not easily seen through. You and Watson would not have been the best of judges, for your opinions could be clouded by emotion and thus cause you to hesitate to point out any defects in my disguise. I needed an independent judge, so I returned to the poulterer whom I visited for an hour yesterday and begged for some scraps. He promptly escorted me out of his shop." Joanna paused and chuckled to herself. "He also bluntly suggested I go back to East London and take my Cockney accent with me.

"The second reason for my secrecy was to keep you in the dark at the Covent Garden market," she went on. "Despite your best efforts you would have no doubt continued to steal glances my way and the workers about the stalls would have noticed this behavior. In their minds, they would see two finely dressed gentlemen eyeing a poor flower girl and think the worst of it. They would have watched my every move and yours as well, so as to serve as my protectors. This would have in all likelihood disrupted my plans to arrange an encounter with Lady Jane's cook. So, all in all, it was best I remained unknown to you. I trust you will forgive my deception."

"You are forgiven," my father said, with a warm smile. "And I must say that Sherlock Holmes would have been most delighted with your disguise."

"From the stories I have read, my father was quite good at improvising disguises."

"He was a master at it and took great pleasure in surprising me, just as you have," my father reminisced. "And he took even greater pleasure in explaining why such a disguise was necessary. Perhaps you will now tell us the main reason you went to such extraordinary lengths to conjure up such a magnificent disguise. It had to be more than just to keep John and me in the dark."

"It was indeed," Joanna said. "I needed the disguise in order to go places that a lady of standing would never gain entrance to."

"Such as?"

"The world of Lady Jane's cook."

"Exactly what in the cook's world merited so much of your attention?"

"Why, Lady Jane's secrets, of course."

My father and I drew in closer to Joanna, so as not to miss a word.

"You see, everyone has their dark, deep secrets that they guard zealously. This holds true particularly for the aristocracy, who would not divulge their secrets, even if questioned a thousand times. After poverty, disgrace is the very worst affliction they could ever suffer. But such secrets are often known by the household who keep it to themselves and their peers for obvious reasons."

"How could you hope to pry such information from the cook?" I asked. "After all, you were neither friend nor peer."

"That took a bit of doing," Joanna replied. "But my task was made easier once I learned the cook also spoke Cockney. With my rather pronounced Cockney accent, we immediately became sisters in arms who would delight in trading juicy gossip. I provided her the story of a royal couple who had a rather odd sexual fetish involving the great toe. Good manners prohibited me from mentioning the family name, to which the cook nodded her approval. This tale set the stage for her to return the favor by revealing romantic encounters—real or imagined—that circulated amongst Lady Jane's household."

"Really, Joanna!" my father protested mildly. "This all seems so beneath you."

"When dealing with sordid matters, one has to be prepared to sink to a lower level," Joanna said, with an indifferent shrug. "In any event, by all accounts Lady Jane goes shopping at Harrods several times a week on a regular schedule. She steps off her carriage at the front entrance, enters the store, and promptly exits via a side door. You see, although her carriage remains in front, a close friend of her driver parks his carriage on a side street, and it is he who witnesses Lady Jane's rather hurried departure. She moves quickly in a direction away from Brompton Road and returns an hour or so later, again using the side entrance. Now, considering Lady Jane's past, what do you make of this?"

"She has strayed again," I answered at once. "She is meeting up with a secret lover."

"Or with a German agent," my father suggested.

"Or both," I ventured, but then I had second thoughts. "On the other hand, we may be making too much of her adventure. It could be quite innocent."

A mischievous smile came to Joanna's face as she asked, "Suppose I told you these disappearances cease when her husband, Lord Oliver Hamilton, returns home from sea duty."

"She is straying," I said resolutely.

"But why and with whom?" Joanna pondered. "Those are the important questions that need to be answered."

"How do you propose we go about this task?"

"By following her," Joanna replied.

"I am afraid your flower girl outfit will not serve as well in that regard," said I. "You would stand out like a sore thumb in the fashionable Knightsbridge area."

"I would indeed," Joanna agreed. "It is for that reason we must hire someone inconspicuous to do the following for us."

My father nodded. "They would have to melt perfectly into the background."

"And have an air of innocence about them," Joanna said, and reached for a bell to summon Miss Hudson. "By the way, was there any exchange of notes between the poulterer and the cook?"

"Absolutely not," my father replied.

"I too had my eyes on the pair the entire time and saw no such exchange," I agreed.

"Did you notice the cook offered no payment for the goose?" Joanna asked, and waited for a reply that was not forthcoming. "The goose was certainly not free, which would indicate an invoice was placed within the wrapping. Such a sealed invoice would then be promptly handed to Lady Jane. Could there be a more innocent way for the Germans to send instructions?"

My father and I exchanged glances, both of us with the same thought. Joanna was so much like her father, Sherlock Holmes, for whom a single trivial clue could lead to a significant conclusion.

"One would never have guessed at Lady Jane's involvement," my father said, shaking his head dolefully.

"It is best not to guess," Joanna cautioned. "It is a habit of the worst sort. One should wait for the clues that will remove all guessing."

With a rap on the door, Miss Hudson called, "Yes?"

"I have a note to be delivered," Joanna said. "Please send for a messenger straightaway."

12

The Baker Street Irregulars

They sounded like a herd coming up the stairs, stomping on each step as if to make their presence known. Unlike our earlier encounter with the Baker Street Irregulars, there were three of them rather than two, and each was clad in their Sunday best, clean and smart, head to toe. Closing the door behind them, they stood silently and awaited Joanna's inspection. One could not help but be impressed with their transformation to the middle class, for they all had started out and still dwelled in some of London's poorest neighborhoods.

According to my father, there was an extraordinary history behind the Baker Street Irregulars. Holmes had somehow gathered up a gang of street urchins that he often employed to aid his causes. They consisted of a dozen or so members, all streetwise, who could go anywhere, see everything, and overhear everyone without being noticed. For their efforts each was paid a shilling a day, with a guinea to whoever found the most prized clue. Since Sherlock Holmes's death, more than a few of the original guttersnipes had drifted away or become

ill, but Wiggins, their leader, remained and took in new re-
cruits to replace those who had departed.

Standing before us, Wiggins appeared even thinner than
when last seen. There was a look of hardness about him, with
his hollowed-out cheeks and dark eyes, which made him seem
older than his twenty years. By contrast, the two members beside him had angelic faces. Little Alfie, whom I recalled from
our last adventure, was small for his fifteen years, with tousled brown hair and an air of innocence that made him look
even younger. Next to him was a thin, dark-complected girl
of no more than ten whom I did not recognize.

"Here we are, ma'am," Wiggins said. "Dressed to the nines
and dapper as can be. The clothes for Little Alfie and Sarah the
Gypsy come to a pound extra for each."

"Well spent," Joanna said, and peered down at the young
girl. "And what role will Sarah the Gypsy play?"

"She and Little Alfie will be the team that follows your
fine lady," Wiggins replied. "In addition, Sarah has a sixth
sense that tells her when she is being watched or if there is a
copper nearby. More importantly, when people see her they
feel sorry for her rather than threatened. This is doubly necessary when a snatch is about to occur or is in progress."

"She puts people at ease, I would imagine," my father said.

"That she does, guv'nor."

Sarah remained quiet, but watched every move with her
doelike eyes. She seemed to be assessing some characteristic we
possessed. Beneath her innocence there was cunning, I suspected.

"Now, ma'am, please give us the particulars on this lady
we are to follow," Wiggins requested.

"She is an elegant lady who resides on Curzon Street in a
quite splendid house, the address of which you will have
shortly. You are to go there by yourself and keep your eye on

the door in a most inconspicuous manner. An exceedingly attractive woman, tall with flowing brown hair, will depart from the house and stroll to her waiting carriage. You are to memorize her face, but do not follow her."

"I take it you know where the lady's carriage is headed," Wiggins surmised.

"To Harrods where she will enter via the front entrance. Minutes later she will leave the store, using a side door that opens onto Hans Road. From there she will travel southward away from Brompton Road, and it is at this point she is to be followed."

"Will she be accompanied?"

"No."

"Or carry packages?"

"None."

"Will a carriage follow her?"

"If it does, you have picked the wrong woman."

Wiggins carefully considered the matter before inquiring, "That neighborhood is quite fancy, yet it is not usual for ladies to stroll alone down a side street. Are you certain she will not have a protector watching over her?"

"She is being very secretive, so I would think not."

"To be sure, Sarah will be on her toes, won't you, ducky?"

Sarah nodded, her expression unchanged. "I'll pick him out faster than you can sneeze."

"Now, I will need the exact address to which she goes," Joanna instructed them. "Make certain to survey the entire building to determine if there is a rear or side door from which she could depart. Once you are certain the lady is remaining in the house, learn who she is visiting. A crown for his description, a pound for his name."

"And if we overhear their conversation?"

"Another pound."

"And actually witness the goings-on between the two?"

"A fiver."

Wiggins's jaw dropped at the offer. Five pounds was a great sum to the lower class, equivalent to a hundred shillings, which translated into the pay for three months' labor. Wiggins exchanged pleased glances with the other Irregulars, all eager to pocket the enticing reward. Their expressions indicated they would go to any length to learn every detail of Lady Jane's visit.

"There will be some added expenses," Wiggins said.

"Such as?" Joanna asked.

"We will require jackets of different colors for Little Alfie and Sarah," Wiggins explained. "Changes of color make for a different appearance. A little girl in blue looks different from one in red. Then we'll need packages for them to carry that can hide their faces. And books would come in handy as well."

"To what end?"

"Children carrying books are seen as middle class or better straightaway. You see, Little Alfie and Sarah must fit well into the neighborhood."

"All well and good then," Joanna agreed, and motioned to the door. "Now, be on your way. Keep in mind, the quicker you return with the information, the better."

As soon as the Irregulars departed, Joanna lighted a Turkish cigarette and began pacing back and forth across the drawing room. It appeared her conversation with Wiggins had brought some important matter to her mind, and she was now dwelling on it.

"Something is of concern to you," I said, as she stopped by the window and peered out to Baker Street.

"It is the five pounds I offered as a reward," Joanna replied. "It may be too great of an enticement and cause the Irregulars to take unwarranted chances."

"They are in a risky business," I reminded.

"Nevertheless," my father joined in, "five pounds seems an extraordinary amount."

"Not if it saves the life of Alistair Ainsworth," Joanna said, and went back to pacing the floor.

13

St. John's Wood

We waited impatiently for news from the Baker Street Irregulars, although we knew it could be days before their service bore fruit. Our stalemate, however, came to an end with a phone call from Inspector Lestrade. An important clue had surfaced regarding the location of the German agents, and the inspector wished us to join him on his way to the site.

"I am surprised at his generosity," Joanna remarked. "In dramatic instances such as this, Lestrade prefers the limelight to be on Scotland Yard alone, for it greatly enhances their reputation."

"I suspect it is not his generosity that beckons us, but his need for an investigator who is fluent in German," my father said. "Moreover, it sounded as if the idea was as much Dunn's as his."

"You may wish to bring along your service revolver, Watson."

"But surely Dunn and the inspector will be armed."

"But your aim is quite excellent, and at this point a wounded German agent would be of far greater use than a dead one."

Fifteen minutes later we were seated in Lestrade's four-wheeler, racing for St. John's Wood. We moved along at a good speed until we departed Baker Street and turned onto a wider avenue where we were slowed by an accident involving two large transport lorries. With the additional time, Lestrade reviewed the details of the fortuitous encounter that might well lead to the rescue of Alistair Ainsworth.

"A gardener overheard a conversation that was going on at a nearby house that he knew had been recently leased," Lestrade told us. "Now, with the war on everybody's mind, anti-German sentiments are running high. So, when the gardener heard what sounded like German being spoken, he moved in for a closer look. In the back, hidden garden of the leased house, a pair of Teutonic-appearing fellows were having an animated chat. One was pointing to his stomach and saying the word *smearhar* over and over. He could make no sense of it, but it sounded very suspicious to him, so he promptly called Scotland Yard. And we of course notified Lieutenant Dunn at once. We both recalled from the case of *A Study in Treason* that you are quite fluent in German, which would come in most handy at the moment. Indeed, we are wondering if the gardener had misheard, for we could find no word resembling *smearhar* in the German dictionary."

Joanna thought for a moment before asking, "And the gardener stated the man was pointing to his stomach when the word was spoken?"

"So I was told," Lestrade said. "But then again, there is a question whether he heard the word correctly."

"He heard it correctly," Joanna said as our carriage came to a halt.

We alighted to find the area swarming with the forces of Scotland Yard. Near a stand of oak trees were a dozen uniformed constables, along with armed sergeants who had their holstered weapons on display. At the rear was Lieutenant

Dunn surrounded by several naval officers. Upon seeing our arrival, Dunn broke away from the other officers and hurried over to us.

"Thank you for coming so promptly," he said. "Allow me to give you the latest details. The furnished house was recently leased for six months, all paid in advance. The neighbors saw nothing out of the ordinary, other than the newcomers kept entirely to themselves. There were no noises, disturbances, or unusual visitors. It is the gardener's report that the new occupants spoke German that brings us here."

"I should like to speak with the gardener," Joanna requested.

"This way." Dunn led us to a nearby fence, beside which stood a portly man with a ruddy complexion and protuberant abdomen. The gardener seemed to be enjoying the attention he was receiving.

Joanna approached him directly and said, "You stated the neighbor was motioning to his stomach when he spoke the strange German word."

"Yes, ma'am. He most certainly did," the gardener replied. "He did it several times to make his point."

"Can you remember his words exactly?"

"Only one, and I heard it clear. It was *smearhar.*"

"Could it have been *Schmerz hier?*"

"That's it! Like I said, *smearhar.*"

"Thank you for your keen observation," Joanna said and walked away, with the rest of us hurrying to catch up.

"Well?" Dunn asked.

"*Schmerz hier* translates to *pain here,*" Joanna responded. "So, with the German gesturing to his abdomen, he was stating where the pain was located. And this of course was the location of Alistair Ainsworth's discomfort that forced the German agents to summon Dr. Verner."

"It would appear Ainsworth was gesturing that his pain persisted or may now be even more intense," I concluded.

"Or so he wished the Germans to believe," Joanna said.

A uniformed constable sprinted up to Lestrade and, after catching his breath, said, "Sir, the house is completely surrounded, front and back, with no means of escape."

"Inform the sergeants they should have their weapons drawn," Lestrade ordered, then turned to Dunn. "Would you care to do the honors?"

Dunn reached for a megaphone and strode to the front gate of the stately house on Wellington Road. In a stern voice he called out, "You in the house at seven-two-five. You are surrounded by Scotland Yard and have exactly one minute to show yourselves. If you choose not to surrender, you will be taken by force."

We waited anxiously and hopefully, but there was no movement in the house or the surrounding garden. As the seconds slowly ticked by, Lestrade and Dunn checked their weapons, as did my father. He was a true marksman from his soldiering days in the Second Afghan War and had kept his aim sharp by practicing at an enclosed firing range. Despite his age, my father's distant vision was excellent.

"Try not to kill," Joanna said quietly. "A wounded agent can provide information that a dead one can't."

"Your point is well taken," Dunn said, and glanced at his watch. "Their minute is up. I favor the front entrance."

"As do I," Lestrade said, and called over to a group of well-proportioned constables. "We shall all rush the front entrance, with the lieutenant and I a step behind. You are to quickly kick the front door open, then move aside."

The constables tightened their chin straps and readied themselves while awaiting the inspector's command.

Ten more seconds passed before Lestrade cried out, "Now!"

A force of five sprinted for the front door, with Lestrade and Dunn keeping their weapons trained on the curtained windows. My father had his Webley No. 2 pistol aimed at the upper floor should shots be fired from there. With powerful kicks, the front door was made to fly off its hinges and land inside the house with a crash. Lestrade and Dunn dashed in, followed by the constables. There was no sound coming from within.

More police rushed into the house while others tightened the circle surrounding the garden. The sergeants beside us had their revolvers pointed at the front entrance. Another minute passed before the call of "All clear!" rang out.

We entered the stately house and were guided into a large drawing room that was handsomely appointed. The furnishings were Victorian in style except for two sturdy, leather-upholstered chairs near a brick fireplace. There were opened pages of a newspaper strewn about the floor next to the chairs. An overturned cup of tea had badly stained the front page of the *Standard*.

"Rather messy," I commented.

"Obviously," Joanna said, and strolled over to the fireplace. Using an iron poker, she stirred the still-hot ashes and watched scattered cinders turn bright red. Next she leaned over and touched the tea stain on the newspaper. She used her handkerchief to remove the wetness from her fingertips.

Dunn came into the drawing room, shaking his head angrily. "They have gotten away and left no clue behind."

"Clever devils," Lestrade groused. "They have somehow managed to outwit us again."

"They were warned," Joanna said. "They knew we were coming and would be here shortly."

"Perhaps the gardener inadvertently tipped them off," Dunn surmised. "He may have been foolish enough to snoop around."

"But he was told in no uncertain terms to stay away from the house when he called Scotland Yard," Lestrade said.

"When were these instructions given?" Joanna asked.

"An hour or so ago," Lestrade answered, then rubbed at his chin pensively. "He could have gone back for yet a second look and that would have most certainly alerted the Germans."

"Well, whatever the reason, they are gone," Dunn said unhappily. "And they've taken Alistair Ainsworth with them."

Joanna went back to the fireplace and, using a poker, pushed a well-burned log aside. Beneath it were more ashes and cinders, but nothing recognizable. At the rear of the fireplace, tucked under a protruding brick, however, was a partially scorched slip of paper. Joanna plucked it out and, with her magnifying glass, studied it carefully.

Dunn moved in quickly and asked, "Are you able to make out the writing?"

"It appears to be a receipt from a restaurant called François," she replied.

"I know it," my father said at once. "François is a quite pricey restaurant located on Portobello Road. It is frequented by tourists, so the Germans would not seem out of place."

"They are burning every trace of their trail, being ever so cunning to leave nothing behind," Lestrade grumbled.

Joanna restudied the receipt, front and back and against the light, before placing it on a nearby table. Using the iron poker, she again stirred through the ashes and cinders, without finding anything of value. With Lestrade's assistance, she pulled out the single, remaining log and rolled it out onto the wet newspaper. There were no clues attached to it.

"Another dead end," Lestrade growled.

A uniformed constable dashed into the room and held up a map of London's train stations. "Sir, we found this item glued by the toothpaste to the rear of a bathroom mirror."

Lestrade quickly reached for the thin map that appeared to be relatively new, yet had torn edges. He took a moment to remove flakes of toothpaste from his fingertips before opening the guide and spreading it onto a nearby table. The only remarkable sign was a circle drawn in black around Waterloo Station. "This map must have come from Ainsworth."

"But why did he circle Waterloo?" Dunn asked promptly. "Certainly the Germans would know that it, like all major train stations, is under close surveillance."

"Perhaps there are other clues on the map that might only be uncovered by experts," Lestrade said, then appeared to second-guess himself. "Assuming of course that Ainsworth drew the circle and hid the map."

"Who else would?" I asked.

"Any number of people," Lestrade replied. "But particularly the Germans themselves who wish to lead us on an errant chase."

The remainder of the house was searched top to bottom, without anything of value being discovered. Lestrade and Dunn remained behind to requestion the nearby neighbors, which Joanna assured us would be unproductive. The Germans were simply too skilled to let themselves be seen close up and would avoid any contact with the neighbors. As we approached our carriage, Joanna spotted the gardener who had called Scotland Yard, and strolled over.

"Thank you for your assistance," she said. "Your sharp eyes and ears have proven to be quite useful."

"I hope they catch those bloody bast—" he said angrily before catching himself. "I mean those bloody Germans."

"As do I," Joanna went on. "Allow me to ask one final question. After calling Scotland Yard and being instructed to stay away from the house, did you do so?"

"Oh yes, ma'am," the gardener replied without hesitation.

"I walked to the corner garden and worked there until the police arrived. I didn't want to give the Germans even a hint I
was on to them."

"Well done," Joanna praised, and strolled away. Then
abruptly she turned and asked the gardener, "Where did you
find a phone to call Scotland Yard?"

"At the pub down the way, ma'am."

"Very good."

As we rode back to Baker Street, Joanna closed her eyes and
leaned back, oblivious to everyone and everything around her.
This was her posture when assembling clues and placing them
in an order that allowed her to reach a conclusion. She nodded
at one notion, then at another, before opening her eyes.

"We have a true, well-hidden traitor in our midst," Joanna said at length. "This traitor warned the Germans we were
on our way, and they made haste to escape."

"It still might have been the gardener," my father countered. "He could have been too obvious in his first sighting
and thus alerted the Germans."

"The timing does not fit that line of reasoning, Watson,"
Joanna said. "Permit me to give you the sequence of events as
the evidence so informs us. First, the gardener called Scotland
Yard an hour ago, but he initially saw the Germans at least a
half hour in front of that. You must take into account that prior
to making the call he had to carefully observe the Germans,
then find a phone to use. The closest phone available to him
was the pub we passed on our ride in. That pub is a good
twenty minutes' walking distance away. Thus, an hour and a
half had transpired since the initial contact between the gardener and the Germans."

"It is still possible the gardener's presence made the Germans suspicious," I said.

"But that would not have caused such a hasty exit that

occurred only thirty minutes before our arrival," Joanna elucidated. "The Germans are such orderly people, yet we found newspapers strewn about the floor and an overturned teacup atop a front page. These skilled agents were obviously so surprised by the warning that they jumped up from their chairs, with the newspaper flying and their cups of tea overturning."

"But what evidence indicates their exit occurred only thirty minutes before our arrival?" I asked.

"The hot ashes and sparks in the fireplace suggest this to be the case," Joanna answered. "In addition, the tea stain on the newspaper was still quite wet and showed no signs of drying. Over the course of an hour and a half, the tea would have surely begun to dissipate and dry, particularly in front of a warm fireplace."

"But to where does this sequence lead us?" my father asked.

"To the traitor," Joanna replied, as a Mona Lisa smile crossed her face. "And our search may well be facilitated by the receipt found in the fireplace."

My father shrugged. "It simply stated that a meal was enjoyed at François."

"Oh, it revealed much more than that," Joanna went on. "Had you the opportunity to study the receipt closely, you would have noted that it was dated the exact same day that Alistair Ainsworth disappeared."

My father stared at Joanna quizzically. "Are you saying that the receipt may somehow be connected to the cryptographer's disappearance?"

"Only if my assumption is correct."

"Which is what, pray tell?"

"That the receipt belonged to Alistair Ainsworth and not to the Germans."

14

The Secret Companion

We arrived at François at the latest possible hour, having wished to be amongst the last to dine and thus the last to leave. Our intention was succeeding nicely, for as the clock struck ten there were only two other tables occupied in the upscale restaurant. Near the window was a young couple signaling for more coffee, while an elderly gentleman at an adjacent table studied his bill.

"How shall we determine which of the waiters served Alistair Ainsworth?" I asked quietly.

"It is not the waiters but the maître d' we should concern ourselves with," Joanna whispered back. "He will know the most."

My father asked, "And what will be the topic of your conversation? Obviously you must be somewhat circumspect for the maître d' will be reluctant to share information on an aristocratic patron."

"We shall talk of the excellent food at François," Joanna replied.

"Which requires no exaggeration," I interjected.

The dishes we had ordered—both the chicken cordon bleu and the coq au vin—were truly superb in every aspect, particularly when topped off by a delicious but far too expensive Chablis. The restaurant itself had a definite French feel to it, with its quaint tables upon which rested long, elegant candles that gave off gentle illumination. The low lighting seemed perfect for the engravings by Renoir and Monet that decorated the walls. Despite the charming atmosphere, our collective minds remained focused on Alistair Ainsworth and the fate that awaited him.

I asked Joanna in a whisper, "Why are you so convinced that it was Ainsworth and not the Germans who visited François on the day of his disappearance?"

"Because foreign agents do not dine at expensive, popular restaurants," she replied. "Nor do they hold on to receipts for days and days. They immediately destroy all items that might leave a trail behind."

"But Ainsworth may have dined here for lunch, long before he vanished," I argued mildly.

Joanna shook her head at the notion. "Recall that Mary Ellington saw him at lunch with Roger Marlowe and Lady Jane Hamilton on that very day."

"The same Roger Marlowe who was said to have had dinner with Ainsworth at Simpson's-in-the Strand that evening," I commented.

"The very same."

"Strange business here," my father remarked.

"Or quite revealing, if we can determine who Ainsworth had dinner with on that fateful night," said Joanna.

"What is the evidence that he had company?"

"The scorched receipt, which listed two separate entrées."

Over by the window, the elderly gentleman had paid his bill and was preparing to leave, while the young couple watched their coffee cups being replenished before returning to their deep conversation. The waiters began dousing the candles on unoccupied tables.

"Now," Joanna said in an undertone and signaled to the maître d'. The tall, thin man, with a perfectly trimmed moustache, hurried to our table.

"Yes, madam," said he.

"I must tell you that your food far exceeded our expectations," Joanna lauded.

"Thank you, madam."

"The chicken cordon bleu was superb."

"As was the coq au vin," I interjected.

With a half bow, the maître d' stated, "Those are the two dishes most favored by our patrons."

"Our good friend Alistair Ainsworth did not overstate when he called François the best French restaurant in all London," Joanna remarked.

"Oh, Mr. Ainsworth is a true connoisseur, whom I had the pleasure of serving this past week."

"Was he accompanied by our mutual friend Mr. Roger Marlowe, who also happens to be a connoisseur of French cuisine?"

"Oh no, madam. He brought along the same charming woman he always dines with."

"Then the rumors are true."

"Rumors?"

"Indeed. As you may know, Alistair Ainsworth is a lifelong bachelor and his family has feared he will remain so. But, as of late, some say he is attached to a most charming lady, which gives the family hope."

"They did seem to enjoy one another's company," the maître d' said, then lowering his voice, added, "as evidenced by their gaiety and touching of the hands."

Joanna nodded, with a smile. "So they appeared to be romantically involved."

The maître d' nodded back. "They made no effort to hide
their affection for each other."

"Good show!" Joanna said approvingly. "Perhaps there is
a wedding in the offing after all."

"Perhaps, madam," the maître d' agreed, but hesitatingly
so. "You should know that there is an obvious age difference,
with Mr. Ainsworth being her senior by a good twenty years."

Joanna shrugged indifferently. "In these days and times,
that does not matter as much as it once did."

"Happily so."

"Well, enough of such talk, let us now turn to dessert and
indulge ourselves with your crème brûlée."

"An excellent choice."

"And please ask your chef to stop by our table, so we can
praise his delicious dishes."

"With pleasure, madam."

My father waited until the maître d' was out of earshot,
but still spoke in a quiet voice. "Well done, Joanna!"

"But we require more information on the woman, which
I hope to gain from the chef," said Joanna. "She is the key
here."

"How can the chef who spends all of his time in the kitchen
be of assistance?" my father asked.

"Keep in mind that Alistair Ainsworth is a gourmet cook
and a connoisseur of fine foods," Joanna replied. "I can assure
you he had more than a few conversations with the chef that
almost certainly took place in the presence of the woman."

"But, for the most part, they would have spoken of food."

"As did I with the maître d'," said Joanna, before uttering
in a whisper, "Shhh! The chef approaches."

The middle-aged man looked the part. Short and stout,

he had a round, pleasant face that was accentuated by a traditional chef's hat that rested low on his forehead.

"You wished to see me, madam?" he greeted.

"What I wish to do is inform you that your chicken cordon bleu was quite simply the best I have ever eaten. It was beyond superb."

"Merci beaucoup, madame," the chef said, with a half bow.

"Now as I have some knowledge of the makings of a chicken cordon bleu, one must ask if it is the type of cheese you use that allows for such a distinctive taste?"

"You are correct, madam," the chef answered, with another half bow. "In most kitchens, the chicken is wrapped around Swiss cheese. We use a tasty, complex cheese that gives the bird a richer flavor."

"But I would think one has to be careful here, for according to Alistair Ainsworth, if the cheese is too strong, it may dampen the flavor of the ham."

"Not to worry, madam. If one uses a salty prosciutto, it will hold its own against any of the cheeses."

"As I recall, I believe Alistair preferred a nicely smoked Polish ham."

"Many gourmet cooks do, in that it blends so well with the cheese."

"Particularly when a touch of Dijon mustard is added."

"Aha! So Alistair shared the secret ingredient with you," the chef said happily. "He is truly a gourmet cook, with whom I am delighted to trade recipes."

"I am told that his female companion is also a connoisseur of French food."

The chef uttered a dismissive sound. "She is not so well informed, madam. She dared to compare my veal cordon bleu to that of a restaurant in Heidelberg. Heidelberg, mind you!"

Joanna's brow went up. "Is she German?"

"I do not think so," the chef said, after a moment's thought. "Her English is very good, and the restaurant in Heidelberg was one she had visited as a student some years ago. Perhaps it was there she acquired the bad habit of ordering a Riesling to go with the veal cordon bleu."

"A poor match," said Joanna.

"Indeed. A hearty Bordeaux Sauvignon is much preferred by most."

"When we return then, we shall have the veal, with a fine Bordeaux that I trust you will help us select."

"It would be my pleasure, madam," the chef said, stepping away as the crème brûlée arrived.

We rode back to Baker Street in a motor taxi, for another storm was under way, with strong winds and a heavy downpour that threatened to flood the streets. No mention was made of our journey to François and our new but tantalizing clues, for we wished not to be overheard by our driver. Upon reaching our rooms, we changed into more comfortable attire and settled in front of a blazing fire to enjoy snifters of Napoleon brandy.

"I had no idea you were so familiar with French recipes," my father remarked to Joanna.

"I had little such knowledge until this afternoon when I read several texts on the subject," she replied. "When in a foreign land, you do well to speak their language. And in an upscale French restaurant, food is the singular, sacred language spoken."

"But how did you determine they would be so familiar with Alistair Ainsworth?" I asked.

"That was fairly simple," Joanna answered. "We learned from several sources that he is a gourmet cook, who even went to the bother of selecting his own birds for the oven. When such an individual visits a fine restaurant, you can bank on him visiting with the chef. You see, they both feel they belong to a rather select group, and are more than happy to chat with one another."

"So you had to walk the fine line of knowing some but not too much about French recipes."

"Everyone loves to converse about their particular area of expertise, and the chef at François was no exception. Of course he readily recognized his knowledge was superior to mine, which made him even more eager to discuss his dishes." Joanna swirled the brandy in her snifter before taking another silent swallow. "But one must be careful and always cloak your questions with inquiries about food. Thus, when asked about Ainsworth's companion's knowledge of various French dishes, the chef was only too happy to tell us of her lack thereof, and the apparent German influence on her choice of wines."

"Do you believe her to be German?" I asked at once.

"It was not possible to tell with certainty," Joanna replied. "But I doubt very much that she was a visiting student who spent only a brief time in Germany. Such students have a limited income and do not frequent expensive restaurants in Heidelberg, nor do they order veal cordon bleu, which is always a high-priced item on the menu. And preferring a Riesling to go with the veal is a German taste and not an English one."

"If she is German, how do we connect her to Ainsworth's disappearance?" my father queried. "Could she in fact be a German spy?"

"Why not?" Joanna asked in return. "Spies come in all shapes, sizes, and genders. Moreover, I am always a bit suspicious when I see a match between a man and woman with a wide difference in their ages. Of course she could be attracted to older men or to his wealth and social status. But this does not explain his reluctance to introduce her to his sister and friends. He lies to his sister and informs her that he will be having dinner with Roger Marlowe, all the while sharing a clandestine dinner with the woman at François. Even Roger Marlowe lies for him."

"Could it be that Ainsworth is ashamed of the age difference between the woman and himself?" I wondered.

"Unlikely," Joanna said. "Most middle-aged men are delighted to be seen with much younger women. They consider it a sign of virility and charm."

"Let us return to the premise that she may be a German spy," I proposed. "What role could she play?"

"A guide as to what Ainsworth was doing at a given time," Joanna answered. "Allow me to give you an example. On the evening of his disappearance, there was no certainty he would be visiting Ah Sing's. Since they were dining together, one might assume they would be spending the entire evening together. But if the woman learned he was to later visit Ah Sing's, she could have well notified the Germans once she left Ainsworth and the restaurant."

"The agents could have been in a carriage a block away and never be seen."

"Indeed."

"But does that role not seem somewhat unlikely, with the obvious feelings of affection they had for one another?"

"I suspect their relationship was quite platonic."

"Why so?"

"Because Alistair Ainsworth came home to his sister at night without fail."

"So we are faced with yet another riddle within a riddle."

"Which can only be unraveled if we know who the woman truly is," my father remarked.

"And how do we accomplish that feat?" asked I.

"By learning why Alistair Ainsworth went to such lengths to hide their attachment," Joanna said and, after finishing her brandy, retired for the evening.

15

A Coded Message

There was a mood of gloom at the Admiralty Club the following morning. It was now evident that Alistair Ainsworth had been broken and at least one of the deciphering mechanisms revealed.

"We must redouble our efforts," Dunn beseeched all those gathered. "For it appears that our decoding system will shortly be entirely compromised, and at that point Ainsworth's life will be ended and the fate of England put at great risk. The former would be unfortunate, the latter a disaster."

"May I ask how you came to know that a deciphering mechanism had been broken?" Joanna asked.

Dunn hesitated at length before saying, "We intercepted a wire from German Naval Intelligence instructing their submarines to vacate their positions immediately. I shall leave it at that."

"You must give me the details, Lieutenant," Joanna insisted. "I need to know what the Germans know."

"That information is so sensitive I cannot—"

"Oh, Bloody Christ!" Marlowe interrupted. "Tubby's life

is at stake here, and we have no time for your silly games. Either you provide her with the information or I shall."

Dunn gave Marlowe a stern look as his face closed. It took a moment for him to regain his composure, and only then did he turn to Joanna. "You should keep in mind that what I am about to reveal is highly classified."

"Get on with it," Marlowe demanded.

"Last month," Dunn began, "a coded message was sent to our fleet, warning that a number of German U-boats were spotted in the waters off Scotland's Orkney Islands. We have a major naval installation in that area, and ships moving in and out would be prime targets for submerged U-boats."

"I require the entire message," Joanna said.

"Oh, I remember that one," Montclair recalled. "There was a group of U-boats roaming about the innermost of the islands, which placed them near one of our critical harbors."

"Was the particular island named?" Joanna asked.

Montclair closed his eyes, as if thinking back. "That was not mentioned. However, that would not be unusual since the Orkneys are an archipelago consisting of seventy islands, most of which are uninhabited and unnamed."

"So now," Dunn concluded, "our destroyers, which have been endlessly scouring these waters to hunt down the U-boats, will have been sent out on a meaningless mission. And those same U-boats are no doubt currently at an undisclosed location, waiting to inflict damage and death on us."

"But no harm has been done yet," Joanna said. "There were no ships sunk and no lives lost. Furthermore, the communiqué caused the Germans to withdraw their U-boats and now your critical harbor is safe."

"Are you suggesting Ainsworth did us a favor?" Dunn asked sharply.

"I am suggesting that Alistair Ainsworth purposely selected this message for us to decipher," Joanna replied.

"To what end?"

"The message was not of great strategic importance, but it gave the German agents a taste of things to come, thus ensuring that Ainsworth will be kept alive. In essence, I believe Ainsworth is simply buying time and hoping we will eventually come to his rescue."

"That is a possibility," Dunn agreed.

"Allow me to present another possibility," Joanna continued. "Remember, Ainsworth is an accomplished chess master who thinks two or three steps ahead of his opponent. With this in mind, perhaps he is doing much more than simply buying time."

A smile came to Mary Ellington's face. "Tubby may be sending us a message within a message!"

"Precisely," Joanna said. "That is why the exact wordage of the intercepted dispatch is so important."

Dunn reached into his attaché case for a thick file and opened it. "The German communiqué reads as follows: 'Three U-boats off innermost Orkney Islands discovered. Vacate area immediately.'"

All in the room went silent as we gave the matter long, concentrated thought and tried to decipher a code within a code. Marlowe and Mary Ellington jotted down the message, while Montclair closed his eyes and appeared to be summoning his memory bank. I wondered if we should consult with Sir David Shaw, the renowned codebreaker who might be of assistance here. But it was a certainty Dunn would not allow any further outsiders into the group.

"If it's there, it is well hidden." Mary Ellington broke the silence.

"Tubby would have it no other way," Marlowe said. "He had to design a code that was impossible for the Germans to notice, which in turn makes it difficult for us to decipher."

Mary counted aloud up to ten. "There are only ten words in the message, with one number and no symbols or apostrophes to provide a hint."

Montclair opened his eyes. "Something is a bit off in Tubby's message. I can't put my finger on it, but there is something that feels out of order."

"With a single word or the message itself?" Joanna pressed.

"I am not certain," Montclair said, with a shrug. "Perhaps I am confusing it with another communiqué."

Joanna asked, "Did you work with Ainsworth on this particular message?"

"Only to a limited extent," Montclair replied. "As I recall, our original coded message to the fleet was based on a biblical passage of some sort."

"Which passage?" Joanna asked quickly.

"Tubby never mentioned it because he was too consumed recoding the dispatch so the Germans could not decipher it. To that end he used a nursery rhyme."

"Do you remember the rhyme?"

Montclair shrugged again. "Only that it included a lot of numbers, with each number representing a letter in the alphabet."

"That does not appear to be the case here," Joanna said.

"It can't be that complicated," Montclair opined. "Most likely there is only a single word or two that is the key to the message."

"We need to come up with answers here," Dunn urged. "Please keep in mind that your colleague's life is on the line, and that line grows shorter with each passing minute."

"We were so close yesterday," Marlowe groused. "If the

troops had arrived at the home in St. John's Wood just a bit sooner, Tubby would be sitting with us this moment."

"I am surprised you were not invited to join in yesterday's pursuit," Joanna said to Marlowe. "Your knowledge of German and Germany might have been quite useful."

"I tried to convince Lieutenant Dunn of that, but he insisted I stand back," Marlowe explained. "He uttered some sort of nonsense about me being too valuable to put in harm's way."

"I can assure you my superiors would have never allowed it," Dunn said firmly. "Now let us move on." He walked over to a nearby desk and pointed to the opened map of London's train stations that had been glued behind the bathroom mirror at the last house the Germans inhabited. "Have you had any luck with the map?"

There was no response from the group.

"Can you attach any meaning to the circle drawn around Waterloo Station?"

"There are at least a dozen interpretations," Marlowe replied. "None of which brings us any closer to Tubby."

"List the two or three you believe most promising."

Marlowe reached for his sterling silver cigarette case and lighted a Player's Navy Cut. "Each of us shall give you our best choice and the reasoning behind it. But please keep in mind that at this point we are only stating our best guesses."

"Yes, yes," Dunn said impatiently. "But nevertheless, let's have them."

"First, we have to assume that Tubby did the circling to leave us a message," Marlowe began. "Secondly, we must believe that he had overheard or otherwise come by information that indicated the Germans' next move. This would be the critical message he wished to transmit to us. That being the case, I suspect Tubby was not referring to the train station, which would be far too obvious, but to Waterloo where the historic battle between the French and British troops took place. Now we all know that Tubby was multilingual, but his weakest language was French. Because of this, he kept a French-to-German dictionary in his desk and actually penned important notes in it. I believe some notation in that dictionary will tell us where the Germans are headed next."

I could not help but be impressed by Marlowe's creative and lateral thinking. How could one possibly go from a train station in London to a French-to-German dictionary was far beyond me. But then again, that was his skill and that was what made him so valuable to His Majesty's intelligence service.

Montclair squinted an eye, then added, "As I recall, Tubby kept a copy of the Old Testament in his desk as well."

"Is he of the Jewish faith?" Joanna asked.

"Tubby is of no faith," Montclair replied. "His interest in the Old Testament involved a peculiar code we solved together. There was a passage in which God polluted the Nile River with blood, thus turning it red, to punish the Egyptians. But I doubt the Old Testament is in any way related to our current puzzle. I think we should concentrate on Tubby's French dictionary, for it is clearly linked to the word *Waterloo*."

"Agreed," Dunn said. "What say you, Mrs. Ellington?"

"I too am under the impression Tubby was pointing to the Battle of Waterloo," Mary said. "But from there, I traveled in a different direction. The French were of course commanded by Napoleon who was married to the enchanting Josephine. On a whim I investigated to see if there is a Josephine Street in London, and there is one located in Reigate. We are currently determining if any houses in the district were leased over the past year, with all rents paid in advance."

"If such leases are uncovered, it would be important to learn if the lessees had Teutonic features," my father advised.

"That would be the second question asked," Mary assured.

"And you, Montclair, have other ideas crossed your mind?" Dunn asked.

"We should not overlook the British side at the Battle of Waterloo, where our troops were under the command of the Duke of Wellington. Tubby may be directing us to the monuments that were built in honor of this celebrated hero. As you know, there are two of these. The first being the statue at the southeast corner of Hyde Park where all is very busy and wide open, and, for the most part, commercial. That would not be a locale the Germans would select. The second monument is much more likely. The duke is entombed in a crypt at St. Paul's Cathedral, and the residential neighborhood could readily meet the Germans' requirements. We are at this moment scanning the entire area for recently leased houses." Montclair rocked back and forth in his chair, then added, "I am also considering the possibility there is a connection between the message Tubby decoded and the one he left for us behind the mirror. Now, wouldn't that be clever of old Tubby?"

"I do not see how the two could be connected," Dunn said. "One is attempting to tell us his location, the other simply buying Ainsworth more time."

"So it would seem, but that does not exclude their linkage," Montclair argued. "You might be interested to know that in chess there is a strategy called the combination, in which a planned series of moves gives you the advantage and leaves your opponent in a weakened position. Tubby knows this gambit all too well, Lieutenant. Do not underestimate his ability to outwit the Germans."

"Then you had best work your hardest on both coded messages," Dunn implored. "If even the barest of clues suggests where the Germans are located, please bring it to my attention immediately. We have the manpower to cover all possibilities, no matter how remote."

The phone on Roger Marlowe's desk rang. Dunn picked up the receiver and quickly brought it to his ear.

"Dunn," he said curtly, followed by, "When?"

Dunn listened carefully, then replaced the receiver and reached for his attaché case. "It would appear you have all been off the mark on the last message Ainsworth left us. A suspected German agent was just taken into custody at Waterloo Station."

16

Waterloo Station

Led by Lieutenant Dunn, we hurried up the metal steps and entered the train where the German spy awaited us. The car itself was vacant except for two constables and a solitary figure seated by the window and shrouded in a wool blanket.

"The spy?" Dunn asked, pointing to the figure.

"Yes, sir," replied a constable.

"Why is he covered?"

"Because he is dead, sir."

Dunn was taken aback for a moment, then quickly recovered. "How did this happen?"

The constable shrugged. "I do not know, sir. We had placed him in handcuffs when he smiled at us, then took a last gasp and was gone."

"Did you harm him in any way?"

"We arrested him without a struggle and applied the handcuffs. Nothing more was done, sir."

"Remove the blanket," Dunn ordered.

The figure was uncovered and revealed a heavyset man,

in his middle years, with a strong jawline and bright red hair. His suit was well made and unsoiled, as were his shoes and the hat on his lap.

"The bomb planner himself," Dunn murmured to himself and moved in for a closer inspection of the corpse's hands and face. "There are no signs of violence to explain his sudden death."

"Perhaps he had a fatal heart attack," Lestrade suggested.

"Individuals do not smile while experiencing a myocardial infarction," my father rebutted.

"Nor do men such as this one die unexpectedly, even when placed in the most challenging of situations," Dunn said, and came back to the lead constable. "I need to know every detail, from the moment he was spotted until his capture. Leave out nothing, for the smallest happening may be of consequence."

The second police officer stepped forward and introduced himself. "I am Constable Harrison, sir. It was I who first noticed the suspicious man and gave chase. Officer Bates actually followed him into the train and made the arrest."

"What made you suspicious of him?" Dunn asked.

"His red hair, but only after he tripped over a pram," Harrison replied. "I was mingling amongst a group of departing passengers when I saw a man hurry by and trip over a moving pram. He lost his balance and, in the process, his hat became dislodged and revealed his very red hair. As he readjusted the position of his hat, I heard him utter a German-sounding word."

"Do you recall the word?" Joanna interrupted.

"It was *achtgeben* or something quite close to that."

Joanna nodded. "It is German and it means to be careful or watch your step."

"That would fit, madam," Harrison agreed.

"Get on with the chase," Dunn implored.

"I shouted for him to stop immediately, but he fled and I

sounded my whistle to alert the other constables. The exits were quickly secured and, having no other recourse, the suspect ran across the tracks and into a train from which passengers were alighting. At this juncture, it was Constable Bates who was close on the suspect's heels and followed him into the train. I raced to the exit at the other end of the car and thus blocked any chance of his escaping. He gave up without a struggle. He had no identification papers and this of course made him even more suspicious—that together with his shocking red hair, sir. It was only moments after his arrest and having been placed in handcuffs that he smiled at us and promptly died."

Joanna addressed both constables. "Did either of you see the suspect reach into his pockets after he was obviously cornered, with no hope of escape?"

They shook their heads simultaneously, but it was Harrison who spoke. "Because of fear that he was armed, we kept our attention focused on his hands while he was in the process of being captured. His hands were visible at all times and he made no attempt to go for his pockets."

"One last question," said Joanna. "You mentioned that it was the suspect's red hair that alerted you initially. Why was that so?"

Constable Harrison looked to Inspector Lestrade, who nodded his permission to answer. "We were given a bulletin instructing us to keep a sharp eye out for a redheaded German agent who was most dangerous."

"When was this bulletin issued?"

"Weeks ago, ma'am."

"Thank you for the helpful information," Joanna said, and gave my father and me a knowing look, for the agent was most certainly Rot, whose name Verner had heard shouted out at the Germans' residence.

Lestrade stepped forward to praise the constables. "Both

of you are to be commended for your fine work, which will be duly noted in your records. Now, I should like you to arrange for a gurney and transport to carry the corpse to the morgue at St. Bartholomew's. You are both to stand by the remains at all times and make certain it is not touched or in any way disturbed until I give further instructions."

"Very good, sir," Harrison said.

"And finally, there are no doubt many onlookers outside the train at the moment. Please disperse them and have a constable posted to keep the curious clear of this car."

The constables gave Lestrade a brief salute and hurried to their tasks. Once they had departed, Lestrade quickly searched the suspect's clothes. As expected, the spy had no wallet or identification papers, nor were there any labels to indicate where his suit was made. There were two five-pound notes in a pants pocket, but no foreign currency. The heels of his shoes were worn and showed no markings that might have revealed their country of origin.

"Please see if the heels contain a secret compartment," Joanna requested.

"To what end?" Lestrade asked while determining no such secret space existed.

"For the poison he used to kill himself."

"May I inquire what brings you to that conclusion?"

"There is no other explanation," Joanna answered. "When a man dies with a smile on his face, he is expecting death or may even be relieved that it is coming. Thus, I believe it is fair to say he somehow brought about his own demise."

"There are ways to inflict sudden death other than poison," Dunn countered.

"Such as what, pray tell?"

"Swallowing an object that would completely occlude one's airway."

"But that would have induced an involuntary choking seizure, which did not occur here," Joanna refuted. "Nor would it have brought a smile to his face."

"And where would he obtain such an object?" I interjected. "Keep in mind the constables watched his every move and saw no such act committed."

"Well put, John," Joanna said with a nod. "We can also exclude blows to the head and neck because there is no evidence any were administered and, unless repeatedly applied, would not induce death."

"Nor would a concealed, self-inflicted knife wound," my father chimed in. "Which, in any event, would have been quite impossible with his hands handcuffed behind him."

"All of which leaves us with poison," Joanna concluded.

"But how was it given?" Dunn asked.

"That is what we must determine," replied Joanna and turned to me. "We should have my husband examine the corpse to see if there are any telling signs. John, please be good enough to look for injection sites on the arms and parts of tablets in the corpse's oral cavity."

"But the constables kept their eyes focused on every move of his hands," Lestrade argued. "Surely they would have seen him inject himself or reach for a tablet to swallow."

"I am afraid you give them too much credit, Inspector," Joanna responded. "You must remember that the spy fled into this car ahead of the constables and for a brief moment was alone and unobserved. That is when he could have swallowed a tablet or injected himself."

"If he injected himself, where then would the needle be?"

"He could have discarded it so that it is currently out of sight, or hidden it in his clothes, which were only examined in a cursory fashion."

"All reasonable possibilities," Lestrade said before gesturing to me. "If you would be so good as to lend us your expertise, Dr. Watson."

I began my examination with a careful inspection of the corpse's fingertips. A hidden needle, dipped in a curarelike poison, could easily pierce the skin of his fingers or palms, but no such injection site was to be seen. Nor were any pinprick marks present on the forearms or in the antecubital fossa where a rich supply of veins would rapidly carry the poison into the bloodstream. The oral cavity revealed good dental hygiene and again no injection sites. I lifted the tongue to search for particles of a tablet that had been administered sublingually, but found none. Moving in closer to examine the back of the pharynx, I detected a familiar scent.

"Cyanide!" I announced to the group. "His mouth has the aroma of bitter almonds."

Lestrade stepped in for a deep sniff. "Blimey! It is cyanide. But how did he manage to do it?"

I reexamined the oral cavity and saw no mucosed pockets where the poison might have been hidden. The gingival tissues were clear as well, and the tongue revealed no tears. But one of the molars at the very rear appeared to be cracked open. The other teeth were in fine condition and showed no such abnormality. Then I saw the telltale sign. Wedged into the cracked tooth was a particle of a capsule that solved the problem. "We are looking at remarkable German ingenuity."

"How so?" asked Lestrade.

"They hollowed out one of his molars," I described. "Then they placed a capsule of poison within it before capping the tooth. All the spy had to do was grind his teeth together, which would disrupt the cap and release the poison. Which in this case was cyanide that produced instant death."

"No hands required," my father added.

Joanna moved in near to the corpse and studied its face at

length before asking, "What was so unique about this spy that he had to avoid capture at all costs?"

"He was a master spy who sat at the very top of our most wanted list," Dunn replied. "In a recently decoded message, we learned that Rot's primary mission was to plot and select the major sites in London to be bombed by the Germans' zeppelin fleet. These dirigible airships were responsible for hundreds upon hundreds of British deaths. Should he have been taken prisoner, I can assure you he would have been treated quite harshly and beyond a doubt executed."

"But why was Rot at Waterloo Station, which he would have known was under close surveillance?'

"Perhaps it was a site he was selecting," Lestrade suggested.

"That would be most unlikely," Joanna said. "Please recall that the zeppelin raids always occur at night when the station would be virtually empty. To bomb a vacant station would go against the airship's main purpose, which is to terrorize the civilian population."

"Then why was he here?" Lestrade wondered.

Joanna shrugged. "All we can say for certain is that he was here and Alistair Ainsworth circled Waterloo Station on the map."

"Are you connecting the two?" Dunn asked at once.

"I have not excluded that possibility, nor should you. Keep in mind that Ainsworth may have known of Rot, in that both occupied the house that Verner had been taken to." Joanna stepped away from the corpse and gestured to Lestrade. "You may wish to carefully reexamine the corpse's clothes to see if there are hidden clues that could help us in this regard."

Lestrade emptied each of Rot's pockets one by one, turning them inside out. All the search uncovered was a soiled handkerchief, a half-crown coin, and a broken toothpick enmeshed in lint. The buckle on his belt had no secret compartment.

"Nothing," Lestrade announced.

"Perhaps the postmortem examination will be more revealing," said I.

"He may have swallowed a note or some item he wished to conceal," I replied. "Thus, the contents of his esophagus and stomach will be carefully scrutinized."

"Also please determine if his shoes show any traces of chloroform," Joanna requested.

"But certainly any aroma that may have been on his shoes would have disappeared by now," Dunn argued mildly. "As I recall, the odor of chloroform is quite evanescent."

"Ah, but the chemists at St. Bart's may well have a test that can detect the barest traces of chloroform," Joanna rebutted. "And chloroform on Rot's shoes would place him in Verner's office and connects him beyond any doubt to the disappearance of Alistair Ainsworth."

The four of us carefully inspected the train car, searching under the seats and in the compartments above for items the master spy might have discarded. Nothing of value was discovered. Dunn remembered a case in which an important clue on a train was hidden beneath the ashes at the bottom of an ashtray. Thus, each of the ashtrays was emptied and inspected, but to no avail.

The two constables returned to inform us that a transport for the corpse would arrive shortly and that the authorities at St. Bart's had been notified and instructed on how the body was to be kept. To make certain the instructions were adhered to, Lestrade directed the constables to accompany the corpse to the morgue and stand guard over it until the postmortem examination was under way. After a final glance around the car, he ordered the corpse to be re-covered and the shades on all windows drawn. We waited for the commands to be followed before departing.

The large crowd that had earlier gathered outside the train had been dispersed, and uniformed constables were stationed to assure it remained so. It was now near noon and the station appeared filled with passengers, arriving and leaving, all of whom seemed to be talking at once. The loud hum of combined conversations drowned out any attempt for us to speak further about the strange events surrounding this most unusual case. But in an instant, everything went silent.

Down the platform and approaching us was a small funeral procession. It consisted of an expensive, polished casket being pushed along on wheels by porters on each side of the carriage. At the front was the funeral director, dressed entirely in black, with a most solemn expression on his face. To the rear was a rather tall woman, likewise attired in black, with a matching veil that hid her face. As the cortège neared us, I took note of the small bell atop the casket, to which was attached a cord that dropped into the casket itself. This arrangement was instigated by the widespread fear of being buried alive, for a few such cases had been publicized during last year's cholera epidemic. The ringing of the bell would alert all that the person within was alive.

But Joanna's attention was fixed on the veiled woman at the rear of the procession. I saw nothing unusual about the woman or the polished coffin, with its brass fittings, that she accompanied. I doffed my hat out of respect for the departed, as did the others around me, including the officers from Scotland Yard.

Joanna quickly turned to Lestrade and said, "Please stop the procession, Inspector."

Lestrade gazed at her oddly before asking, "For what purpose?"

"To prevent Alistair Ainsworth from slipping away under our very noses."

In an instant Lestrade spun around and moved the onlookers in front of him aside. He dashed over to the funeral director and brought the cortège to a halt. Interested onlookers moved in for a closer view and to possibly overhear any conversation that might explain the odd interruption.

"Is there something amiss?" asked the funeral director.

"Perhaps," Lestrade replied. "I should like you to answer all questions asked by my associate."

"Of course, sir."

Joanna stepped forward, but her gaze was focused on a narrow rubber tube that exited the casket an inch beneath the edge of its lid. Like the bell, this apparatus was based on fear of being buried alive. It provided a supply of fresh air should the presumed-dead individual within the casket suddenly awaken.

Joanna asked the funeral director, "When did the departed die? And please be exact."

"Just over three days ago."

"And the destination of the remains?"

"To Shoreham."

"Did you yourself place the body in the casket?"

"No, madam. His family performed the task, and it was done in total privacy."

"Most unusual."

"Quite," the director agreed. "But I was informed it was a strict family custom that only close relatives were allowed to touch the deceased."

"And I take it they secured the lid in total privacy as well?"

"That too was insisted upon, madam."

Joanna leaned forward and brought the rubber tube exiting the casket to her nose. She quickly dropped the tubing in disgust. "Open the casket at once!"

"But, madam, I—"

"It is a sham funeral!"

The woman at the rear of the procession suddenly bolted.

"Stop him!" Joanna cried out.

"Who?" Lestrade shouted back.

"The mourner dressed as a woman!"

The tall mourner fled into the gathered crowd to seek concealment, but his head was clearly above those around him. Thus we could follow him as he shoved onlookers aside and trampled over the ones who remained in his way. He appeared to take a circuitous route before suddenly veering off and dashing into the ladies' water closet where he was met with a chorus of screams and shrieks. But these sounds were soon muted by gunshots and the noise of shattering glass.

"Outside!" Joanna called out above the commotion. "He is escaping through the window!"

Uniformed constables and Lieutenant Dunn sprinted for the entrance to the station while Joanna raced into the ladies' water closet, with Lestrade, my father, and I only a step behind her. Pale, frightened women were huddled together off to the side, well away from the shattered glass window. On the floor near the window was a torn black dress, and atop it a wig and dark veil.

"With his head start, we will never catch him," Lestrade said disheartedly.

"I should have discovered him earlier," Joanna grumbled. "The clues were there, staring at me and waiting to be discerned."

"Pray tell, what were these signs that the rest of us overlooked?" asked Lestrade.

"First, the mourner's body size," Joanna elucidated. "Did you not notice the tall height and broad shoulders, which would be most unusual in a woman? Then there was the thick veil that hid the face completely. The vast majority of mourning veils will hide a woman's tearstained cheeks, but not her most prominent features, as this one did. You could see nothing behind it, which would effectively conceal any masculine characteristics. And the final clue was the noxious odor emanating from the rubber tube that originated from within the casket. The deceased had only been dead for three days and it requires eight to ten days for putrefaction to occur. Thus, the malodor could not have come from the corpse."

"So what then caused the awful smell?" Lestrade asked.

"Oh, there are a number of ways to accomplish that," Joanna replied.

"But it still could have been a woman," Lestrade insisted. "There are ladies who are tall and broad shouldered, and the mourner may have used the dress, wig, and veil to disguise her true identity."

"All true," Joanna agreed. "Except when he bolted, I noticed that his shoes and heels were those seen only on men. A woman would never wear them."

We hurried out of the ladies' water closet and returned to the casket, which Lestrade ordered to be opened at once. The gathering of onlookers, which had increased to twice its original size, was urged to step away, but few did. Most stood on their tiptoes for a better view.

When the last screw was removed and the lid opened, a terrible stench arose from within the casket. Lying atop sacks of sand was a long-dead cat, with its insides gutted. The lid was hurriedly closed.

"A trial run." I stated the obvious.

"A dress rehearsal in full regalia to iron out any flaws in their plan," said Joanna. "If there were defects, better to find them now rather than later, when a drugged Alistair Ainsworth would be inside the casket."

"But why the dead cat?" asked Lestrade.

"That was a nice touch," Joanna explained. "Had anyone demanded the casket be opened, simply cracking the lid open would have released a most putrid odor and, in most instances, necessitated immediate closure. I can assure you a cargo inspector would not have wished to look further."

I had to admire the ingenuity of the foreign agents. Like the true Germans they were, they rehearsed every step of the funeral down to the smallest detail. And except for a redheaded spy tripping over a pram, they might well have gotten away with it. I nodded to myself as yet another part of their clever plan came to mind. Thinking aloud, I said, "In all likelihood the train's destination to Shoreham was not some random choice. Shoreham-by-Sea is a small port where a German U-boat could easily slip in unnoticed during the dark of night and transport a most valuable cargo back to Germany."

"So cunning," my father remarked.

"Oh, they are beyond cunning, Watson," said Joanna, as a thin smile crossed her face. "A foreign agent of such clever thought is one I would be eager to do business with."

Dunn, with a pair of constables at his side, ran up to us and grimly announced, "He has gotten away scot-free. Of course, the entire surrounding area will be thoroughly canvassed and searched, but the chances of finding him are virtually nil."

"So we are back to square one and the Germans remain one step ahead of us," Lestrade said unhappily. "We have gained nothing despite our cleverness."

"Oh, I believe we have gained some much-needed information," Joanna informed.

"Pray tell, what?" Lestrade asked.

"The Germans now know we will closely surveil every train station within a fifty-mile radius, so they can no longer move their cargo by train," Joanna replied. "They are thus forced to travel by motorcar or carriage to reach their desired destination."

"That gives us no advantage," Lestrade argued. "It is quite impossible to block all roads leading out of London, and we most certainly cannot search every vehicle that wishes to pass."

"We must think moves ahead if we are to counter their next step," Joanna advised. "It is not their way out of London that we should be concerned with, but rather their destination."

"How can we possibly determine that?"

"By deduction, Inspector, which goes as follows," Joanna went on. "John is correct in his reasoning that their ticket to Shoreham was not a random choice, but one that takes them to a small port where, in all likelihood, a German U-boat will await them."

"But surely they will not return to Shoreham now," said Lestrade. "Particularly since they know we are aware of their train's destination."

"I would not rush to that conclusion," my father cautioned. "Perhaps the Germans in their cleverness now believe we will pay little attention to Shoreham and thus proceed with their original plan."

"Very good, Watson, for you are now beginning to think as the spies would," said Joanna. "Of course, another very real possibility is that Shoreham-by-Sea was never their intended port of departure. It, like the funeral procession, may have been false. For obvious reasons they would keep their final destination secret until the very last moment."

Lestrade pondered the dilemma at length before asking, "Are you suggesting we must cover hundreds of small ports on the east coast of England?"

"It can't be done," Dunn said firmly. "We do not have the manpower to undertake such a task, and the local police are not clever enough to measure up. If these foreign agents can outwit us so easily, it would be no problem for them to outmatch a small district constabulary."

"There are ways to narrow down the list of ports from which the Germans might depart," Joanna told us. "We now know they cannot transport their cargo by train, which restricts their movement to roads. In all likelihood they will have a bound, drugged Alistair Ainsworth in their motorcar or carriage, which necessitates them traveling in the dark of night to avoid curious eyes. They cannot stop at an inn or hotel, and thus would be obliged to ride straight to their destination. By car or carriage, a single night's journey would be limited to seventy-five miles or less. We can further reason that they will not travel south to the Southampton area, which is England's major port and whose waters are closely guarded by His Majesty's warships. No U-boat would dare come near. When all is said and done, I think it fair to say that the Germans plan to depart at a port seventy-five miles or less north of London."

"There are dozens of such ports, some of which are mere villages with hidden docks and wharfs," Dunn countered. "Moreover, we must consider the possibility that the Germans have a safe house along the way outside of London. Here, they could rest and delay their departure for a more suitable date."

"I think your latter point is unlikely," Joanna responded. "The Germans must be very exact in their escape, which no doubt was planned in advance. They would be on a strict schedule—as would the U-boat—that dictates how and when the transfer of Alistair Ainsworth would occur. To be successful, these types of maneuvers must be carried out on a precise timetable. We can therefore assume that, on leaving their current location, the next move is to go directly to their port of departure. Nevertheless, your description of the small villages with their secluded docks and wharfs is well taken and could present a surveillance problem. Yet, with the forces of Scotland Yard and Naval Intelligence, you should be able to find a way to cover them."

"We shall give your suggestion our closest attention," Dunn said. "But we should realize that, even with our best efforts, surveillance of all the inlets and estuaries would be next to impossible."

"Nonetheless we should try," Joanna persisted.

"And we shall."

We paused briefly as hospital personnel entered the train car to retrieve the body of the German spy. Moments later the covered corpse was wheeled away, with strands of his bright red hair protruding out for all to see.

"Perhaps we should concentrate on the dead spy," my father proposed, as the door to the car closed. "Does his presence here give us any clues that could lead to the whereabouts of the other German agents?"

"You assume that he is connected to the sham funeral," Dunn said. "There is no evidence to associate the two. One must consider the possibility that it was a random, unplanned encounter."

"Spies do not do *random,*" Joanna said. "There is a purpose behind every action they take, and that was certainly the case here."

"But where is your proof to back up such an assertion?"

"Let us begin with the premise that two of Germany's most skilled foreign agents show up at the same place at the exact same time," Joanna elucidated. "And this takes place during the rehearsal of a plan to smuggle Alistair Ainsworth out of London. What is the chance of these events simply being coincidental?"

"None," I replied at once. "Absolutely none."

"Exactly."

Lestrade asked, "But what was Rot's purpose?"

"A number of possibilities come to mind," Joanna answered. "He might have been an uninvolved observer who was there to oversee the plan in action and determine if there were any flaws. Or he could have been here as a protector for the actors in this play. And then there is a third, more likely reason that could tie Rot to the other German agents. Perhaps he was at Waterloo Station to conduct business that required a face-to-face encounter with the others."

"But would he have taken such a risk, knowing the station was under close surveillance?" Dunn challenged.

"The risk was not as great as one might think," Joanna replied. "Rot would have melted into the crowd without notice had he not tripped and exposed his red hair. And no one would have ever considered the woman in mourning to be the recipient of a spy message."

"But all eyes would have been on the funeral procession," Dunn persisted.

"Not initially," Joanna responded. "Arrangements for moving the casket would have been carried out in a private room where Rot could have stopped in to pay his condolences. I can assure you no one would have paid his visit the least bit of attention."

"But why take the risk at all?" Lestrade asked. "Why not send the information by wireless?"

"They would have been concerned the vital message might have been intercepted and decoded," Joanna told him. "The safest and most secure method would be a hand-to-hand transfer, and this indicates how very important the message was."

I inquired, "Do you have any idea what was in the message that made it so vital?"

"Here we must depend on logic and ask ourselves the following question. What was Rot's singular mission while stationed in London?"

"To select the sites to be bombed by the zeppelin fleet!" I cried out.

"Precisely," said Joanna. "That is what made the message so important. And I suspect the information was meant to be transferred to a U-boat, along with Alistair Ainsworth, and sent on its way to Germany."

"If we assume the list was in his possession at the station, the possibility exists that he chewed and swallowed it prior to his apprehension," I surmised. "That being the case, parts of the message may yet be in his esophagus and gastric juice."

"And his clothes must be torn apart thread by thread to search for additional notes that could lead to the operatives holding Ainsworth," my father proposed.

"This is all supposition," Dunn warned. "And if no such notes are found, we might justifiably conclude that no such transfer was ever intended."

"Or it might indicate that the transfer had taken place prior to Rot's apprehension," said Joanna.

On that unhappy note we hurried out of Waterloo Station and into our carriages, all headed for St. Bart's, where we hoped the postmortem examination on Rot would reveal hidden clues that could help us unravel this most perplexing case that so threatened England.

17

Lady Jane

Later that afternoon my father and I settled in front of a warming fire to search the evening newspapers for any happening that might apply to the disappearance of Alistair Ainsworth. Periodically I glanced up to watch Joanna pace back and forth across our parlor, smoking one cigarette after another as she attempted to assemble the available clues into a recognizable order. She would nod at one piece of evidence and flick her wrist at another, all the while muttering to herself, which further indicated the degree of difficulty in solving the problem. To add to our predicament, the postmortem examination of Rot turned up nothing of consequence. Carefully sewn into the shoulder pads of his suit were two hundred dollars in American currency and a false Portuguese passport, as one might expect of a spy. He was also quite ill, with prostatic cancer that had painfully spread to his pelvic bone, which might have accounted for his readiness to take his own life. No chewed items or notes were found in his esophagus and gastric juice nor any clues uncovered that might lead to the whereabouts of the other German agents. It would seem we had reached a dead end in our search for Alistair Ainsworth, but the Admiralty Club believed otherwise. They were of the opinion that Waterloo Station circled on the train map held a second meaning that indicated where Ainsworth and his German captors were located.

"Do you also think that Ainsworth had a double entendre in mind when he circled Waterloo?" I asked, breaking the silence.

"That is the most likely case, for that is how the brain of a cryptographer would work," Joanna replied. "It is the best of hidden messages, with one being obvious and the other obscure."

"So it is the obscure you are searching for."

"I will leave that to the Admiralty Club," Joanna said, as she crushed out her cigarette. "It is the second message Ainsworth sent that draws my attention."

"The one that tells us of the U-boats off the Orkney Islands," I recalled. "Do you believe it points to the method by which the Germans will move Ainsworth to Germany?"

"I think not," Joanna replied. "Allow me to take you through my line of reasoning, and if by chance you detect any flaws, please do not hesitate to interrupt. Let us begin with the well-founded premise that the first message—the circling of Waterloo on the map—was meant to inform us of Ainsworth's location, either in the train station or at a street address."

"But how could he possibly predict we would see through the funeral ruse at the station?" I questioned.

"It might not have been a ruse to Ainsworth," Joanna answered. "The plan he overheard may not have mentioned a rehearsal."

"And that was how Ainsworth learned he was soon to be smuggled out in a casket and transported to Germany by U-boat," I thought aloud.

"Which was the obvious reason for him to circle Waterloo Station on the train map," Joanna went on. "But there was always the chance that his initial message would not be interpreted correctly or perhaps interpreted too late. With this in mind, he had to devise a second coded message that would lead to his rescue."

I attempted to think through the meaning of the second message without success. "How could the position of U-boats off the coast of Scotland possibly reveal Ainsworth's location?"

"That is the point, dear John," Joanna said, and began pacing again. "It may well be that the second message does not refer to location, but rather to information of another sort that will lead to Ainsworth's captors. I further suspect that the critical information is contained in a single word, for—as Geoffrey Montclair mentioned—the code is just a little off from one sent earlier. And that is what so draws my interest to the second message."

"Perhaps the answer is more straightforward than you believe," I opined. "Could it be that the last message is simply telling us that he will shortly be spirited out of the country on a German U-boat and that the Royal Navy should be put on immediate alert?"

"Oh, it runs deeper than that," Joanna said. "I believe there is a hidden message here that is meant for our eyes only."

"Another puzzle within a puzzle," my father remarked.

"So it would seem."

Our conversation was interrupted by the return of the Baker Street Irregulars who, after a brief rap on the door, entered unannounced. They were all dressed every bit as smartly as before. The only difference was that Little Alfie now carried a large, gift-wrapped package, whilst Sarah the Gypsy clutched a pair of new books.

"The lady came and went just as you said she would," Wiggins reported.

"I take it she was not in any way protected?" Joanna queried.

"All alone, she was. But she walked a bit uneasy, not like she was on a Sunday stroll, you see. Every half block or so she glanced around, but tried to cover it."

"How so?"

"She would look like she was sneezing into a handkerchief or shading her eyes from the sun, but all the while she was peering about and behind her."

"But Little Alfie and Sarah remained unnoticed. Correct?"

"The fine lady never knew we were there," Little Alfie replied. "She was more interested in keeping her head down as carriages passed by."

"Was she recognized by anyone?"

"She gave no sign of that."

"Good," Joanna approved. "Which of you followed her initially?"

"I did, ma'am," Sarah the Gypsy said, and stepped forward. "Like Wiggins told you, she kept to herself and tried not to be seen. She walked on the inside of the footpath and pulled her bonnet down when anyone approached."

Sarah's vocabulary was not that of a ten-year-old, but more on a level with Little Alfie, who had some education as I recalled. She was probably near his age as well, but her growth and maturation had been stunted by a harsh upbringing.

"Did the lady make any stops along the way?" Joanna asked.

"No, ma'am," Sarah replied. "Not until she reached her destination."

"So you followed her the entire time?"

Sarah shook her head. "We played the now-you-see-me, now-you-don't game. I would follow her for a block, then move off to put on a different coat brought along by Wiggins. All that while, Little Alfie was trailing her from the footpath on the other side of the street."

"How far did the lady travel?" Joanna inquired.

"Just over five blocks, ma'am. She continued straight on until she came to number twenty-five Ovington Street where she entered."

"Describe the house."

"Two stories, made of brick, and opened onto the street."

"I need to know every step she took from the moment she arrived at the Ovington address."

"At that point, ma'am, Little Alfie was closer than I."

"I take it you were on the other side of the street when she entered."

"Yes, ma'am. But Little Alfie wasn't."

"Held my package up high, I did, like a proper carrier on the rush." Little Alfie picked up the story. "But I slowed to catch ongoings. She rapped on the knocker twice and the door opened quicker than a hiccough. She hurried in, without so much as a hello, and the door closed."

"Did you have a look at the person who greeted her?" Joanna asked at once.

"Not even a glimpse, ma'am," Little Alfie answered. "It happened too fast, like in a half second."

"We must learn who the lady visited in that house," Joanna urged.

"She was with a gent," Little Alfie said without hesitation. "Appeared upper class, he did, with his black frock coat and pearly-gray trousers."

"But you told us you could not see him because the door closed too quickly," Joanna contended.

"That is a fact, ma'am. But I had a better look when I slinked down the alleyway and peeked into a side window."

"Excellent!" Joanna lauded. "I would like you to describe every feature of the man, down to the finest detail."

"Mind you, I was looking through a dirty window and the couple was a good ten feet away."

"The couple, you say!"

"They were embracing, ma'am."

"A close embrace?"

"About as tight as you can make it, and still have room to kiss."

"Tell us about this man."

"I saw him only in profile, but he appeared handsome enough, with moustache and neatly trimmed beard. No spectacles or monocle that I could see."

"Was he taller than her?"

"By a good six inches."

Joanna turned and nodded to us, as the same thought went through our collective minds. It was a certainty that Lady Jane Hamilton was not meeting Roger Marlowe. "Well done!" she said, returning to Little Alfie. "After the kiss, were you able to notice anything else of interest?"

"No, ma'am. I had to move on down the alleyway, for fear of being seen. However, on my trip back to the street, I took one more peek into the room. The couple seemed to be studying papers of some sort. I then returned to Ovington to continue our watch, for you told us the lady would stay for an hour."

"How was this watch accomplished?"

"From a distance, with me and Sarah taking turns parading up and down on the opposite side of the street. Wiggins made sure we were wearing coats of different colors on each pass-by."

"Did the lady stay the entire hour?"

"Just about," Wiggins replied. "Then Little Alfie and Sarah

followed her back to the side entrance of Harrods. I stayed in place in case the gentleman made a move, and he did. Shortly after the lady left, the gentleman came out, smoking a cigarette in a holder. He opened an umbrella, although there was hardly a drop of rain falling. By my reckoning, he was using the umbrella to cover his face. Did a good job of it, I might add. He then strolled to a nearby tobacco shop and walked out clutching two packages of cigarettes. The gentleman lighted up yet another cigarette on his return to twenty-five Ovington."

"Could you determine what brand he smoked?" Joanna asked.

"Player's Navy Cut," Wiggins replied. "On his way to the shop, he stamped out the one he was smoking. I picked up the stub and read its label."

"Did you note the time at that moment?"

"Just after three."

Joanna nodded, obviously pleased with Wiggins's observations for reasons that were beyond me. "Tell me," she went on, "were there any features about the gentleman that Little Alfie did not mention?"

Wiggins pondered the question briefly. "Nothing in particular, except for his military posture. Ramrod straight, it was."

"Very good," Joanna said. "Now, I have further work for you, if you feel up to it."

"Involving the lady?"

"Involving the lady."

"Day or night?"

"Both."

"Then we must increase our fee to two shillings each."

"Done," Joanna agreed. "I need you to keep a watch on twenty-five Ovington around the clock as well. See who comes and goes, and if on foot, follow them."

"There will be added expenses, ma'am, for food and drink and other clothing."

With a nod, Joanna said, "Be off with you then, and report back with the very first sighting."

Once the Irregulars had departed, Joanna rubbed her hands together gleefully. "The chase now becomes even more interesting. There is nothing more tantalizing than a case in which everything goes against you."

"Were you not disappointed the man was not Roger Marlowe?" I queried.

Joanna waved away the notion. "That was never a serious consideration. They are close friends and need not steal away to some pricey Knightsbridge house to conduct their romantic affair. They could have easily used Marlowe's home or the home of confidants or a dozen less conspicuous places."

"Do you believe the man is a German agent, then?"

"That is a possibility," Joanna said.

"Particularly since Little Alfie saw them reading or exchanging papers," I added. "That would not be the first thing on the minds of secret lovers."

"Your point is well taken," Joanna said, with a mischievous smile that quickly faded. "But until we know who the gentleman is and what papers were of such interest to the couple, I am afraid we are guessing, which does not help our cause. It is a capital mistake to theorize before one has the data, for it tempts one to twist the facts to fit the theory."

"So what steps do you propose we take next?" I asked.

"Why, the obvious. We must identify the man who holds the key to the mystery surrounding Lady Jane."

"Which the Baker Street Irregulars will provide for us."

"No, John. They will see, but cannot identify. That is a task we alone must accomplish."

"And how do we go about that?"

"By visiting Knightsbridge."

"Shall I arrange for a carriage?"

"A motorcar will suit our purposes better."

From outside came the distinct sound of hammers breaking stone that was shortly followed by several dull thuds. Joanna hurried to the window overlooking 221b Baker Street and stared out as the hammering grew even louder. Slowly her head began to move up and down, as if tracking some moving object.

"What so holds your attention?" my father asked.

"Danger," Joanna replied.

"Imminent?"

"Quite."

The door to a bedroom opened and Johnny, holding a small blackboard with hieroglyphics written in chalk upon it, dashed out and over to his mother's side. My father and I were only a step behind. Across the street in a light rain, workers were busily removing the stone parapet from a sturdy brick building that rose up three stories. We watched as large pieces of stone were dismantled, a few of which fell off the roof and toppled to the footpath below.

"Should they not close off the footpath, Mother?" Johnny asked.

"They have," Joanna replied, and pointed to the wooden barricades a half block away that people ignored and walked around.

"Flying stones can cause terrible injuries," my father remarked. "Such blows to the head can be fatal."

"Particularly when they are descending at a rate of thirty-two feet per second per second," Joanna noted.

"How do you know they fall at that speed?" asked Johnny.

"It is a law of physics and one worth remembering."

Johnny gave the matter momentary thought and shrugged. "If it falls rapidly, it falls rapidly."

"No, no," Joanna rebuked mildly. "The rate of descent is most important, for it once determined whether a witness was in fact telling the truth."

"How so?" Johnny asked, now keenly interested.

"A witness, who was a gardener, claimed that he saw a man leap to his death from a three-story building, with his arms flailing wildly in the air. The problem with his account was that the witness was nearsighted and needed spectacles for distant vision. At the moment the victim supposedly leaped from the window, the gardener was not wearing his spectacles."

"But surely he put them on to view the fall," Johnny said at once.

"It required five seconds for him to reach into a coat pocket for his spectacles, place them on, and look up," Joanna delineated. "The Watsons and I actually timed how many seconds the act would have consumed. Now, recalling that a three-story building is thirty-two feet tall, the poor man who fell would have struck the ground in one second. Thus, there is no way the gardener could have witnessed the event."

"Why would he lie?"

"That is not the point," Joanna went on. "The point is the gardener could not possibly have seen the fall and therefore his story was false. And it is all based on a law of physics that states that an object falls through space at a rate of thirty-two feet per second per second. You would have certainly learned this in your physics class."

"But, Mother, I am not scheduled to enter physics until next year."

"Then should you return to Eton, you must take a seat at the very front of that particular class."

"Do you truly believe the study of physics will be to my advantage in the profession I have chosen for myself?"

"You should ask Dr. Christopher Moran."

"Who is he?"

"The man who murdered his friend and pushed the body off a three-story building."

Johnny allowed the new information to set in before asking, "Was the crime uncovered because of a gardener who could not possibly have seen a body fall thirty-two feet to the ground?"

"It was a major clue that eventually led to the arrest and conviction of Dr. Moran."

"And where is this doctor now?"

"He is awaiting hanging at Pentonville."

"Thirty-two feet per second per second," Johnny uttered solemnly and, with his blackboard in hand, returned to his room to continue the study of Egyptian hieroglyphics.

18

The Mysterious Gentleman

We were seated in the rear compartment of a hired motorcar half a block up from 25 Ovington Street. Outside, our driver had the bonnet of the vehicle opened and appeared to be inspecting its engine. It was all theatrics designed by Joanna to give us a clear view of the entrance to the brick house Lady Jane Hamilton had visited the day before.

"What makes you confident our unnamed gentleman will visit the tobacconist today?" I asked.

"Two reasons," Joanna said. "First, he is a heavy smoker, quite addicted to cigarettes. During his short stroll to and from the tobacconist, he consumed two cigarettes. At that rate, he will easily go through two packages a day, which is the number of packages he bought at the shop yesterday. Thus, he will be driven to replenish his supply this afternoon."

"But he might have taken the walk much earlier or do so much later in the day. Yet you are somehow convinced he will make his move at three o'clock. How could you possibly predict that?"

"Because like most of us, he is a creature of habit," Joanna replied, her eyes fixed on the house down the street. "In addition, according to Wiggins, our man has a ramrod posture that suggests a military background. Those individuals are the most regimented of all. You may recall that Wiggins recounted the time of the gentleman's stroll. He did so yesterday at three; he will do the same today."

My father glanced at his timepiece. "It is ten after three, Joanna."

"His nicotine urge will prompt his departure momentarily."

Despite Joanna's confidence, I feared we were in for a prolonged wait that would take up precious time of which we had so little. The investigation into the disappearance of Alistair Ainsworth had come to a stalemate in every sense of the word. Lestrade had informed us that to date no progress had been made by Scotland Yard in tracking down addresses that could have been related to the Waterloo Station circled on the train map. All possible locations that might be linked to the Battle of Waterloo were being carefully looked into, without success. Inspectors and constables were scouring Josephine Street in Reigate and the neighborhood surrounding St. Paul's, but to no avail. There was nothing to suggest a German presence or influence. Moreover, the mystery of the second U-boats message remained unsolved. The only bit of good news came from an intercepted note from the German high command that stated their zeppelin fleet was awaiting further orders before taking to the air again. We all wondered if the agent Rot had handed the list of selected bombing sites to Ainsworth's captors and whether the German command was waiting for it, along with Ainsworth, to be delivered. And then the bombing would be resumed.

"There he is!" Joanna cried out, and rapped on the side window of the motorcar.

Our eyes went to the doorstep of 25 Ovington Street from which a tall, well-dressed man was departing. He was attired in a tweed suit and derby, but had no umbrella as the weather was cloudless. In his left hand was a walking stick, in his right a cigarette in a holder. He kept a hand on the holder as he smoked, thus obscuring most of his face.

Our driver hurriedly closed the bonnet of our hired motorcar and drove us toward a tobacco shop two blocks down. We stared straight ahead, not daring to even steal a glance at the walking man as we passed by. Our driver was instructed not to wait outside the storefront, but rather to circle the neighborhood and return every few minutes.

From the outside, the tobacco shop of Thomas Duvane and Sons appeared well appointed, and the interior did not disappoint. The air held the sweet aroma of cut tobacco, with all the shelves and paneling done in polished wood. There were elegant displays of fine pipes, cigars, and cigarettes that were obviously meant for the well-to-do.

Joanna immediately went to the nearest section where a most excellent variety of pipes were on exhibit. Her focus was directed to a long-stemmed cherrywood that was beautifully shaped.

"Look, Watson! Here is a type of pipe my father so enjoyed," Joanna noted.

"Indeed it is," my father said. "That, along with a blackened clay, were his favorites."

"I read he gravitated to the clay pipe when in a disputatious mood."

"Which occurred with uncommon frequency. Because of this, I often referred to that particular pipe as Holmes's disputable clay."

"Which of course was the one he favored when involved with a three-pipe problem."

A short man, slight in figure, with neatly combed gray hair and a gentle face, came over to greet us. "What type tobacco did your father favor, may I ask?"

"Common black shag, coarsely cut," Joanna replied. "He enjoyed a most vigorous smoke."

"And one that left a dense, blue cloud behind."

"Quite," the tobacconist said. "I am Thomas Duvane and would be happy to be of service to you. Is it the long-stemmed cherrywood that is of interest?"

"Not at present," Joanna said. "But come next Christmas I shall return, for there are people close to me who would be delighted to receive such a gift."

"I would think so. The best of the cherrywood are now a seven-shilling pipe."

"And well worth it," Joanna went on. "The person I have in mind is happiest when smoking his cherrywood while reading the newspaper. We know that the cherrywood pipe has a flat bottom that allows it to stand on its own when placed down. This of course allows the reader to rest his pipe and keep both hands on his newspaper."

"I have more than a few customers who purchase the cherrywood for that very reason."

Joanna reached for a briar pipe and examined it carefully. "But I am told that those of briar absorb the moisture from the tobacco better than the cherrywood, which gives the former a more flavorful smoke."

"I have heard that as well, but in my opinion the cherrywood holds its own in that regard."

"I value that opinion and will keep it in mind."

Duvane gave Joanna a half bow. "It is a pleasure speaking with someone so informed about pipes. May I ask where you acquired this knowledge?"

"From my father," Joanna replied.

"Does he enjoy cigars as well?"

"Havanas on occasion."

"A man of excellent taste."

"Who unfortunately is no longer with us."

"My condolences," Duvane said sympathetically.

"Thank you," Joanna said. "I should also like to thank you for the new information, which I will find most useful. And now I would very much like to purchase three packages of Player's Navy Cut."

"Of course, madam," he said, and walked to the shelves that held the cigarettes.

"Why have you asked for Player's when you have always smoked nothing but Turkish cigarettes?" I asked quietly, following Joanna to the cigarette section.

"How many packages of Player's do you see on the nearby shelf?" Joanna replied in a whisper, motioning with her head.

"Three."

"There is your answer."

"Why are you buying the last?"

"To empty the shelf when the approaching gentleman comes in for his two packages. If there are no more in stock, I will generously offer to share and thus strike up a conversation with the unnamed man."

"Clever," I remarked.

"I try to stay ahead of the game," Joanna said with a smile.

But the smile quickly left her face when the door to the shop opened and the tall, well-dressed gentleman entered. Joanna hurriedly turned away and moved back to the pipe section. In a low whisper she said, "John, stand between me and the new arrival. Position yourself so that his view of me is blocked. Watson, step to my right and hide my profile, which I do not wish him to notice on his way out."

My father and I rapidly followed Joanna's instructions and

appeared to be focusing on the display of fine pipes, but our ears were concentrated on the conversation taking place on the counter behind us.

"Your two packages of Player's, sir?" Duvane proffered.

"If you would be so good," the man replied in clipped English.

"The Dutch Masters you ordered should arrive tomorrow morning."

"Quite popular, are they?"

"The blunts are in constant demand, sir." Duvane reached for two packages of Player's Navy Cut. "As are the Player's that are by far our most preferred brand."

The transaction was completed without further conversation and the well-dressed gentleman departed. The tobacconist hurried behind a curtain at the rear of the shop and returned with a fresh supply of Player's Navy Cut. As he placed them on a mid-level shelf, Joanna strolled over and asked, "Would it be too much of a bother to change my order to Turkish cigarettes?"

"No problem at all, madam."

"Thank you."

"Three packages, then?"

"I think two for now, for they are a stronger smoke."

"With more intense flavor, I might add."

"Quite so," Joanna said. "Would you also be good enough to replenish my father-in-law's supply of Arcadia mixture? I think three ounces would suffice."

"Very good, madam," the tobacconist said and once again disappeared behind the curtain at the rear.

My father said quickly, "But, Joanna, I have an adequate supply of Arcadia mixture at home."

"We need time to make certain the gentleman is well away, for I recognized him and he may recognize me."

"How do you know him?"
"Through his wife."
"Who is?"
"Lady Jane Hamilton."

19

The Unexpected Death

We did not retire until the late hour that evening, all the while trying to unravel the mystery of the strange meeting between Lady Jane Hamilton and her husband. My father and I finally went to our bedrooms at midnight, and left Joanna pacing the floor and smoking one cigarette after another as she grappled with the unsolvable problem. When I entered the drawing room the next morning, Joanna was still pacing through a dense haze of cigarette smoke.

Opening a window for fresh air, I said, "I take it the mystery remains."

"I have the knot partially untied," Joanna said. "It is the end equation that continues to elude me. But it too will come into view when I acquire the singular, most important piece of the puzzle."

"Which is?"

"The papers that Little Alfie saw Lady Jane and her husband studying. Show me their contents and everything immediately falls into place. Nothing else begins to approach their relevance."

"But I would think that Lady Jane and her motive are the key."

Joanna flicked her wrist at the suggestion. "She is but a carrier or go-between. She either brought the papers to her husband or he had them waiting for her arrival."

"Where would she have gotten the papers you speak of?" I queried.

"A dozen places or more," Joanna replied. "They could have been handed to her by Roger Marlowe at their luncheon meeting, or delivered during her walk through Harrods where we had no eyes on her, or even placed in the wrapped goose from the poulterer. But then again, it is equally possible that her husband provided the papers. After all, Sir Oliver Hamilton is a high-ranking officer in His Majesty's Navy and has access to the most sensitive documents."

"Surely you don't suspect him of treason."

"I suspect everyone until they are proven innocent."

My father entered the drawing room, neatly dressed and already smoking his first pipeful of Arcadia mixture. "Through my opened door I heard your conversation and wondered if all three of those you mentioned were somehow involved. In particular, could Lady Jane be a go-between for both her husband and dear friend Roger Marlowe?"

"Capital, Watson!" Joanna exclaimed. "That very thought crossed my mind as well and cannot be easily discarded. It is a most convenient triangle in which Roger Marlowe decodes the message, hands it to Lady Jane who then rushes it to her husband, and who in turn decides if it is important enough to transmit to the Germans."

"But why would a titled, distinguished naval officer resort to treason?" I asked.

"Uncover the perpetrator and I will give you the motive,"

Joanna responded. "Nevertheless, there are difficulties with this line of reasoning. In particular, it does not explain why husband and wife must meet in a secret location and avoid being seen together. Such a transaction could have taken place in their home and no one would have been the least bit suspicious. Also, recall that Lady Jane's disappearance for an hour only occurred when her husband was supposedly at sea. Why the need to make him absent when it serves no apparent purpose here?"

"Yet, as you just mentioned, we cannot totally disregard their involvement," I opined.

"Nor do I plan to," Joanna said. "But we must keep our focus on the Admiralty Club where most of the naval codes are broken and devised. That is where the traitor is. All the others, if implicated, are simply coconspirators. Bear in mind, our traitor knew Alistair Ainsworth well, was aware of his work and unique skill as a decoder, and was cognizant of his habits. Only those belonging to the Admiralty Club meet all these requirements. Thus, the traitor must reside within this group."

"That being the case, I would favor Roger Marlowe," my father said. "As Joanna has pointed out, his earnings can't begin to cover his lavish tastes. There must be an outside source of income."

"The years he spent in Germany at the University of Heidelberg would also cast a shadow," I added.

"Indeed," my father agreed. "And his closeness to Lady Jane makes her the perfect go-between for Roger Marlowe."

"Should we then not concern ourselves with Geoffrey Montclair and Mary Ellington?" Joanna asked.

"Not at all," I said. "I am still concerned with Montclair's somewhat feminine features. If he does have sexual peculiarities, it would make him a most tempting target for blackmail."

"I am certain his past was carefully scrutinized before he was allowed into the Admiralty Club," my father argued mildly. "Surely they would have discovered any such doings."

"Even if they did, perhaps they were willing to overlook them," I countered. "Remember that talents like Montclair's are not easy to come by."

"Particularly his photographic memory," Joanna recalled. "That unique characteristic makes him invaluable when deciphering multiple codes."

"Thus, both Roger Marlowe and Geoffrey Montclair are suspects, but certainly we can exclude Mary Ellington," I concluded. "After all, she has lost a son in the war and must hate the Germans for that reason alone."

"Or perhaps she holds a similar grudge against England for sending her son off to a war she disapproves of," Joanna said.

"How do you know she disapproves of the war?" I asked.

Joanna shrugged. "I don't. I was simply raising the possibility."

"You must admit that is highly unlikely," I said.

"Do not overlook the unlikely, John," Joanna cautioned. "For at times, it is the unlikely that shines a light on the likely."

"The other side of the same coin," my father noted.

"Precisely," Joanna said. "Recall the case of *A Study in Treason* in which a most expensive Havana cigar was reportedly purchased by a stable boy who had a salary of far less than a pound a month."

"So then, all things considered," my father concluded, "we now have three suspects and at least two coconspirators. But alas, that does not bring us any closer to Alistair Ainsworth."

The telephone on our desk rang and my father picked up the receiver, saying, "Watson here."

He listened intently, then slowly replaced the receiver. A

grim expression came to his face. "It seems our list of suspects at the Admiralty Club has been narrowed to two. Geoffrey Montclair has been found stabbed to death."

We arrived at the Admiralty Club just as a homicide team from Scotland Yard was departing. Fortunately, the body of Geoffrey Montclair had not been moved and was in the exact position when first discovered. According to Inspector Lestrade, the body was discovered by Lieutenant Dunn on his arrival at 7:45 A.M.

Montclair's corpse was slumped over his desk, his bloodied right hand extended and resting on the keyboard of a typewriter. There was a large, pearl-handled dagger plunged so deep into his back its blade was not visible. The blood spread over his back and shoulders was well clotted and blackish maroon in color, indicating the stabbing had taken place hours earlier.

"He never saw it coming," Lestrade proclaimed. "All evidence strongly suggests he was sitting at his desk, working away on his typewriter, when he was attacked from behind. You will note he made no effort to turn or resist, which I believe tells us the murderer crept up silently on his victim. Death must have come quite quickly."

"There is obviously no sign of a struggle," Joanna said.

"None whatsoever," Lestrade agreed. "But there is clear evidence the motive was robbery. You will note that the drawers in the victim's desk are opened and have been rummaged through. More importantly, Montclair's wallet and gold timepiece are missing."

"Were the desks in the other offices rummaged through as well?" Joanna asked.

"Not that we could see," Lestrade replied. "We believe the thief was in too big a hurry to depart. After all, he had just committed murder and had no idea if other coworkers might be returning shortly."

"Was the main door locked?"

"There was no sign of forced entry, if that is your question."

Dunn stepped forward and said, "I am afraid that the members of the Admiralty Club all too often leave the door unlocked in the late evening, although repeatedly warned not to do so."

Joanna moved over to the desk and motioned to the items atop it. There was a leather card case, a silver fountain pen, and some loose coinage. "And these?"

"They were found in the victim's pockets," Lestrade replied.

"Strange."

"How so?"

"That they were left behind," Joanna said, and turned to the group who was gathered just outside the door. "Who was the last to see Montclair alive?"

"I was," Roger Marlowe answered. "It was almost seven when I said good night to Geoffrey and traveled down to the pub for a quiet drink."

"Did you lock the door after you?"

"I do not recall, but it is my usual custom to do so."

"At the time of your departure was Geoffrey Montclair working on the message in his typewriter?"

Marlowe nodded. "As he had been for most of the day. He felt certain there was something amiss within Tubby's last message that was of critical importance."

"Are you referring to the one he decoded for the Germans?"

"Yes."

"Did Montclair give any hint as to what he was searching for?"

"He continued to state that something was off," Marlowe answered. "Apparently some fact tucked away in his photographic memory seemed to contradict the current message."

"Was it common for Montclair to remain after the others departed?"

"That was most unusual, for he always seemed to have other engagements for the evening," Marlowe said. "But in this instance, he thought he was very close to the answer and wished to pursue it, rather than break his line of concentration."

"So death could have occurred any time between then and now," Joanna concluded.

"Unfortunately that is so, for we have no way to time the event with precision," Lestrade said. "Nevertheless, the coldness of the corpse would suggest death happened some hours ago."

"Perhaps my husband could be of assistance here," Joanna suggested.

"We would be most grateful for his expertise in this matter."

I began my examination from a distance and purposely avoided the fatal wound, for not to do so can distract the examiner from other less obvious clues that may be equally important. The slumped position of the corpse over his typewriter and the failure to see blood elsewhere indicated the death blow was administered while Montclair sat at his desk. There were no defensive wounds about his hands and wrists, which was additional proof that Montclair was caught totally unawares. I glanced down at the corpse's groin and saw no blood or evidence of sexual mutilation which at times occurs when the victim is killed in a bout of homosexual rage. The muscles of the arms and face were only beginning to show signs of rigor mortis. Finally I inspected the knife wound that penetrated so deeply into the thorax it would have caused injury to or perhaps severed a great artery. Grasping the knife's handle, I attempted to move it side to side in order to gauge the knife's depth, but found it quite fixed in place. My gaze went back to the victim's bloodied hand, and I wondered how the blood arrived there. There were no wrist or arm wounds to account for this.

Joanna asked, "Tell me, John, what so draws your attention to the victim's hand?"

"I was trying to determine how the blood reached it."

A Mona Lisa smile came to Joanna's face. "Curious, isn't it?"

Lestrade stepped in for a closer look and said, "He was probably reaching back in an attempt to extract the knife."

"The wound would have been quite painful," my father interjected.

"My reasoning as well, Dr. Watson," Lestrade said. "The thief steals up on Mr. Montclair, stabs him in the back, and allows him to briefly struggle against the wound before removing the victim's possessions and fleeing."

"Such a waste," Mary Ellington declared. "He had such a fine mind. And he seemed so close to solving the coded message now in his typewriter. As a matter of fact, he called me last evening just before nine to confirm the exact number of Orkney Islands. He seemed to think that might be an important clue."

"Were you able to give him the answer?" Joanna asked.

"I confirmed there are seventy islands in the archipelago," Mary responded. "He said he would add the number into his equation, whatever that meant."

"Well then, we can now state with certainty that the

victim was murdered some time after nine in the evening," Lestrade said.

"Can you be more precise than that, John?" Joanna asked.

"Death occurred approximately five hours ago," I answered. "Rigor mortis is now setting in more completely and involves the muscles of the jaw, neck, and upper extremities. In that the body was discovered at seven forty-five this morning and rigor mortis requires five hours to show itself, we can estimate he was murdered at two forty-five."

"At which time the pub below was closed," Joanna said unhappily.

"Of what significance is that?" Lestrade asked.

"Possible witnesses," Joanna replied. "Of which we currently have none."

"We are now scouring the neighborhood in that regard," Lestrade said. "Although I must admit that I am not optimistic."

Joanna went over to the window and attempted to open it, but it was securely fastened. Next she gazed at the door and the transom over it. "Tell me, Lieutenant Dunn, is this facility not kept under some sort of surveillance late at night? After all, important, sensitive documents pass through these rooms."

"There is no need," Dunn said. "As I mentioned earlier, the documents you refer to are secure in Whitehall at that hour. No personal items are left behind either."

"And that is why our common thief found nothing of value in Montclair's desk," Lestrade noted. "But his mistake may have been in taking Mr. Montclair's gold timepiece. He will no doubt attempt to pawn it, and we will alert all pawnshops to be on the lookout for the timepiece, which, by the way, we are informed has Montclair's initials engraved on its back surface."

"Do you believe the thief is that stupid?" Joanna asked.

"Most of them are, madam."

"Well then, we shall leave you to your investigation," Jo-anna said, taking a final glance at the typewriter and the blood-ied hand that rested upon it. Something about the message within the typewriter seemed of particular interest.

Lestrade followed her line of vision before saying, "I trust you will inform us if any further clues come to light."

"Rest assured I will."

As we stepped into the central area of the Admiralty Club's rooms, Mary Ellington raced after us. She was holding up a folded slip of paper. "Mrs. Watson, I believe this just dropped from your purse."

Joanna took the slip and, without looking at it, returned it to her purse. "Thank you," she said warmly. "I sometimes make little notes to myself."

"As do I," Mary said, and retreated back into her office.

Once we had carefully climbed down the wet back stairs and were seated in our carriage, Joanna sighed deeply to her-self. "This is obviously not the work of a common thief."

"Surely you do not think the German agents performed this dastardly deed," I said.

"Of course not," Joanna said. "Such an adventure would have been far too risky for them. If they wanted him silenced, why would they endanger themselves by coming to these rooms? There are a dozen other places they could have dis-patched him without raising suspicion."

"Who then?"

"The traitor."

My father and I leaned forward, both of us wondering what signs we had missed.

"There is no other explanation, and all clues point to that singular conclusion," Joanna elucidated. "Let us begin with the supposed common thief. He is tall and no doubt powerfully built, yet he enters Montclair's office unnoticed. With Montclair's desk facing the door, surely the thief would have been seen."

"How did you determine the thief was both tall and powerful?" my father asked.

"From the angle of the knife, which was at forty-five degrees," Joanna explained. "Thus, it had to be delivered by someone who loomed above Montclair's upper thorax. A short man could have never performed such a feat."

"Is your observation that the murderer was powerfully built based on the depth of the knife wound?"

"That and John's inability to move the position of the blade," Joanna replied, and turned to me. "It was rather fixed in place, was it not?"

"Indeed," I said, then recited the obvious. "It was either embedded between the ribs or jammed into the vertebrae of the spine. Only a powerful man could have delivered such a blow."

"So we have a tall, well-built thief who passes within touching distance of Montclair, yet his presence goes undetected," Joanna continued on. "This would have been highly unlikely, and even more unlikely is the conclusion that a common thief would kill Montclair. There was no need for murder. The thief could have easily overcome Montclair with a single blow to the head. Also, keep in mind that even stupid thieves will avoid murder at all costs, for if caught, robbery lands them in prison for five years, while murder assures them the gallows."

"You raise good points," my father said. "But they are hardly conclusive."

"Ah, but the list goes on. What sort of thief takes a gold timepiece and wallet, yet leaves behind a leather card case and fountain pen that can easily be pawned? And there were four shillings in Montclair's pocket that our thief overlooked or ignored. It is also striking that he didn't bother with the ring on Montclair's finger that would have brought a pretty price on the black market."

"I too saw the ring, but did not place great significance to it," I admitted. "Pray tell what made it so valuable?"

"Its Freemason symbol, which consists of a Masonic square and compasses, with the letter *G* in its center," Joanna described. "No thief worth his salt would ever leave it behind. You see, after money, thieves search meticulously for the next most valuable item, which is jewelry. Finally, your attention should be drawn to the position of the corpse's hands. Do you observe anything in that regard, Watson?"

My father took several puffs on his cherrywood pipe as he considered the question. "There was a bloodied hand resting on the typewriter."

"A *single* hand," Joanna emphasized. "Now, I ask you, who sits at a typewriter with only one hand on the keyboard? The answer is no one. He had a hand on the typewriter in a final effort to point to the sheet of paper it possessed. He even smeared his blood on the sheet so we could not help but notice it."

"Perhaps it was simply a random motion of a dying man," my father suggested.

Joanna shook her head at once. "Highly skilled codebreakers, like Montclair, do not make random moves. Every act they take has a purpose. Thus allow me, if you will, to reconstruct the last moments of Geoffrey Montclair's life. Someone he knows enters his office, causing no alarm. That person gazes over Montclair's shoulder at the sheet in the typewriter and becomes aware that Montclair is close to uncovering the traitor's identity. The person then stabs Montclair in the back and attempts to make the scene appear that of a common robbery. He leaves the office, believing Montclair is dead, but the code-

breaker still has a breath of life in him. With his last move on
the face of the earth, Montclair dips his finger in his own
blood, which is pouring out from the wound just below the
neckline, and points to the sheet in the typewriter. You may
recall that people facing such a death often try to leave a message behind that names the murderer. Thus, the message on
that sheet will tell us who murdered Geoffrey Montclair and
who the traitor is, for they are one and the same."

"Which narrows the list of suspects to Roger Marlowe and
Mary Ellington," I concluded.

"With Marlowe being the most likely by far," my father
asserted.

"So it would appear," Joanna said as she reached in her
purse for the folded slip Mary Ellington had retrieved.

"I was unaware that you wrote notes to yourself," I remarked.

"I don't," Joanna said.

"But you accidentally dropped a slip of paper from your
purse."

"I lost nothing from my purse," Joanna said. "I was simply covering for her."

"Covering what?"

"Her rather clever way of sending me a message."

Joanna unfolded the slip. It read:

THE POETS' CORNER AT NOON

20

Westminster Abbey

At noon, Westminster Abbey was overflowing with tourists, many of whom were congregated in the Poets' Corner to pay homage to England's greatest poets and writers. We found Mary Ellington standing over the tablet in the floor bearing the name Alfred Lord Tennyson.

"Is Tennyson your favorite poet?" Joanna asked quietly.

"My very favorite," Mary answered. "His haunting lines in 'The Charge of the Light Brigade' continue to resonate in my mind. You may recall how they read: 'Theirs not to reason why, theirs but to do and die'. Those few words remind us of the futility of war in a most powerful manner."

I did remember the famous lines that commemorated the tragic loss of life in the Battle of Balaclava during the Crimean War. It brought to mind that Mary Ellington had also paid the terrible price of war, having lost her only son in battle just months ago.

Mary sighed sadly and strode over to the William Shakespeare memorial. She waited for a group of tourists to depart before saying in a low voice, "What do you think of the message in the typewriter?"

"It needs to be deciphered," Joanna replied.

"Oh, you think more than that. I could not help but notice how intently you studied it. Be good enough to inform me what so drew your attention."

"Notes left behind by the deceased can be quite revealing," Joanna said. "When an individual commits suicide, the note will speak of despair and an occasional good-bye. Those in a case of murder are often an attempt to identify the person who perpetrated the crime."

"This is certainly not suicide, is it?"

"Not unless you can describe the mechanism by which one plunges a dagger into one's back."

"So we can conclude that Geoffrey Montclair was trying to name his murderer."

"That is a reasonable assumption."

"It is also reasonable to assume I remain high on your list of suspects."

"Why do you think so?"

"Because you considered the possibility that my invitation might be a trap of some sort," Mary said tonelessly, then gestured with her head at the entrance to Poets' Corner where my father was stationed. "Is he armed?"

"Of course."

"Better safe than sorry."

"But I must say you are not very high up on the list of likely suspects."

"I should hope not, for time is now of the essence," Mary said in a voice meant only for us. "With that in mind, let us return to the heart of the matter, which is the coded message within the message. I am your only chance to decipher it and that is why you are here."

"Roger Marlowe could be of assistance," I suggested. "Particularly since he was quite close to Alistair Ainsworth."

Mary shook her head at once. "Roger is far too high on your list of suspects for obvious reasons. So you must either trust me or walk away now."

Joanna and I remained in place.

"Let us begin with Geoffrey Montclair," Mary continued. "He knew something was amiss with the message in the typewriter and wondered if the critical clue was the number three or some variation of it. For example, could it refer to every third letter in the message or such? Or to the square root of three or a multiple of it? Now, with Roger Marlowe being the mathematical wizard, Montclair went to him for ideas. Roger tried a variety of equations, but could not apply the number three to the remainder of the message. They both began to believe that the number was not the key and had little relevance in deciphering the code. I believed otherwise and still do, but find myself at a stalemate. Which brings us to the purpose of this meeting. At this point I require outside assistance to unravel the code. I need to know everything the police know about the life of Alistair Ainsworth outside the Admiralty Club. In particular, please focus on the number three, as in Tubby's address, phone number, passport, appointment times unrelated to work, and the like. I am certain therein lies our answer."

"Might I inquire how a street address could be useful?" I asked.

"Permit me to give you a simple example," Mary replied. "Let us say the number in question is twenty-five and the person lives at twenty-five or two-five Iron Road. The two or second letter in the address is *r*, which is followed by an *o*. The five or fifth letter in the address is also an *r*, followed by an *o*. Thus, we have *ro* mentioned twice, and we recall that the first name of the prime suspect is Robert, and so the finger of guilt points directly at him."

"Or the *ro* could signify the name Roger," I thought aloud. "As in Roger Marlowe."

"Good," Mary approved. "Now you begin to see the light."

"Do you consider him a prime suspect?"

"Don't you?"

"There is one consideration we have not yet discussed," Joanna said, then paused as a well-dressed couple strolled by in front of us. "That being the message itself. Are we certain the line—'Three U-boats off the innermost Orkneys'—is correct in every regard?"

"To the best of my knowledge."

"Is there more written in the original message sent out to the Royal Navy?"

Mary furrowed her brow in concentration, obviously thinking back. "Of that I cannot be certain. But the line you quoted is the essential one."

"We must have the entire message," Joanna beseeched. "The number three or a variation thereof may point to other letters in less important lines. It would also be helpful to have all messages that relate to U-boats off the Orkney Islands."

"I very much doubt Lieutenant Dunn will let us pry into those," I said. "Obtaining the complete first lines from him earlier was akin to pulling teeth."

"But I may have some of that information in my notes at home," Mary volunteered. "Assuming I have not tossed them into the fireplace as is my habit when done."

"But Dunn specifically told us that members of the Admiralty Club were not allowed to take documents and notes from their offices," I recalled.

"When in heated pursuit of a code, we do not concern

ourselves with Lieutenant Dunn's instructions," Mary said.
"Nevertheless, I am not optimistic I have the entire message
in my possession."

"But you must search," Joanna implored. "We should keep
in mind that Alistair Ainsworth is a master cryptographer, and
he would be aware that most people would expect the key to
the code to be located in the first line. That of course may not
be the case."

Mary nodded at the notion. "That would be very much
like Tubby. That is, let your opponent concentrate on the first
line, while you orchestrate your move on the second."

"Or the third," Joanna suggested. "As in the number
three."

"Indeed."

I could not help but be impressed with Joanna as she
matched wits with one of England's finest codebreakers. But
then again, I recalled her deciphering a most confusing code
that consisted of only slanted lines. It was of such complex-
ity that it even baffled Sir David Shaw who was knighted for
his codebreaking accomplishments.

"In addition, it would be most useful if you could obtain
the sheet of paper that was secured in Geoffrey Montclair's
typewriter," Joanna requested.

"That might be quite impossible, for I am certain Scotland Yard will wish to hold on to it as evidence," Mary said.
"But I can copy it word for word if you like."

"No, no. It is the original I require, and it must be gotten
at all costs."

"What makes the sheet itself so important?" Mary asked.

"The blood upon it," Joanna said and, taking my arm,
strolled away from the Poets' Corner.

21

A Strange Meeting

We spent the entire afternoon trying to decipher Alistair Ains-worth's message, but to no avail. The singular significance of the number 3 in the coded communiqué continued to elude us. It did not refer to the third letter of the alphabet, *c*, nor to the ninth letter, *i*, 9 being the number 3 squared. Neither the combination of the *c* and the *i* nor the reverse revealed any hidden meaning. There were no symbols or apostrophes, the latter being of great importance since they are always followed by the letters *s, t, d, m, ll,* or *re*. We even employed the Caesar shift using the number 3. In this sophisticated code, you shift the alphabet a certain number of spaces in one direction. For example, using 3 as a guide, *a* becomes *d*, *b* becomes *e*, and so on. Thus, the word *boat* would be decoded as *erdw*, which made no sense. As darkness fell and our fatigue set in, we decided to adjourn for dinner and start afresh in the morning.

Taking our seats in front of a nicely burning fire, we enjoyed a richly flavored amontillado while Joanna gave us the detailed history of this fine sherry.

"It is named after the town of Montilla in Andalusia, the

region of Spain where its grapes are grown," she told us. "The grapes are often dried up to twenty days prior to fermentation, which is known as the *soleo* process. The actual aging in casks can vary for different varieties, but all must be stored away in oak casks. The sherries are naturally sweet for the most part, but in some instances the winemaker adds ingredients to make it so."

"Is all sherry from Spain?" my father asked.

"Without exception."

"But how did it become so popular in Great Britain?"

"There is a merry history behind that," Joanna said as she replenished our glasses. "It became quite popular after Sir Francis Drake sacked the city of Cadiz in 1587. At the time, Cadiz was a major port, and Spain was preparing an armada there to invade England. Among the spoils brought back by Drake after destroying their fleet were two thousand nine hundred barrels of sherry that had been waiting to be loaded onto Spanish ships. This event popularized sherry throughout the British Isles."

I was aware that Joanna was well versed in any number of subjects that were related to crime and criminal investigation, but on occasion she surprised me with her considerable knowledge of other, unconnected topics. Nevertheless, I wondered if perhaps her enlightenment on sherry served some investigational purpose. "Why this insight into sherry?" I asked. "Was there something that spurred your interest?"

"I delved into the subject after reading Edgar Allan Poe's short story, 'The Cask of Amontillado.' It was not so much a mystery as a tale of horrific murder."

"Was the cask of sherry the murder weapon?"

Joanna shook her head with a smile. "It was the enticement."

There was a brief rap on the door and Miss Hudson peeked

in. "I am sorry to disturb you, Dr. Watson, but the street urchins have returned and insist on being seen, even at this late hour."

"Please show them up," my father said. "We shall not take long."

"I should hope not, for the goose you brought me is nearly done."

"Which we so look forward to."

As the door closed, Joanna said, "Something of the utmost importance must have transpired."

"New and unexpected visitors?" I wondered.

"Most likely," Joanna replied. "And they must have some unusual features that could not wait until morning to be reported. Keep in mind that, although the Baker Street Irregulars are young, they are streetwise and not easily moved. It is either the individual or an event instigated by that individual that has brought the Irregulars here at this unusual hour."

We heard racing feet coming up the stairs and quickly finished the last of our sherries. The trio of Irregulars sprinted into our drawing room, with Wiggins leading the way. He was dressed in workman's clothes, while Little Alfie and Sarah the Gypsy were still in their Sunday finest.

"What a tale we have for you, ma'am!" Wiggins exclaimed, catching his breath.

"I want every detail," Joanna said. "Start from the very beginning and leave not a syllable out."

"Well now, we took our positions early on, we did," Wiggins began. "Little Alfie and Sarah paraded the street, while I pretended to be a laborer seeking a day's wages."

Joanna asked, "Did that not make your presence obvious?"

"No, ma'am. There was plenty of workers about the neighborhood—roofers, plasterers, painters, and the like. It was not easy to find a nearby position, but luck struck as the sun began to fall, for a crew appeared to repair the cracks in the cobblestones. I landed a job pushing a wheelbarrow and that gave me a good view of the house. And it was then that a carriage arrived at the house and the lady stepped out."

"What lady?"

"Why, the fine lady you had us follow a few days back. Got right off, she did, without so much as a glance around, and entered the house."

"Did she make any effort to conceal her arrival?"

"None that I could see. Pranced right in, like she had no concerns."

"Did Little Alfie manage to peek into the house once again?"

"I did, ma'am," Little Alfie said, stepping forward. "They met in the parlor as before, but this time there was no embrace or kissing. It was all business, it was, with serious talk. Then the phone rang, which I could hear through the glass window. And they just stared at it a bit, before picking up. It was most solemn, I would say. I did not stay longer, for fear of being seen."

"We thought that was the end of it." Wiggins continued the story. "But we could not have been more wrong. For fifteen or so minutes later, a mighty military man arrived in a bloody big limousine."

"Mighty, you say!" I exclaimed.

"And then some, with his uniform all covered with ribbons and decorations. He also had one of those gold strands across his shoulder, indicating he was of high rank. I would guess the couple inside the house knew he was coming because the door opened for him without a knock."

"I need an accurate description of the naval officer," Joanna implored.

"He was a big man, with broad shoulders, and he carried himself very well indeed. His face looked royal, with high cheekbones and the like. I am guessing he was in his fifties because he had gray hair and thick, gray sideburns but no moustache."

"Was his head covered?"

Wiggins nodded. "With one of those strange, peaked navy hats that sit high."

Joanna turned to Little Alfie. "Were you able to sneak a peek after the officer entered?"

"That was a bit tricky, ma'am, for the officer's driver remained standing by the limousine, like a man keeping a careful eye out. But I got around him with Sarah's help. She walked by him, with a painful limp, which took his attention away from the alleyway, so in I went. It was quite dark by then, so I felt I could stay a bit longer without being seen. And there was this small crate in the alleyway that I could stand on, and this gave me an even better look."

"How many people were in the drawing room?"

"Three," Little Alfie reported. "The gentleman and the fine lady from earlier, and the new man in uniform who Wiggins just described for you. Now the talk continued to be quite serious. There were no smiles or handshakes nor any sort of refreshments. Then the old man in the uniform pulls out a map, and they all gather around it."

"Could you make out the details on the map?" Joanna asked quickly.

"I was too far away for that, ma'am. But I can tell you it was a bloody big map, for he had to open and hold it with both hands."

"I take it that it was impossible to overhear any of the conversation."

"Only two words, ma'am, and that was because the old gent shouted it out."

"And the words?"

"Damned spy!"

Joanna's eyes narrowed abruptly. "Are you certain?"

"Loud and clear it was, through the glass," Little Alfie replied. "And the old gent was bloody mad too. He had a tightly clenched fist to go along with his raised voice. Then, in a huff, the lady and old gent left. They were most unhappy, I can tell you that."

"The lady went directly to her carriage, and the naval officer to his limousine," Wiggins continued. "There was no exchange of words that I could see."

"Was anything said or done to identify the naval officer?" Joanna asked.

The three Irregulars shook their head simultaneously.

Joanna thought for a moment before asking, "Wiggins, you mentioned the officer had ribbons and decorations on his coat. Could you make any of them out?"

"No, ma'am. I was across the street at the time and the light wasn't all that good."

"I did see some sort of scroll on his sleeve," Little Alfie recalled. "When the gentleman was holding up the map, I had a clear view of his black sleeve. Near the cuff was a thick band of gold, with a circle atop it."

"Was the gold circle part of the band?"

A puzzled look came to Little Alfie's face. "I am not sure what you mean, ma'am."

"Now think back," Joanna urged. "Was the circle partially buried into the top of the gold band or was it placed separately atop it?"

"It was a bit buried," Little Alfie replied.

"Very good," Joanna said. "You must now return to the house on Ovington Street and report all comings and goings without delay."

Once the Irregulars had departed, Joanna lighted a Turkish cigarette and began pacing the floor, obviously lost in thought. For some reason, she concentrated best while on the move, much like Sherlock Holmes according to my father. From outside came a loud clap of thunder, followed by cracks of lightning, which Joanna paid no attention to as she continued to pace back and forth. Finally she stopped and, on tossing her cigarette into the fireplace, said, "This goes to the very highest level of government."

"Is this based on the appearance of a naval officer in a limousine?" my father asked.

"It is based on his rank," Joanna said. "The insignia on his sleeve denotes a rear admiral in the Royal Navy, and such a man does not make clandestine meetings in the dark of night unless the need is urgent."

"That is obvious from the words *damned spy* being shouted by the officer," my father noted.

"Oh, it goes much deeper than that, Watson. We have Lady Jane Hamilton sneaking away to visit her husband who is supposedly at sea, yet resides on Ovington Street in Knightsbridge and remains out of uniform so as not to be noticed. Does that not strike you as being odd?"

"But she made no effort to conceal herself this evening," my father argued mildly.

"That is because it was already dark and there was little chance she would be recognized. In addition, she was apparently in a rush and had no time to bother with unnecessary concealments. So we have Lady Jane Hamilton hurrying in the night to visit a hidden-away husband who should be at sea. Now, if that is not strange enough, add to the mix a rear admiral dashing in, carrying a large map and shouting 'Damned spy!' What a most odd confluence of events that needs to be explained."

"Apparently they are all involved in uncovering a spy," I surmised.

"Why would that require a rear admiral racing over to share such secretive information with Lady Jane?"

"Because she is close to Roger Marlowe," I replied at once.

"And who is Roger Marlowe close to?"

"Alistair Ainsworth!"

"And so the circle tightens," Joanna pronounced. "There is a common link among all these individuals and the events they are tied into."

"But what is the link?" I asked.

"That remains to be uncovered, John. For therein lies the answer to the disappearance of Alistair Ainsworth."

"But everything seems so disconnected."

"It is not as disconnected as you believe," Joanna said, reaching for a poker to stir the fire. "I only require one more piece of the puzzle and all will fall into place."

"Where is this piece to be found?"

"In Geoffrey Montclair's typewriter."

22

Hyde Park

My father awoke the following morning with his arthritic knee acutely inflamed, so he required assistance as we climbed into the carriage and traveled to see a rheumatic specialist whose office was located just off Park Lane. The specialist had devised a new topical treatment for such flare-ups, using heat and a cream that contained a high concentration of aspirin. This treatment was well suited to my father, for the increasing doses of aspirin he had been taking orally was causing him gastric distress. Rather than wait in the specialist's office for my father to be seen, Joanna, Johnny, and I chose to cross Park Lane and take a leisurely stroll through Hyde Park.

It was a surprisingly warm winter's day, with a clear sky and a gentle breeze coming off the Serpentine Lake. Dozens of people were out and about in the park, enjoying the glorious weather that we knew would be all too brief. Ahead of us, Johnny seemed to be in constant motion, glancing from side to side as if in search of something.

"Why does your son gaze around so?" I asked.

"It is a game we have played since he was a little boy,"

Joanna replied. "He searches for a scene at a distance and attempts to discern what is transpiring. We then compare our observations and match wits."

"With you winning, I would imagine."

"Yes, but the day will come when he is my equal."

"I truly doubt that."

"Watch," Joanna said, and gestured for her son to come join us. "What in this park so interests you, Johnny?"

"The two men by the lake who appear to be having a heated discussion."

"Do you envision it leading to fisticuffs?"

"That is unlikely, Mother, for there is a woman standing close by."

"Perhaps she is attempting to intercede."

"Perhaps, but there is a dog near the woman and it does not seem concerned," Johnny noted. "Dogs are very keen at anticipating trouble and would not simply sit back on their haunches and watch such an event."

"Pay attention to the dog and why it is not concerned with the obvious goings-on."

Johnny studied the scene once again before sighing under his breath. "I see a small hand feeding the dog. There is a child behind the woman, and were there the slightest hint of trouble the mother would quickly depart with her child in hand. Yet she stands in place, for the argument is apparently a friendly one."

"Well done, Johnny."

"I must learn to observe more carefully."

"You shall."

I asked, "Precisely how does one learn to observe more carefully?"

"By seeing the obvious, but not concentrating on it," Joanna replied. "You must then direct your study to the periphery where more clues await, which will allow you to see the whole picture rather than only a portion of it. Using this practice, you may well be able to connect all the clues and reach a sought-after resolution."

We walked across the expansive lawn until we came to the magnificent equestrian statue of the Duke of Wellington. It rested upon a tall stone pedestal, with only the name WELLINGTON engraved into it. Joanna slowly strolled around the statue and studied its every aspect, paying particular attention to the engraving.

"Do you note anything of consequence?" I asked.

"Nothing that will tell us why Waterloo was circled on the map."

Johnny inquired innocently, "Was it a map of Belgium that indicated where the battle was fought?"

"Are you familiar with the battle?" Joanna queried, evading the reason for her interest in Waterloo.

"Quite," Johnny replied. "And even more familiar with the Duke of Wellington who stands as one of England's greatest heroes."

"Which every English schoolboy will proudly state," said I.

"Yet with all their knowledge about the duke, not one in ten can tell you his given name."

"Which is?"

"Arthur Wellesley."

Joanna smiled at her son. "I was unaware."

"And not one in a hundred can name the horse the Duke of Wellington rode into battle," Johnny went on.

"Which is?"

"Copenhagen."

Joanna and I exchanged knowing glances, for the names Arthur Wellesley and Copenhagen should be brought to the attention of the Admiralty Club. It was indeed possible that

Alistair Ainsworth had those names in mind when he circled Waterloo on the train station map. What a stroke of luck that would be for all concerned!

Joanna asked, "May I inquire how you came about all this knowledge?"

"I learned of it from my tutor at Eton," Johnny answered. "He is considered to be a recognized authority on the subject, having written his thesis on the Duke of Wellington."

"Would you have ever learned these hidden facts from a private tutor we might have to hire?"

"No, Mother, for that information is not known by most."

"So we can conclude there is something rather special about your tutors at Eton."

"Oh yes, they are in every way special."

"Do you believe we can easily find their equal here in London?"

Johnny stared out at length and watched the ripples crossing the Serpentine Lake, for the wind was now picking up. Birds flew overhead, but made no sound. "Mother," he said finally, "I think it is in my best interest to return to Eton."

"A wise decision."

We turned as the group Johnny had studied was gaily strolling toward us. The adults were smiling and laughing, while the little girl led her dog on a merry chase. It was clear that the observations made by Joanna and her son were correct, yet they showed no delight in their achievement. Indeed, Johnny paid only scant attention to the approaching group before dashing off in search of more challenging scenes to be considered and discerned. I could not help but wonder if I was witnessing yet another reincarnation of Sherlock Holmes.

23

Exodus

That afternoon, with my father's knee much improved, we were summoned to the Admiralty Club where the news was dire. Alistair Ainsworth had been broken completely. The Germans were now aware of Exodus, a plan to blockade Kaiser Wilhelm's navy and all the shipping lanes into Germany's major ports. It was a disastrous blow to Great Britain's war effort.

Dunn's face was haggard as he spoke to us in a most grim voice. "The plan was to shortly deploy a squadron of ten ships from His Majesty's Navy to the North Sea where they would patrol the waters off the mouth of the Baltic Sea. From this position, they could hinder German warships entering the Atlantic and stop all the merchant vessels heading for German ports. Thus, Germany would not only have been deprived of a strong naval presence in the North Sea, it would have also been denied vital raw materials they need so desperately. Now that the Germans *have been informed of our war plans*, they will put their ships into the North Sea at once, have their U-boats swarm the area, and of course stockpile critical raw materials."

"We know that Germany has learned of our plan because

of a communiqué that was intercepted by Naval Intelligence," Dunn continued on. "It read simply 'Exodus broken.' Needless to say, it is a devastating hit and we fear the worst is yet to come. As I mentioned earlier to you, the Germans have been keeping on file all of our messages and communiqués, much like we do with theirs. Up to the present, our messages have for the most part been undecipherable, but all that changes now. With Ainsworth broken, the German intelligence unit will provide their navy with information of the greatest value. They will have detailed knowledge of our fleet, including the number and whereabouts of our ships, our naval strategies, and our alliance with other navies. It will put us at the greatest of disadvantages. With this in mind, I must ask you to redouble your efforts to locate Alistair Ainsworth before even more damage is done."

"Are we certain that Tubby gave them accurate information on Exodus?" Marlowe asked. "Perhaps he only gave them the name of the plan, with otherwise false information."

"That is wishful thinking," Dunn said. "Naval Intelligence has confirmed that a squadron of German warships has departed from their home ports and is currently passing through the Kattegat Strait, heading for the Atlantic Ocean. Yet additional warships are being prepared to make sail. These moves indicate they know the details of *our naval strategy*. There is no question that Ainsworth has been broken, and at this point we must attempt to salvage whatever we can. Thus, our first and only order of business is to find Ainsworth and learn what other information he might have shared with the Germans."

Dunn took a long, worrisome breath before gathering himself. "That is my directive and I mean to carry it out. So let us return to Ainsworth's first message, which was the Waterloo train station circled on a map. I need to know if any of your ideas have offered even a glimpse of a clue. Now, what about the French dictionary in Ainsworth's desk? Anything there, Marlowe?"

"Nothing of value," Roger Marlowe reported. "It contained numerous notes scribbled in the margins that dealt with nouns of no relevance. I could not find numbers or symbols that might lead to a cryptic message or location."

"Did you examine his copy of the Old Testament?"

"In detail, but I could find no hidden messages or clues. I of course concentrated on the book of Exodus this morning, but saw no inscribed markings, arrows, or symbols. I could see nothing to indicate Tubby had employed that section of the Old Testament to break or construct codes."

"Was there no writing at all?"

"Not on those pages."

"You must continue your search of the two books unless you uncover a better avenue to investigate," Dunn ordered, then turned to Mary Ellington. "As I recall, you also believed that the circled Waterloo somehow referred to our epic battle with France. In particular, you thought Ainsworth could be pointing to the emperor Napoleon who led the French forces."

"Tubby would have never been that direct," Mary said. "As I mentioned earlier, it was far more likely he was referring to another feature of Napoleon, namely his lovely wife Josephine. There is a Josephine Street in Reigate that Scotland Yard is currently investigating."

"With little success," Lestrade interjected. "No Germans or individuals with German-sounding names live there, nor have any houses been leased recently. We are now extending our search to other limits of the Reigate district."

"And what of Geoffrey Montclair's notion that the word *Waterloo* was intended to direct us to monuments built in honor of the Duke of Wellington?"

At this point Joanna raised the possibility that Ainsworth's

coded message was referring to Arthur Wellesley or Copenhagen, and told of their connection to the Duke of Wellington. The Admiralty Club knew of the duke's family name,
but were unaware that his horse was called Copenhagen and
deemed it worth studying.

"Nevertheless, we are continuing to investigate both monuments," Lestrade said, consulting his notepad. "It is our belief that the St. Paul's area is the more likely since it contains
several large residential pockets, in contrast to the neighborhoods surrounding Hyde Park. We have had no success to
date, but our investigation is not nearly completed."

"You may wish to double the manpower to that area,"
Dunn recommended. "If need be, draw on the police forces
from outlying districts. When asking about recent leases, how
far back in time did you go?"

"Six months."

"Extend it to a year," Dunn said. "These types of operations by foreign agents require great planning that takes far
more time than one might think."

"Then more men will definitely be required."

"Draw as many as you deem necessary. Better too many
than too few," Dunn said, then waited for others to speak.
When none did, he added, "I am open to further suggestions."

Joanna asked, "Does it not surprise you that Ainsworth
gave away such a valuable plan, when he could have chosen
one of lesser importance?"

"Perhaps they threatened him with death should he not
do so," Dunn surmised. "With a knife at one's throat, one's
resistance tends to disappear rather quickly."

"That is a possibility," Joanna agreed. "But allow me to
raise another. Perhaps he chose the plan called Exodus to provide an additional clue to his whereabouts. After all, the Ger-

mans would not have known of the plan's name unless Alistair Ainsworth so informed them."

"That is correct," Mary said at once. "Only we knew the name of the plan, yet the Germans mentioned it in their communiqué. Thus, Tubby must have purposely given it away."

"But what would its significance be?" Dunn asked impatiently.

"Exodus is the first book in the Old Testament," Joanna replied. "The answer may lie therein."

"The Old Testament!" Marlowe cried out. "Exodus could have a religious connotation, which might tie into the St. Paul's neighborhood. St. Paul's, of course, is Christian, while the Old Testament is the Jewish Bible. Is Tubby telling us there is a Jewish temple or synagogue near St. Paul's, and his location is between the two?"

"Quite possibly," Dunn said, and gestured quickly to Lestrade. "Please look into that, Inspector."

"Done!" Lestrade said.

"There is yet another possibility that needs to be raised," Joanna went on. "Perhaps there is a passage in the book of Exodus itself that holds Ainsworth's message."

"Are you familiar with that particular book?" Dunn asked promptly.

"I am about to be," Joanna answered.

"Perhaps we should bring in a theologian," Lestrade suggested.

Dunn shook his head dismissively. "We require a codebreaker, not a worshipper."

"Tell me, Joanna, what sort of passage in Exodus would you look for?" Mary asked.

"Any phrase or word that could relate to modern London," Joanna replied. "For example, if Pharaoh had a tower where prisoners or hostages were held, it could point to the Tower of London, which is located on the north bank of the Thames in central London."

"Or to Moses's journey up Mount Sinai," Mary added. "We should see if there are any synagogues or temples near St. Paul's that bear the name Mount Sinai."

Lestrade hurriedly copied down notes in his small notepad, writing on one page after another. "It might be wise to look into all Mount Sinai and Sinai synagogues, and not only those near St. Paul's. After all, the Germans may have moved yet again."

"Indeed," Dunn approved. "You should focus on those situated in residential neighborhoods."

"And those located on streets that have French- or German-sounding names," Joanna advised.

"Quite right," Lestrade said, and jotted down another reminder.

"Are there other ideas?" Dunn asked and, when none were forthcoming, he walked over to a large window and peered out at the tourists gathering in Trafalgar Square. He appeared lost in his thoughts for a long moment before turning back to the group. "Let us redouble our efforts, for so much is at stake here."

As we strolled through the central area of the Admiralty Club, Joanna motioned with her head to the now vacant office of Geoffrey Montclair. On his desktop was the typewriter containing the bloodied message.

"We need that typewriter," Joanna muttered under her breath.

"Perhaps the bloodied sheet can be retrieved," I hoped.

"But I require it to be in the typewriter," Joanna whispered. "That is of the utmost importance."

Outside, the day was clear and brisk, so we strolled over to Nelson's towering monument and found a space free of tourists. Nevertheless Joanna glanced around to make certain no one was within hearing distance.

"We are running out of time," she said in a concerned voice. "I fear that Alistair Ainsworth will shortly be out of reach."

"Surely they will not attempt to move him to Germany so quickly now," my father asserted. "Not with the English ports under such close surveillance."

"At this juncture a rapid move would be the smart move," said Joanna. "The Germans have already had several close encounters with us, and will not wish to push their luck further. They are very much aware that the longer they remain on British soil, the greater the chance they will be apprehended."

"It would still be a dicey maneuver," my father noted.

"But worth the risk," Joanna insisted. "Imagine the immense value of having Alistair Ainsworth imprisoned in Germany. Not only could he decipher all the coded messages they have on file, he could decode all future communiqués as well. Ainsworth would become a never-ending font of information."

"It would be a nightmare for the Royal Navy."

"From which they might never awaken."

"But even if this transfer were to happen, you assume that Ainsworth would continue to cooperate with the Germans."

"Once a man is broken, he stays broken."

"Your point is well taken, but I continue to believe the German agents will bide their time and await a more opportune moment to carry their catch to Germany."

"To the contrary, they will now move with haste."

My father gave Joanna a most serious look and asked, "What indication is there to show this will occur?"

"The word *exodus,* which means to go out or go forth," Joanna said. "Alistair Ainsworth is telling us that the Germans are about to depart, with him in tow."

24

The Deciphering

On returning to our rooms at 221b Baker Street, we immediately retrieved Sherlock Holmes's copy of the Old Testament and gathered around the fireplace as Joanna read from the book of Exodus. The initial reading revealed no clues, but the second was more productive.

"Perhaps the number ten is important here," Joanna ventured. "Ten is mentioned twice in this passage. The first being the tenth plague in which God threatened to kill all the Egyptian firstborn. The second refers to the ten commandments that Moses received on Mount Sinai. Thus, we have two tens, which may or may not be relevant."

My mind went back to the instructions given to us some time ago by Sir David Shaw, the curator at the British Museum who was a master codebreaker. He had stressed the importance of a particular number in deciphering coded messages. "Sir David would tell us that ten could represent *j*, the tenth letter in the alphabet, or the number ten could be one-aught, with the one being the letter *a* in the alphabet, followed by aught or the letter *o*." I shrugged my shoulders at the possible variations of *j* or *ao*. "But neither makes sense here."

"Do not discard the relevance of the number ten so quickly," my father advised. "For there is yet another ten to add to the equation. Recall that in the coded naval message a squadron of ten British ships was to be deployed to the projected battle area."

"Can you somehow relate that to the message sent by Alistair Ainsworth?" I asked.

"Sadly, I cannot," my father said. "Perhaps Joanna can help us in that regard."

Joanna shook her head. "The permutations are endless. Furthermore, now that I give the matter second thought, if the number ten is so important, Ainsworth would have inserted it in the original message he decoded for the Germans. He could have said that there were ten rather than three U-boats off the Orkney Islands. This would not have raised suspicions with the Germans, in that their major concern would have been the submarines themselves being detected, not their exact number. They might have even enjoyed the British exaggeration of their strength."

"So we have reached yet another dead end," I said.

"When it comes to numbers we have," Joanna concurred, then furrowed her brow in thought. After a long pause, she said, "Perhaps we should not be searching for some deeply hidden passage, but for a key that is rather obvious."

"But Alistair Ainsworth is a master of codes," I challenged.

"That is my point, dear John. Because he is such a master, we have assumed he would use this unique skill to send his message. But that may not be the case. You must consider the dire situation in which Ainsworth finds himself, with time being of the essence. He had to communicate quickly, using a code that could be obvious to his colleagues, but not to the Germans. The key word here is *obvious*. He would not transmit a message that would require days and days, if not weeks, to decipher."

"How can you be certain your assumption is correct?" my father asked.

"By putting myself in his place," Joanna replied. "It is the avenue I would have taken under the circumstances."

"But we know every word in the message Ainsworth sent," I argued. "Yet we remain in a quandary."

"That is because we do not have the complete original message to compare with the one in Montclair's typewriter."

"I am having difficulty finding your line of reasoning."

"Allow me to explain," Joanna went on. "We have an individual who studied the original message and the one sent by Alistair Ainsworth, and that individual is now dead. And it was Montclair who insisted there was a difference between the two messages, but could not recall it. His exact words were 'Something was amiss, something was off.' Now please be good enough to place all these indisputable facts in order and tell me what conclusion you draw."

My father and I tried to connect all the facts, but to no avail. We gave each other puzzled glances.

"Come now!" Joanna urged. "Concentrate on the difference that Montclair was pursuing."

My father's cherrywood pipe dropped from his grip as the answer came to him. "Montclair was murdered because he remembered the difference!"

"Spot on, Watson! Somehow the traitor learned of it and had no choice but to dispatch Montclair." Joanna reached down for my father's pipe and handed it back to him. "And I will go a step further. The message itself was no longer of value to us or the Germans. Dwell on it for a moment. The message stated there were U-boats off the innermost Orkney Islands. The secret was out. We knew, the enemy knew. So why kill Montclair over an already decoded message?"

"As we discussed earlier, the message must be pointing to the traitor," my father replied.

"And now you see the importance of us having both the original message and the one in Montclair's typewriter," Joanna continued. "It is the difference between the two that is of paramount importance, for it will disclose who the traitor is."

"We should ask Lieutenant Dunn for the original message in its entirety," I urged.

"Which may or may not be forthcoming," Joanna said. "There might well be other sections of the message that are not meant for our eyes. Even our sworn oath to the Official Secrets Act will not prevail if the document was classified as top secret."

"In which case it would be heavily redacted before being shown to us," my father noted.

"And thus would be of little use to us," Joanna agreed.

"But we should still ask for it," I insisted.

"So we shall, but we should be prepared for disappointment," Joanna said, reaching for a Turkish cigarette, which she studied at length. "And we face another problem in that obtaining the sheet from Montclair's typewriter will be no simple matter."

"Surely Lieutenant Dunn will allow us to examine it," I said.

"It will not be in his hands, but Lestrade's," Joanna reminded us. "Montclair's death is now a murder case, and Scotland Yard will have complete jurisdiction and consider the sheet prime evidence."

"Then Lestrade will have no objection to our reviewing the bloodied sheet."

"But it will in all likelihood have been removed from the typewriter."

"Is that of such great importance?"

"Any move that alters or distorts the crime scene is important." Joanna rose to light her cigarette and began pacing the floor. She continued to do so for several minutes, all the while ignoring us. Then she abruptly turned and, with a firm nod, said, "I still believe the word *exodus* has the most relevance here. Why else would Ainsworth go to such lengths in order to bring it to our attention?"

"Should we again read that particular section of the Old Testament?" I asked.

"The answer is not in a single passage or line," Joanna replied. "Ainsworth is directing our attention to the word *exodus* or something closely attached to it. Using that scheme, it would have to be relatively obvious, yet still hidden."

"Such as?"

"Blood," Joanna replied. "Therein must lie the answer, for Montclair used his own blood to point to something on the sheet in the typewriter."

"Perhaps his blood was the only inklike material available," I suggested.

"That is not the case," Joanna said. "Remember that among Montclair's personal possessions was a fountain pen. It would have been far easier for him to use it, rather than reaching to the stab wound in his back for blood. That, my dear John, was done on purpose. Montclair is literally screaming 'Blood!' from his grave."

"Blood is mentioned several times in the book of Exodus," my father recollected.

"Actually twice," Joanna said. "It was used in the first and tenth plagues."

I rapidly turned the pages to the section in the Old Testament that described the ten plagues. "I shall begin with the part that deals with the first plague, and read it word for word."

Joanna waved away the idea. "It would be best if you simply summarized it for us. The answer is not in a given word, but in the underlying meaning of a particular passage."

After reading about the first plague that was entitled Blood, I encapsulated the story as follows. "It seems that when Pharaoh refused to set the Israelites free, he was threatened with the plague of blood, in which the waters of the Nile River would turn red with blood and thus be unusable for human consumption. Pharaoh ignored the threat and God polluted the river with blood in full view of the Egyptian leader."

"Does it speak of how the feat was performed?" Joanna asked.

"It only states that God did it."

"No subterfuge, eh?"

"None that was mentioned," I replied. "I suspect there was a reason God performed this mighty act in the presence of Pharaoh. In that fashion, there could be no magic or trickery to explain away the incredible feat."

"A wise move," Joanna said, more to herself than to us. "Let us now turn to the second mention of blood. I believe it occurred just prior to God's threat to kill all Egyptian firstborn."

I quickly went to the tenth plague. "Here," I told them, "God sent the Angel of Death to kill the firstborn, with instructions to spare those of the Israelites. In order to assure that the Jewish firstborn were left unharmed, the head of each such household was ordered to paint the sides and tops of their door frames with lamb's blood. The Angel of Death, on seeing these signs, would pass over the houses of the Israelites, and thus their children would be saved. And this is the origin of the

Jewish religious holiday of Passover, which commemorates this miraculous event," I concluded.

"I can make nothing of it," my father grumbled. "And lamb's blood certainly does not equate to human blood."

"It is not the source of the blood that is important here, but the fact that it was used as a signal," Joanna said, as she continued to pace. "That is the common denominator. In both the tenth plague and in Montclair's message, *blood* was used to reveal identities."

"Yet it remains a puzzle within a puzzle," I said unhappily. "And we have only the word *blood* to go on."

"The answer is in the tenth plague," Joanna reaffirmed. "Ainsworth's message led us to the book of Exodus, and Montclair's message was signaling us with blood, just as the Israelites signaled the Angel of Death with blood."

"Are you suggesting we read of the tenth plague yet again?" I asked.

"We have no other recourse."

My father sighed with fatigue. "Perhaps we should have Miss Hudson prepare an early dinner, for we are certain to be working late into the night."

"A nice glass of sherry would also offer a most welcome respite," I added. "Perhaps two glasses would serve that purpose even better."

Joanna shook her head vigorously. "Every moment we waste brings England closer to disaster. We have no choice but to persevere. Refreshments can wait."

"Does it not strike you as odd that the messages left by the two dead men, Verner and Montclair, were both written in blood?" I queried. "Could there be a revealing connection?"

"The only connection here is that both men used blood as ink to identify their murderers," Joanna replied. "With this in mind, we should focus on the last plague, for therein is the answer to Montclair's coded message."

I wearily turned my attention to the description of the tenth plague. "Shall I begin with the Angel of Death?"

Before she could answer, the phone rang out and Joanna quickly picked up the receiver.

"Yes?" she said in a most curt manner, then listened and responded more gently. "Of course I recognize your voice."

Joanna's brow went up. "You have both?

"Fifteen minutes would be very convenient," she said, and placed the receiver down.

"The tide of fortune is changing," Joanna announced. "The caller was Mary Ellington, and she has found her notes on the original document that she helped Ainsworth decode."

"Hooray!" I shouted.

"Most importantly the message mentions the word *exodus*," Joanna went on. "So in essence, Alistair Ainsworth has pointed to the very word twice."

"Which tells us we are on the correct track," my father concluded. "Yet we still require Montclair's bloodied sheet to solve the puzzle."

"Not to worry," Joanna said, and gleefully rubbed her hands together. "You see, Mary Ellington has that sheet in hand as well."

"But it should be in Scotland Yard's possession, should it not?" my father asked.

"Yes, it should," Joanna said, with a mischievous smile.

"Then how did she come by it?"

"I did not ask, for it is a crime to remove prime evidence from a crime scene," Joanna said, and hurried over to the large table on the far side of the room. "Let us clear the surface, for Mary Ellington will arrive shortly."

The long rectangular table was brimming with materials used by Joanna in her investigations. There were bottles of various reagents, a Bunsen burner, glass flasks, test tubes, and the very same microscope that her father, Sherlock Holmes, once peered through. We closed and pushed aside texts and manuals that dealt with the principles of codebreaking. Despite our careful study, the books had proved to be of no help in deciphering the coded message that lay before us.

Time seemed to drag by as we anxiously awaited the arrival of Mary Ellington. My father checked his timepiece every minute or so, but its hands refused to move faster. Joanna began pacing again, no doubt arranging and rearranging the facts surrounding the coded message. Yet even she periodically glanced at the window, anticipating the arrival of a most important visitor. Finally there came a rap on the door. But it was not Mary Ellington.

"There is a lady downstairs carrying a large package who wishes to see you, Mrs. Watson," Miss Hudson said.

"Be good enough to show her in," Joanna said. "And please see to it we remain undisturbed."

As the door closed, Joanna again happily rubbed her hands together. "Pray tell, what do you think of the large package Mary has in her possession?"

"It could be anything," I replied.

"Oh, you can do better than that, John," Joanna coaxed. "Why would a small lady like Mary Ellington bother to lug around a large package to visit us at this time of evening?"

I had no answer.

"It is the typewriter," Joanna said joyfully. "This Mary Ellington knows the value of evidence that must be taken as a whole. She would make a fine detective, for she realizes the typewriter itself may provide important clues."

With a rap on the door, Mary Ellington entered, holding

on to a quite large package with both hands. "Where shall I place it?"

Joanna motioned to the large table against the wall. "There will do nicely."

Mary carefully put the package down next to Sherlock Holmes's microscope and went about unwrapping it. The typewriter, with the bloodied sheet it contained, appeared exactly as it did in Montclair's office. "Aren't you going to ask how I obtained it?"

"I suspect you simply walked out with it," said Joanna.

"Right you are," Mary said. "Scotland Yard left the crime scene as it was, so they could return tomorrow and complete their investigation. I, shall we say, ah, borrowed it for now and will return it before the detectives revisit in the morning. Since there is a slim possibility they will come back sooner, we should move along quickly."

"Let us begin with your notes on the original message, and then compare them to the message in Montclair's typewriter."

"Not only do I have the notes, I have a complete copy of the document itself that I had taken home."

"I thought that was strictly prohibited," my father remarked. "According to Lieutenant Dunn, that was an absolute rule not to be violated."

Mary smiled slyly. "It was and is, but we often do so when struggling with a particularly difficult code. Lieutenant Dunn's mind works eight to six, while ours must remain powered on twenty-four hours a day."

"Which is much to our benefit at the moment," I thought aloud.

Mary nodded and reached for a folded sheet in her handbag. Unfolding it, she placed it on the table and stepped back for us to see. It read:

4 U-boats off innermost Orkney Islands
Exodus must be delayed

"What the communiqué in fact states is there are four German submarines close to a major naval installation," Mary interpreted. "Thus, the plan to send our warships from this port to the Baltic Sea entrance had to be put on hold for the present. You will also note the obvious discrepancy between the two messages. In the original message, four U-boats are mentioned, while the sheet in Montclair's typewriter speaks of only three. I believe this was Tubby's method of telling us to concentrate on the original message."

"Which contains the word *exodus,* and which he again used in the second message," Joanna emphasized.

"Precisely my point," Mary continued. "Tubby is informing us that is the key to the code or some passage contained therein."

"We reached the very same conclusion and searched through the book of Exodus with diligence, but could uncover no clues," Joanna said. "We are of the opinion that Montclair used his own blood to signal something of utmost importance in the message, much as the Israelites employed the blood of a lamb to signal the Angel of Death to pass over their homes and thus spare their firstborn."

"Ah yes," Mary said, nodding. "The tenth plague, which was inflicted when Pharaoh refused to free the Israelites."

"The horror of killing the Egyptian firstborn," Joanna murmured, leaning in to concentrate on the bloodied sheet in the typewriter.

"It is most unwise to upset the Heavenly Father," Mary remarked.

Joanna carefully removed the sheet from the typewriter

and placed it upon the table, which allowed all of us a clear view of the stained message.

3 U-BOATS OFF INNERMOST ORKNEY ISLANDS

"On examining the blood-smeared sheet, I see where the number three is underlined by a streak of blood," Joanna noted, now using her magnifying glass for a more detailed inspection. "Thus, we can conclude he wanted us to concentrate on the three. Then he left the *u* intact, but smeared out *boats* with blood. Since we know the correct number should be four, let us substitute that for the three. This interpretation of the code reveals the number four, followed by a large *U*, which reads '4 U.'"

"Perhaps the discrepancy in the numbers is simply a signal to draw our attention to a hidden message within," Mary suggested.

"I believe otherwise," Joanna contended, and returned the sheet to its original position in the typewriter. "The discrepancy in numbers must be of greater significance than to simply draw our attention, for the presence of blood alone would accomplish that. There is a deeper reason Montclair went to such obvious lengths to emphasize the number four. He actually underlined it. You must remember he was breathing his last. He had to make every second and every word count. We must therefore concentrate on the number four and what it represents."

"Perhaps it refers to the fourth word in the message," Mary surmised, and counted words on the sheet. "Which is *innermost,* and that is of no help."

"Or it might represent the fourth letter of the alphabet,

which is *d*," Joanna said. "That letter placed next to U–boats spells *duboats*. There is no such word in the German language."

"Nor in French," my father noted.

"Nor in Spanish, Italian, or Russian," Mary said.

Joanna studied the bloodstained sheet once more at length. "Perhaps Ainsworth meant for us to see only the *d* and the *u,* which combines to form the German word *du,* which translates to *you*. But then, it was followed by *boats*. *Youboats off* is nonsensical, as would be the German *duboats off*."

"For some reason, I feel we are on the wrong path here," Mary said. "Tubby would have made it more sophisticated than just moving a few words around. You see, the Germans might have detected that, for their experts no doubt studied Tubby's decoded message with that in mind."

"He would not hide it so deeply," Joanna asserted. "That would take far too long to decipher, and Ainsworth knew time was short."

"Sometimes the most clever codes are the most obvious ones," Mary stated. "The answer can be directly in front of your eyes, yet difficult to see."

Joanna stared at the typewriter and studied its keyboard at length, then the letter itself. Her line of vision went back to the keyboard, upon which was drawn the figure of a hand in chalk. "Who drew the outline?"

"Scotland Yard," Mary replied. "Inspector Lestrade made the drawing just before the body was removed."

"Well done," Joanna said, and placed her right hand over the outline, extending her index finger so that it touched the bloodied sheet. "As I recall, Montclair's index finger was the only one extended. Correct?"

"Correct."

"And he was right-handed. Correct?"

"Correct."

"So we can conclude it would be his writing finger that pointed to the word *innermost* on the sheet."

"And?" Mary queried.

"Perhaps he purposely stopped there."

"To what end? The word *innermost* by itself has no real significance."

My father said, "Perhaps Montclair's finger stopped because death came at that moment."

"Or shortly thereafter," Joanna agreed. "You will note that the blood smear drops off acutely after the *inner* in the word *innermost*."

Mary leaned in for a closer inspection of the letter. "For some reason Montclair underlined the number three that should be a four, and smeared through *boats off.* He then died as he reached the word *innermost,* and at that point the bloodstain stopped and dropped off. So, following this schematic, we have the letters *d* and *u,* and the word *innermost,* which together spell *duinnermost.* It has no recognizable meaning."

Joanna's eyes narrowed noticeably as she read the sheet yet again. Then, using her finger, she began pointing to each individual letter. She performed this act twice before announcing, "All becomes clear."

"But I see only garbled words," Mary said.

"To the contrary, it is a complete message," Joanna asserted.

"Based on what?"

"Passover," Joanna replied. "How clever! How very clever!"

"Please explain," Mary requested. "For you see what I do not."

"Montclair had obviously worked with Ainsworth on the original message and knew it involved the Exodus plan. That was the key Ainsworth was now passing to Montclair and the others in the Admiralty Club, knowing that they alone could decipher the secret message. He did it as follows. First, Ainsworth substituted the number three for the number four, so that the group would be aware that the number four was of critical importance. In this instance, the number four stood for the fourth letter in the alphabet, which is *d*."

"How can you be certain of this?" Mary asked.

"Because I know the remainder of the message," Joanna answered, then continued on. "Thus, we have the letter *d* at the beginning. Following that, the *u* in *U-boats* was left untouched while *boats* was blotted out with blood, which leaves us with *du*."

Mary nodded hurriedly. "Montclair was telling us to pass over the words covered with blood, just as the Angel of Death passed over the Israelite homes marked with lamb's blood."

Joanna nodded back in agreement before saying, "Now, follow the smear as it continues on through *boats* and *off,* and note that it blurs the letter *i* in *innermost* before dropping off. And there you have Ainsworth's coded message."

3 U-BOATS OFF INNERMOST ORKNEY ISLANDS

"And remember the three is a four, representing *d,* which is the fourth letter in the alphabet," Joanna prompted.

Mary Ellington's eyes flew open. "That bloody traitor! Who would have ever guessed it was him?"

"Who?" I asked aloud. "Who is it?"

"Follow my finger, John," Joanna said and pointed to the number 3. "The three is really a four and thus is a *d,* after which comes *u* in that the *boats* portion of *U-boats* has been blotted with blood. So now we have *du*. Then the smear continues through the word *off,* and partially smears the letter *i* from the word *innermost,* leaving *nn.* Now, combine *du* with the letters *nn,* and tell me the result."

"Dunn!" I cried out.

"Our murderer," Joanna said without inflection. "And our traitor."

"We should contact the First Sea Lord immediately," my father demanded.

"I am afraid that may not be possible," Mary said. "The First Sea Lord is currently attending a meeting in Paris."

"How do you come by this information?" Joanna asked.

"My brother told me at dinner last night."

"And he is?"

"The director of Naval Intelligence," Mary replied. "His name is Admiral Lewis Beaumont, Beaumont of course being my maiden name."

"Then you must contact him now."

"At this late hour?" Mary asked. "Would it not be best to wait until morning when we have the full resources of Scotland—"

"Now!" Joanna insisted. "We have not a second to waste, for I fear the word *exodus* represents a double entendre. Ainsworth may also be telling us that the Germans will depart shortly, with our man in tow. This being the case, we shall lose all hope of ever finding them."

Mary Ellington reached for the phone, again muttering "Bloody traitor!" under her breath.

25

A Traitor

There was excitement in the air at the Admiralty Club the following morning. We gathered around Inspector Lestrade and listened intently as he brought the new developments to our attention. A concerned citizen had called Scotland Yard only hours earlier with information that could lead directly to Alistair Ainsworth and the German agents who had taken him prisoner.

"A man walking his dog early this morning noticed some strange activities in a house next door that had been leased to individuals who kept to themselves," Lestrade told us. "The drapes were always drawn and it was difficult to see any activities within, for the lights were rarely turned on. But this morning the man's dog broke from his leash and chased a squirrel into the adjoining garden. It was then that he looked into the house, for there was a narrow opening in the closed drapes. He clearly saw a motionless man in bed who was being shouted at by others. The neighbor is of the belief that the language being spoken was foreign."

"Was he able to describe the men in the bedroom?" Joanna asked at once.

"The one doing the shouting was said to be a large man with broad shoulders, but his face was not clearly visible," Lestrade replied. "However, the neighbor's wife was in her garden a few days earlier and saw one of the household in broad daylight. She could no doubt give us a better description, but unfortunately she was admitted to hospital yesterday with an infection of some sort. She is now being questioned by Scotland Yard and I shall join them shortly. If their story is accurate, we should have both Alistair Ainsworth and the Germans within our sights before noon."

"Was the neighbor able to see the man in bed?" my father asked.

"He was not, Dr. Watson, for the lighting was not good and the men standing around the bed partially obscured the view of its occupant. Thus, at this point we should focus our attention on the man in the garden, and for this I shall ask your assistance. As I recall, you and your colleagues were given a rather detailed description of the lead German agent by Dr. Verner. Are there any particular features other than his facial tic that we should be aware of?"

"Certainly the aroma of chloroform on him is long gone," Joanna remarked.

"Nevertheless we shall ask about it," Lestrade said, and turned to Roger Marlowe. "You and Mr. Ainsworth are lifelong friends, so I was told. Is that correct?"

"From our childhood days."

"Then you should be able to provide essential information we may require. In the event our informant leads us to the whereabouts of Mr. Ainsworth, we shall insist on proof of life. You see, the Germans when surrounded might decide to use him as a bargaining chip. His life for their freedom, that sort of thing. In other words, they threaten to kill him if we do not acquiesce to their demands. Thus, we have to firmly establish that he is alive."

"Speak with him on the phone," Mary suggested. "Tubby has a most distinctive voice."

"But his voice may be altered in his weakened state," Lestrade said. "Furthermore, the Germans may not have installed a phone since they are rapidly moving from one house to another."

"Then have them show Tubby standing before a window," Marlowe said.

Lestrade shook his head. "He could be quite dead and they could have him propped up."

"Could we have an unarmed mediator enter the house and verify?" Mary asked.

Lestrade shook his head once more. "If Ainsworth is dead, the mediator becomes a hostage and the Germans yet have a bargaining chip. The very best way to establish that Ainsworth remains alive is to ask a question he can answer but the Germans cannot. With that in mind, Mr. Marlowe, what information might you and Mr. Ainsworth share that the Germans could not possibly be aware of?"

Marlowe rubbed his chin pensively before saying, "We both enjoy a most expensive Scotch called *Old Vatted Glenlivet*, which is seldom ordered by others."

"The Germans might well know this," Lestrade rejected. "All that would be required is for the Germans to have followed him into a pub."

"It cannot be anything from Alistair Ainsworth's recent history," Joanna added. "It must go back to his childhood days."

"Such as?" Lestrade asked.

"The name of a pet would work nicely," Joanna replied. "Did Ainsworth have a dog when he was a boy?"

"A collie called Ollie," Marlowe recalled. "They were inseparable, even sleeping together in the same bed."

"There is your answer, Inspector," Joanna said. "The Germans could not possibly know this."

Lestrade nodded slowly. "I believe you are correct, but the Germans are very clever. They may have asked Mr. Ainsworth about the names of past pets, with this in mind."

"Would they have inquired where the dog slept?" Joanna asked.

"Most unlikely."

"Then use that as well."

"So we shall," Lestrade said, and quickly glanced at his timepiece. "Now I must hurry to St. Bart's and join in the questioning of the neighbor's wife. She may provide us with even more helpful information."

Joanna cleared her throat audibly. "Inspector, may I make one last suggestion?"

"Of course."

"I think it would be wise—" Joanna stopped in mid-sentence to sneeze. "Ah-choo!"

Immediately she dashed to the coatrack where her purse hung and reached for a handkerchief. She seemed about to sneeze again, but suppressed it and apologized. "I shall rejoin you in just a minute."

"Do not rush, madam," Lestrade said, and used the time to ask Marlowe if Alistair Ainsworth had other pets he was attached to as a child. He was told that there was another dog later on that Ainsworth looked after with care.

As Marlowe spoke of a spaniel with a bad leg, I watched Joanna turn away from the group and face the topcoats hanging on a wall rack. She blew her nose softly and walked over to us while closing her handbag.

"What was the spaniel called?" Lestrade was asking.

"Bella," Marlowe replied.

Lestrade jotted down the name, then came back to Joanna. "Madam, I believe you had one last suggestion before I leave."

"It may not be necessary, but I think it wise to have a sharpshooter with us, in the event a gun battle were to erupt. He could be well hidden and take down the German agents from afar."

"A capital idea, madam," Lestrade agreed wholeheartedly and looked over to Lieutenant Dunn. "Lieutenant, does the navy have sharpshooters in their ranks?"

"Not to my knowledge, but the marines do," Dunn responded. "We are of course speaking of long rifles."

"Of course."

"And the distance for their marksmanship?"

"Fifty to a hundred yards."

"That will present no problem."

"Said and done," Lestrade concluded. "I shall return shortly with all the incriminating information in hand, for I am confident our suspicions will be confirmed. Let us meet here again at eleven o'clock to finalize our plans."

Lestrade and Dunn reached for their topcoats and hurried from the room, closing the door behind them. The group waited for a full minute in silence before speaking in low voices.

"I still cannot believe it is Dunn," Marlowe said quietly.

"Oh, but it is so," Joanna assured.

"Your decoding was a fine piece of work," Marlowe went on. "But it will never hold up in a court of law. If I wished, I could have rearranged the words and letters in the book of Exodus and made Pharaoh the traitor."

"But Pharaoh is not here, and Dunn is," Joanna said.

"There is no doubt Dunn is the traitor," Mary said. "I stayed awake half the night wondering how Geoffrey Montclair had deciphered Tubby's message. After all, he did not have blood smears to guide him. Then I recalled a code he and Ainsworth were devising in which the key word was *off*, meaning to remove as in *hats off*. They inserted the word *off* to inform the reader to blank out the *off*, then proceed to remove letters and/or words next to it until one reached a meaningful message. Thus, in Tubby's message, which included the word *off*, if one removes *boats* from U-boats and the *i* from innermost, you end up with *Dunn*. It is a clever but simple code and Tubby knew that Montclair, with his photographic memory, would remember it."

"Extraordinary," my father said in awe.

"That is still not good enough," Marlowe rebutted. "You must have absolute proof in order to convict him of treason."

"Which I will have shortly," Joanna said.

"And who will provide the evidence?"

"Why, Lieutenant Dunn himself."

"Do you care to share this plan with us?"

"It is best that I do not," Joanna said. "For the smallest slip can ruin the most excellent of plans. Thus, the fewer people who know of it, the better."

"It is as if you do not trust us," Marlowe persisted.

"I assure you that is not the case," Joanna said. "My concern is that you might unintentionally give away our knowledge that Dunn is the traitor."

"Surely we would not speak a word of it to him."

"It is not your speech but your expressions that would give rise to Dunn's suspicions. I could not help but notice the stern, harsh look you gave Dunn when he took the floor to tell us of marine sharpshooters. There was a definite change in your usual expression toward him. He did not detect your animosity, but had he, all could have been lost. So for now, I must ask you to trust me on this matter. You might also soften your expression in his presence."

"And so we shall," Mary said. "But it still escapes me why a trusted naval officer would betray his country."

"I am afraid only Dunn can answer that question," Joanna said.

"Money, perhaps? They say that every man has his price."

"But the price is not always money," Joanna told her. "Blackmail, lust, and revenge can also bring forth the most evil of behaviors."

"But one would expect more from a naval officer."

"Those motives fit all," Joanna said, then walked over to the window and peered out. "I see our good lieutenant is having a rather animated conversation with Lestrade while the inspector's carriage waits."

I came to Joanna's side and followed her line of vision. "It would appear that Dunn is in no rush to arrange for the sharp-shooters."

"A worthy observation," Joanna noted.

"But should he not be hurrying? I would think that sharp-shooters are not readily available on such short notice."

"He is in no rush, for he is certain the house that holds Alistair Ainsworth will be vacant when we arrive."

"How can he be so confident?"

"Because he plans carefully," Joanna replied. "You must keep in mind that Dunn is most clever to have gotten away with his traitorous acts thus far."

"But he is about to be undone."

"Only if he remains unaware," Joanna cautioned, then pointed to the street below. "Ah! Lestrade departs and Dunn hails a taxi."

"And now he appears to be hurrying somewhat."

Joanna smiled humorously. "Does it not strike you as strange that Dunn does not have his own carriage?"

"That is a bit unusual. What do you make of it?"

"The most likely explanation is that he does not wish his customary driver to know where he is about to be taken."

"Should he not be followed?"

"Not at the moment."

Mary asked, "What if Dunn suddenly becomes suspicious and returns here?"

"Then he will find Watson, my husband, and me absent, for we have other duties to attend to."

"But we shall have to explain your absence."

"Be inventive and give him a reason to hurry back to his well-thought-out plans."

"Such as?"

"Inform Dunn that we remembered yet another important feature of the German agent that could be most helpful, and we are racing to St. Bart's to supply Lestrade with the information."

"That will surely spur him on."

"In the event this occurs, do your very best acting. Appear to be worried, but hopeful. Give him no reason to become even more suspicious." Joanna gave Dunn's departing carriage a final glance, then hurried to the coatrack. "And now, we must be off!"

As Joanna put on her topcoat, Mary asked her a last question. "I still cannot fathom how Tubby discovered that Dunn was the traitor."

"The answer to that will have to await our rescue of Ainsworth. But it obviously occurred while he was being held captive."

"Surely Dunn would not expose himself to Tubby."

"That would be foolish and someone as clever as Dunn

does not make foolish mistakes. More likely, Ainsworth either recognized Dunn's voice in an adjoining room or overheard the agents speaking of their spy. I suspect it was the latter since Ainsworth is quite fluent in German." Joanna buttoned her coat and called over to me, "John, please be good enough to open the window and signal our carriage with a wave of your hand."

"Do bring Tubby back alive," Mary implored.

"That is my intent."

We raced down the back stairs and, just as we reached the street, our carriage pulled up to the curb. On entering I was surprised to find an admiral in the Royal Navy, who was dressed in full regalia, seated by the window. He had a distinguished appearance, with chiseled, aristocratic features and silver-gray hair that extended into his muttonchop side-burns.

"Allow me to present Admiral Lewis Beaumont, the director of Naval Intelligence," Joanna introduced. "The gentlemen with me are my husband, John, and his father, Dr. John Watson."

"I am honored, sir," my father said.

"As am I," said I.

Beaumont greeted us with a brief nod, then turned to Joanna. "This is most irregular and were it not for my sister, Mary, I would not be here."

"What is more irregular, Admiral, is that you have a traitor in your ranks."

"You will require more than a weirdly decoded message to prove that assertion."

"Oh, I will prove it to your satisfaction and to the satisfaction of any hard-nosed military tribunal," Joanna assured.

"May I ask what this evidence is?"

"I will show it to you shortly."

At that moment I heard the friendly bark of a dog and looked out to see Toby Two happily wagging her tail. On the other end of her leash was Wiggins, the leader of the Baker Street Irregulars.

"Here you are, ma'am," Wiggins said, handing the leash over to Joanna and watching the spaniel jump into the carriage. "She is all excited to see you again."

"She and I are old friends," Joanna said, and gave the lad a half crown. "You have two more services to perform. The first is to take this glass container and walk quickly down the Mall for a mile, then dispose of it."

I watched Joanna dig into her handbag for a small, cylindrical vial with its top screwed on securely. Toby Two suddenly yelped with joy and wagged her tail furiously. Joanna brought her attention back to Wiggins and said in a firm voice, "Under no circumstances are you to open the container or loosen its top. Understood?"

"Yes, ma'am," Wiggins said obediently. "Shall I toss it into the pond at St. James?"

"No need. Simply place it in a rubbish bin."

"Done, ma'am. And your second request?"

"You are to return here to this very spot and await my return with Toby Two."

"Here I will be."

Joanna held the vial under Toby Two's nose for only a few seconds, which caused the dog's excitement to increase even more. Then, in a quick movement, she gave the vial to Wiggins, saying, "Now be off!"

Toby Two extended her head out of the carriage window and watched Wiggins trot away. Only after the lad had disappeared beyond the Admiralty Arch did she lose interest. Joanna gently pulled the half spaniel, half bloodhound back into the carriage, then patiently allowed for more time to pass.

"Why do we wait?" Beaumont asked.

"For the scent Wiggins carries to completely dissipate," Joanna replied, then held her hand out of the window. "Ah, good! The wind is against us."

"Which means?"

"A great deal to Toby Two," Joanna said, then permitted Toby Two to again sample the air outside the carriage, but away from the Admiralty Arch. Suddenly the dog stiffened, her nose rapidly sniffing the cool air. Then her tail went straight as an arrow and remained perfectly still.

"What does she point to?" Beaumont asked.

"Alistair Ainsworth," Joanna replied.

26

The Trap

With the help of Toby Two's nose, we caught up with Dunn's hansom that had been slowed by heavy traffic. A moment later the hansom did the unexpected. Rather than head north, it turned southward and entered Whitehall before stopping in front of the building that housed the Office of Naval Intelligence. Without so much as a glance about, Dunn hurried up the steps and disappeared behind a set of imposing doors.

"Surely you do not believe Alistair Ainsworth is situated within the Office of Naval Intelligence," Beaumont grumbled.

"You are correct in that assumption," Joanna said.

"But Dunn's hansom has stopped here and your dog continues to point keenly in the direction the lieutenant has taken."

"It is not his direction that so attracts Toby Two, but the scent that Dunn carries with him."

"Which scent?"

"That of a carcass, which all dogs find irresistible."

While we waited for the traitor to make his next move, Joanna told us of the trap she had set for Dunn. During the group's meeting with Lestrade, she had pretended to sneeze and require a handkerchief, which gave her an excuse to visit the coatrack where her handbag hung. Unnoticed by us, she reached into her handbag and, after opening the glass vial containing the smell of carcass, allowed its vapor to seep into the hem of Lieutenant Dunn's naval topcoat. Thus, wherever Dunn went, the scent went with him and so did Toby Two's nose.

"Will Dunn not detect the malodor?" Beaumont asked.

"He will not notice the faint odor, but Toby Two, whose nose is a thousand times more sensitive than Dunn's, will follow it with ease."

"Curious behavior, that," Beaumont said, obviously interested. "Why does the smell of carcass attract dogs so powerfully?"

"No one is certain of the cause, but there are two likely answers," Joanna replied. "First, it may represent a source of food. Secondly, it may well be a clever way to disguise their own aroma. You see, when dogs find the source of the smell, they will often roll about in it. This behavior is believed to be a holdover from primitive dogs that had to hunt for food and wished to hide their scent, so as not to alert their prey."

"Must it be a rotting carcass?"

"That seems to work best."

"Might I inquire as to the source of your carcass?"

"I journeyed to our local poulterer whose shop had a goose that had hung too long and ripened too much. He was happy to oblige me."

Beaumont stared out at the closed doors to the ministry building and said, "Dunn remains inside too long for this simply to be a hasty visit. And the longer he stays in the building, the more my doubt grows that he is the traitor. It may be that he is innocent or, if guilty, has outfoxed us."

"He is not and has not."

"But the passing minutes say otherwise."

"Be patient, for he will shortly appear."

"What makes you so confident?"

"He has ordered his hansom to wait for him," Joanna said, and pointed to the taxi a half block ahead.

We continued to wait somewhat uneasily, but Joanna showed no concern whatsoever. She rested her head back and closed her eyes as she seemed to drift off into one of her pensive moods. Toby Two suddenly yelped as her tail began to wag.

"He comes!" Joanna cried out as Dunn appeared. Quickly she rapped on the ceiling of our carriage to alert the driver. "You must follow at a discreet distance and remain a block or so behind at all times. Do not be concerned if you lose sight of the hansom, for I shall be able to guide you."

My father asked, "Why do you believe he bothered to visit the Office of Naval Intelligence?"

"To arrange for the marine sharpshooters that he knows will not be needed," Joanna replied. "He is a very clever man who is covering his tracks. He performs his duty for all to see, then, like a chameleon, turns to a different color."

With a sudden thrust our carriage began its journey through the crowded streets of central London. As ordered, our carriage stayed well back of Dunn's hansom in the distance. But the wagging of Toby Two's tail told us we were on the correct track. I gazed out at the motorcars passing our carriage and wondered if the odor of burning petrol would interfere with the dog's keen sense of smell. But the same concern had crossed my mind earlier and Joanna had assured me that Toby Two would have no difficulty distinguishing between the two odors. As a matter of fact, scientific studies had shown that dogs could easily differentiate between a hundred different aromas when all were presented simultaneously, thus proving that the nose of a dog was one of nature's most sensitive instruments.

"I am having difficulty believing a British naval officer would be a traitor," Beaumont said, breaking the silence.

"Come now, Admiral," said Joanna. "I am aware you suspected a spy long before Alistair Ainsworth went missing."

"Why do you think that?"

"Because I know of your clandestine meeting with Lady Jane Hamilton and her husband, who was supposedly at sea but wasn't."

Beaumont raised his brow. "Who informed you?"

"I have my sources," Joanna replied evasively. "In the dark corners of our mind, we wondered if Lady Jane and Roger Marlowe had become romantically linked, while her husband was away. Marlowe's close association with the Germans in the past would make him a prime suspect in the disappearance of Alistair Ainsworth, and perhaps he had persuaded Lady Jane to join him. But we learned it was not Marlowe whom Lady Jane was visiting secretly, but her own husband who was residing in Knightsbridge while he was supposedly out at sea. Then, to our surprise, you show up unhappily at the residence late one evening. Putting everything together, Admiral, you were searching for a spy, using Lady Jane as a conduit and her husband as the source of information. You see, with her husband supposedly away, Lady Jane would be free to associate often with Roger Marlowe who, if the traitor, might confide in her or perhaps make a mistake that would confirm your suspicions."

Beaumont breathed heavily. "You would do well in our Office of Naval Intelligence."

"I already have a position, thank you," Joanna said. "Allow me to continue, but do not hesitate to interrupt if my conclusions are in any way incorrect. You too suspected Marlowe and had Lady Jane feed him naval intelligence that of course was given to Lady Jane by her husband, all under your supervision. Whether Lady Jane and Roger Marlowe were romantically involved I do not know and do not care, but she was the perfect conduit and could lure Roger Marlowe while he believed her husband was at sea. Am I correct thus far?"

"Quite."

"Your visit was occasioned when you learned that the secret information being gathered by the Germans was not coming from Marlowe, but from another source. Thus, the traitor was still concealed within the Admiralty and continued to give away sensitive information."

"It was the damned Exodus plan on which so much depended," Beaumont groused. "Of course, Ainsworth could not be the spy and our suspicion of Marlowe had diminished considerably, but not disappeared altogether. With Mary being as innocent as the driven snow and Montclair dead, we had run out of suspects. We never suspected Dunn in the least. He himself was not privy to the coded messages, you see."

"Oh, but he was," Joanna refuted. "He must have had the opportunity to see many of the messages in the late afternoon as they were being placed in the attaché case at the Admiralty Club. And those were the messages that were given over to the German agents."

"All he needed to do was look over Ainsworth's shoulder," Beaumont grumbled.

"Exactly," Joanna said. "Certainly with that in mind, you did not exclude him altogether."

"I am afraid we did, even after reviewing his dossier," Beaumont admitted. "However, in retrospect, there were subtle hints on when and how he might have been turned."

"A woman," Joanna said without inflection.

"How could you possibly know that?"

"The most rigid are usually the most vulnerable to feminine charm," Joanna replied. "But do go on."

"For four years Lieutenant Dunn served as a naval attaché at our Berlin embassy. He became deeply involved with an actress who happened to be the daughter of a high-ranking German naval officer. This occurred in the early nineteen hundreds when relations between our countries were far more cordial."

"Were there any signs that Dunn's relationship with this actress continued after he left his post in Berlin?"

"None that we were aware of, although he made quite a number of official visits to the Continent since returning to England."

"To Germany?"

Beaumont shook his head. "To France and Belgium."

"From where he could have journeyed unnoticed to Germany."

"Ma'am!" the driver called down. "The hansom has come to a stop!"

"Drive by at a steady speed and pay no attention to the hansom or its occupant," Joanna called back. "Once past them, tell us the activity that caused them to stop, then turn right at the next intersection."

"Toby Two will bark," I warned.

"No, she will not," Joanna said, reaching in her handbag for a large dog biscuit that she gave to me. "Feed her this as we approach Dunn's hansom. And now, Admiral, I must ask you to crouch quite low, as shall I, so that our traitor cannot see us."

"Are you certain the biscuit will distract her?" I asked.

"Oh yes, for to a dog nothing supersedes filling its stomach."

My father buried his face in a newspaper while I pretended

to light my pipe and paid no attention to the stopped hansom. Toby Two's eyes and nose were fixed on the dog biscuit, her tail barely wagging.

"Now, John!" Joanna instructed.

Toby Two quickly grasped the biscuit between her teeth and chewed on it vigorously. The part of her that was blood-hound caused her to drool excessively and this appeared to only heighten her appetite. The odor of a dozen carcasses could not have drawn her attention away.

"The empty hansom is stopped in front of a tobacco shop, ma'am," the driver reported.

"But Dunn does not smoke," Beaumont said worriedly. "Has he stopped to have a look about?"

"Most likely," Joanna replied.

"Then he knows us."

Joanna shook her head. "I believe he is simply being careful."

"I am afraid he is on to us."

Joanna shook her head once more. "If he were, he would have immediately turned his hansom around and headed back to the ministry. Clever scoundrels like Dunn take no chances."

"Perhaps he will still do so, after leaving the tobacconist," I wondered aloud.

"I think not," Joanna said. "He will have another look around and, seeing nothing suspicious, will move on to his destination."

As our carriage turned right, Joanna and the admiral sat upright and my father put down his newspaper. Toby Two had finished off her dog biscuit and was eyeing me for another.

"Out the window your nose goes," Joanna said, and reached over for Toby Two.

At first, the dog demonstrated no particular interest, but then her tail began to wag again. Gradually the speed of the wag increased and, with her head now fully extended into the wind, Toby Two yelped happily.

"Onward!" Joanna cried out. "With a right turn at the intersection!"

"Why right?" I asked.

"Because straight ahead narrows and takes a circuitous route before ending in an open park area," Joanna explained. "Moreover, it is a strictly commercial area."

Joanna's prediction proved accurate. We continued on course, using Toby Two's nose and tail to guide us. Dunn's hansom took only one evasive action, in which a complete block was circled before it again headed in a northward direction. Once past the theater district, we drove through Covent Garden and approached Great Russell Street where the British Museum was located.

"Do you believe he will turn for the museum and attempt to lose himself amidst the heavy traffic and swarms of tourists?" I asked.

"Not at this point," Joanna replied. "He cannot afford to waste any more time, for he now has precious little at his disposal."

"But, being the clever person he is, Dunn will certainly try one more evasive maneuver," my father surmised.

"It may not be necessary," Joanna said. "The German house is in all likelihood in a residential area where traffic is light and views up and down the street unobstructed. He would have no difficulty spotting us or anyone else that chose to follow him."

"You seem to know his moves," Beaumont said.

Joanna shrugged. "I am simply putting myself in his place and how I would go about this sordid business."

"And what will his next move be?"

"To alert his German friends so they can make a hasty exit

and thus escape our grasp. Then he will hurry back to the Office of Naval Intelligence to firm up the arrangement for the marine sharpshooters before returning to the Admiralty Club."

"He is a very clever fellow who knows how to hide his tracks."

"Not quite as clever as you might think, for along the way there were clues that pointed to his guilt and that I ignored but should not have."

"What clues, may I ask?"

"A surprising number that I will list for you," Joanna replied. "First, how do we explain the Germans always being ahead of us by just a fraction of time? This occurred both at the house where they tortured Verner and at their next home in St. John's Wood from which they were forced to depart in great haste. Obviously someone from within had to inform them that Scotland Yard would shortly be on their doorstep."

"That individual could have been any member of the Admiralty Club," Beaumont argued.

"Not so," Joanna said. "No one in the group knew of our visit to the first house. But Dunn did. With that in mind, let us go to the next, overlooked clue. With the group now excluded as suspects, another insider had to point out Alistair Ainsworth as the master decoder to the Germans so they could follow him and learn of his habits in order to pick the most opportune time to kidnap him. In this regard, Dunn would have been most helpful. He would be aware that Ainsworth's past had been thoroughly scrutinized before being allowed to join the Admiralty Club. Dunn could have reviewed Ainsworth's dossier and learned of his visits to Ah Sing's in the dark streets of East London. It was the ideal place to take a semidrugged Ainsworth captive."

Beaumont nodded grimly. "Dunn was in charge of vetting the prospective candidates."

"Which indicates he was perfectly positioned," Joanna said. "And this brings us to the third clue that should have drawn our attention. I am referring to the strange death of Geoffrey Montclair. Only an individual known to him could have entered his office late at night without arousing suspicion. That person had to find his way behind Montclair's desk with ease, then stab the poor fellow to death. And that person had discovered that Montclair was about to reveal the traitor."

I raised a hand and interrupted. "But wouldn't Montclair's discovery make him very suspicious of Dunn to say the least?"

"I do not think Montclair knew the answer yet," Joanna replied. "I suspect he was pointing out something in the message to Dunn that caused the lieutenant to believe he would shortly be revealed as the traitor. Thus, Dunn murdered Montclair to prevent him from deciphering the entire content of Alistair Ainsworth's message."

"But how did Dunn manage to see this particular message?" Beaumont asked. "We had strict procedures in place that permitted only members of the Admiralty Club to read the classified material."

"I do not think that presented a problem to Dunn," Joanna replied. "The lieutenant was trusted by all, you see, and could enter the various offices without suspicion and glance over the member's shoulder at what was being deciphered. I suspect that was what Dunn was doing when he realized Geoffrey Montclair was about to expose him."

"It all seems so clear now," Beaumont said.

"It should have been clear earlier," Joanna admonished herself. "I have been blind to the obvious, but it is better to learn late than never learn at all."

Our carriage was now entering the outskirts of St. John's Wood, with its stately houses and lovely gardens. My jaw must have dropped as I realized we were approaching the area in which was situated the last known residence of the German agents. I quickly glanced over to Toby Two. She was still on scent, with her tail wagging happily.

"St. John's Wood," I breathed excitedly. "The Germans never left the area."

We passed through an intersection and continued on, but Toby Two became clearly unhappy. She made a whining sound as the tail dropped and its wagging diminished.

Joanna rapped on the roof of our carriage and called up to the driver. "Return to the intersection and wait for further instructions!"

Our carriage did a slow turnabout and came to a halt at a wide intersection. Toby Two immediately jumped to the opposite window and yelped in a most pleasing manner.

"Turn left!" Joanna ordered the driver.

"Left, you are, ma'am, and onto Wellington Road," the driver called down.

"They are on this street," Joanna said to us without inflection.

"How can you be so certain?" Beaumont asked.

"Because of the map that Ainsworth left for us, on which he circled Waterloo Station," Joanna replied.

A confused look crossed Beaumont's face. "I am at a loss here."

"Ainsworth was also telling us to concentrate on the battle at Waterloo where the Duke of Wellington was the victor," Joanna explained. "He was drawing our attention to Wellington Road where the Germans decided to reside yet again, but in a different house a good distance away."

"Very clever," Beaumont said.

"Very," said Joanna, and called out for the driver to stop, thus giving the carriages carrying Lestrade and his men the opportunity to catch up.

27

Alistair Ainsworth

From a distance and using a handheld telescope, Joanna watched Dunn enter a fashionable two-story house that had an expansive lawn in its front. With the address that housed the Germans and Alistair Ainsworth having been located, Wellington Road was closed off for several blocks in both directions. A few carriages were allowed through, for they carried innocent-appearing Scotland Yard sergeants in civilian attire, who would surround the house to ensure that escape was not possible. The homes on each side of the Germans' abode had been commandeered so that constables could be placed on their second stories to serve as lookouts. The quiet neighborhood was as peaceful as one might find in all England. But this was soon to change.

A sergeant sprinted up to us and reported to Lestrade, "Sir, the men are now in place and await further orders."

"Make certain the drapes are tightly drawn, with only the narrowest of openings," Lestrade said.

"Done, sir."

"I trust you instructed them in the proper use of their whistles."

"They are to sound off loud and clear at the earliest sign the Germans are attempting to escape."

"Well done."

"There is one other precaution I took upon myself, Inspector," the sergeant added. "At the first shot, if there are any, the occupants of the adjacent homes are to retreat to their innermost rooms and lie flat on the floor. I thought this wise in the event of a fierce gun battle, in which shots might go astray."

"A most excellent idea," Lestrade praised. "You may return to your post and keep the sharpest eye out."

"Very good, sir."

I could not help but be impressed with Lestrade's command of the dangerous situation. Whether he had been involved in similar activities in the past, I could not say, but he behaved as though he had. Admiral Beaumont stood by patiently, but had no official capacity, for the intelligence service did not possess the power or authority of police. Nevertheless, Beaumont's presence could be of value should an exchange of prisoners be proposed. As director of Naval Intelligence he knew what could and could not be offered to the Germans.

"However," Lestrade was predicting, "I feel they will fight to the very end, like good German soldiers."

"They may," Beaumont said. "But when given the chance to live and perhaps fight another day, they often change their minds."

"Who would be involved in this exchange?" Lestrade asked.

"Their spies for ours," Beaumont replied tonelessly. "This rather unpleasant task is done under civilian guise in a neutral country such as Portugal."

"I take it they have one of our agents whom we would very much like to bring home," Lestrade surmised.

Beaumont nodded. "A fine young lad from Winchester who was providing us with information on the movement of German warships."

"I trust that Dunn will not be part of any such exchange."

"Dunn will be marched up to the gallows and hanged."

"In total secrecy, I would think."

"It is best not to advertise there is a traitor within your ranks."

Lestrade turned to the street as a carriage slowly passed by. The occupant closest to us doffed his derby twice.

"The house is surrounded," Lestrade announced. "We shall shortly begin our move."

"May I suggest offering them the opportunity to surrender?" Beaumont advised.

"I think it would be of no use and only serve to warn them," Lestrade said.

"But it could work and thus save Ainsworth's life."

"I too would vote for the warning," Joanna said. "For if the battle goes against them and they are down to the last man, he will surely kill Ainsworth."

Lestrade contemplated the matter at length before reaching for a megaphone.

"*Achtung! Achtung!*" he bellowed out in German, which was certain to arouse the agents' attention and further unnerve them in the process. "You are surrounded on all sides by Scotland Yard, with no hope of escape. You must surrender immediately or you will be taken by force. We will allow you one minute to reach a decision."

I concentrated my attention on the windows of the Germans' house, watching for any movement behind them. But I could see none, for their drapes were tightly closed. The roof appeared to be gently sloped, with scattered brick chimneys, but there was no motion there either. Joanna's eyes were on the back garden where there were tall willow trees and flowering bushes.

"What in the garden so grabs your attention?" I asked quietly.

"The most likely escape route," Joanna replied.

"I doubt the Germans would be so bold."

"They may have no choice."

"You have thirty seconds remaining!" Lestrade called out.

To my right I saw a group of sergeants carefully checking the rounds in their service revolvers. Behind them was a smaller group of police constables, holding on to a long, thick spar that was unadorned and resembled a utility pole. There was no nervousness about them, only the steely resolve of brave men about to do their duty.

Lestrade signaled over to the group. In quick order the armed sergeants formed a phalanx around the men now holding the sturdy beam in a horizontal position. The last seconds dragged by in a silence so eerie that even the birds above stopped chirping.

"The Germans will open fire from the second floor," Joanna said in a whisper.

"Why so?" I asked.

"It is the point of greatest advantage."

"But certainly our side will return fire, will they not?"

"It is a well-known fact that it is easier and more accurate to shoot down rather than up," Joanna said.

"Which I can attest to," my father agreed. "For it is so cited in the *Military Manual of Arms*. I can also vouch for this fact from personal experience."

Joanna beckoned over to Lestrade. "Inspector, it might be wise to have your men focus their attention on the windows of the second floor."

"I see no activity there," Lestrade said, after taking a studied look.

"You will once the attack begins," Joanna said. "Have your men train their weapons on the glass panes themselves and be prepared to open fire immediately. Shattering glass, you see, will throw off the aim of even the best of marksmen."

Lestrade quickly passed on the instructions, then brought his arm up and abruptly dropped it as he called out, "Now!"

The constables manning the battering ram charged forward, with a phalanx of sergeants rushing alongside them, weapons drawn. A volley of shots rang out from the second-floor windows of the surrounded house. Two of the advancing sergeants fell, one clutching a bleeding shoulder, the other shouting in pain from a leg wound. Those left standing returned fire with round after round, many of which found their mark. Windowpanes were blasted apart, sending down a shower of shattered glass. For a brief moment there was a halt to the German fire, which gave the men with the battering ram an opportunity to charge once again. On the second try the fortified door crashed with a loud bang. The constables hurriedly stepped aside as a barrage of shots came from within the house. The sergeants, now in shooting positions, gave as good as they got and then some, firing round after round and reloading to fire even more. Suddenly all went quiet. Ever so cautiously the Scotland Yard operatives advanced, with their weapons cocked and at the ready. The sergeants closest to us kept their service revolvers aimed on the blasted-out second-story windows. Those too were now quiet.

Our attention was abruptly drawn to the rear of the house from where we heard a window being smashed apart. A heavyset man, clothed only in underwear, rolled out onto the grass and crawled on his hands and knees to the nearby shrubbery. The sergeants rapidly trained their weapons on the partially clothed man.

"Hold your fire!" Beaumont shouted loudly. "It is Ainsworth!"

Sergeants and constables from all sides converged on the Germans' house, all crouched low and expecting a fight-to-the-death struggle. But it did not occur, for there was neither a shot nor sound coming from within.

It required a full ten minutes for the house to be searched and deemed safe for us to enter. In the foyer, where they decided to make their last stand, lay three German agents. Two were dead with head wounds, the third was gasping and exhaling a bloody froth. As my father examined him to determine if any treatment could be applied, the German agent, with the broad shoulders and facial tic, breathed his last.

"All clear of Germans," a sergeant reported to Lestrade.

"What of Dunn?" Lestrade asked at once.

"Not to be found, sir."

"I want every square inch of this house gone over, cellar to attic," Lestrade ordered, and watched as the officer raced away.

"How could he have possibly escaped?" I wondered.

"The cleverest always have a way out," Joanna said.

"But the house was being watched from all sides at every moment," I argued. "How could he have executed such an escape?"

"There are two possibilities, and I suspect Mr. Alistair Ainsworth will tell us which one is true."

"I will indeed, madam," Ainsworth said, strolling up to us. He was now covered with a blanket and bleeding from dozens of small cuts on his face and arms. "Although I perceive from your tone of voice that you already know the answer."

Joanna gave him a humorless smile. "Dunn presented you with the opportunity to escape."

"Oh, he did much more than that," Ainsworth said. "The German agents had tied me to a chair when they became aware of your presence. They wanted to be certain I could not bolt and make a run for it. When the firing started and the others were preoccupied, Dunn untied me and pointed to the rear window, which was obviously my only avenue of departure. At first, I thought he'd had a change of heart."

Joanna shook her head. "Evil men do not change their hearts; they adapt."

"So I was to learn."

"Were you able to discern the direction Dunn took after freeing you?" Joanna asked.

"He dashed for the stairs while the Germans provided covering fire."

"Did you in fact see him go up?"

"I did not, but I heard him call out to the German agents that he was going upstairs where he could keep Scotland Yard at bay."

"He escaped through the attic," Joanna said, and led the way up to the top of the stairs where a group of sergeants stood. "Where is the opening to the attic?"

"At the end of the corridor, ma'am," the lead sergeant replied. "You will find the opening there, with its ladder down. But the attic is clear, ma'am."

"It is not the attic you should be concerned with, but the roof."

Joanna hurried over to the hinged ladder and ascended it, with Lestrade, my father, Beaumont, and I only steps behind. The attic was dark and cluttered, and had the stale odor that was characteristic of an enclosed space with poor ventilation. Two sergeants followed us in and lighted the attic with powerful torches. Most of the articles were stored in boxes and bins, whilst used pieces of dust-covered furniture were heaped up one upon another in tall columns.

"There!" Joanna pointed to a large couch upon which rested a desk and atop the desk was a wooden stool. She waited for the sergeants to shine the light of their torches to the column of stacked furniture. Behind it was a stepladder of considerable length that went up to a closed trapdoor. Narrow streaks of sunlight clearly illustrated its outline.

"Do you believe the scoundrel is up there, having found a hiding place?" Lestrade asked.

"That is unlikely, for the longer he remains on the roof, the greater the chance he will be discovered," Joanna replied. "The smart move is to keep moving."

"But to where?"

"That is to be determined."

"Let us be certain," Lestrade said, and gestured to the two armed sergeants. "Inspect the roof with the greatest of care. If Dunn is found and resists, do not hesitate to shoot."

As he watched the sergeants scale the ladder, Beaumont suggested, "Perhaps Dunn is attempting to throw us off the track."

"That being the case, he would not have gone to the trouble of hiding it so well," Joanna countered, and began to search the area surrounding the stepladder. Finding nothing of interest, she went to a large wooden crate that was nearby and had its top incompletely closed. She opened it and extracted an officer's coat of the Royal Navy, with its lieutenant insignia clearly visible. "And there is your proof. Of course he would change into civilian attire, for his naval officer's uniform would surely attract attention."

"He was a most careful planner indeed," Beaumont said.

"The best of them always are." Joanna dug deeper into the

crate and found an oversized hammer, with a large, squared head. The metal section of the hammer was coated with white dust. "What do we have here?"

"An old hammer that has been sitting there for quite some time," Lestrade answered, moving in for a closer look.

"Why do you believe it has been in this position for such a long while?" Joanna asked.

"Because it is covered with dust," Lestrade replied.

"The head is, but the handle is not," Joanna observed. "The wooden handle is clean and spotless, which indicates it was used recently."

"But how do you explain the dust?" Lestrade argued.

Joanna reached for her magnifying glass and studied the head of the hammer. "It is not dust, but a powdery substance filled with small particles. Thus, it would seem this hammer was used to strike stone or plaster."

"To what end?"

"I believe the answer to that question lies on the roof."

"All clear!" a sergeant shouted down from the open trapdoor.

We followed Joanna up the stepladder and onto a broad slate roof that was bordered by a stone parapet approximately three feet in height. The roof itself was somewhat sloped, with a multitude of brick chimneys, so we walked with care.

The two sergeants rushed over to us, with their weapons holstered. "Nothing," one of them reported. "There is no place to hide nor any stairs or steps leading to the ground."

"I would not have expected to find those, for he would have been visible to the constables while climbing down," Joanna said.

"But during his stay on the roof, he had to conceal himself from the lookouts," Lestrade opined.

Joanna studied the slate roof at length before turning to me. "John, please be so good as to stroll over to the eastern-most edge of the roof that overlooks the adjacent house and tell me what you see."

I walked over to the eastern parapet and gazed out at the nearby house and the activities in its front courtyard. "There is nothing remarkable about the house itself, but in the court-yard I can see the wounded sergeants being attended to."

"Excellent!" Joanna cried out. "Now wait a moment, then turn around and describe my whereabouts."

I did as instructed and saw the entire group of men— Lestrade, his two sergeants, the admiral, and my father—but Joanna had disappeared. "Has she gone back downstairs?"

"No, I have not," Joanna answered, and stepped out from a pair of brick chimneys. "I simply slouched low where Dunn must have, and was thus hidden from the view of Lestrade's lookouts."

"But where did he go from this point?" Lestrade asked. "He was trapped unless you believe he was capable of flying away."

"That is a talent he does not possess," Joanna said, and once again studied the entire roof until her eyes came to a halt on a large willow tree whose slender limbs were touching the rear section of the parapet. She hurried over and stopped abruptly in front of a leaf-covered limb. "Here!" she called to us and gestured downward.

We dashed over to the area of the parapet that acted as a barrier to the smoke discharged from the close-by chimney. The slate roof adjacent to the parapet was covered with a thick layer of soot and ashes, in which resided two handprints and two round smudges made by Dunn's knees.

"He crouched down on his hands and knees at this posi-tion, and waited for his chance," Joanna said. "As soon as

Alistair Ainsworth crashed through the window, all of our eyes went to him, and that was the moment Dunn escaped."

"But this is a willow tree and its fragile branches could not begin to support a man of Dunn's weight," Lestrade contended. "And its trunk is well away from the roof and would require an exceptional jump to be reached."

Joanna inspected the tree and its nearby limbs at length, then moved in closer to the parapet and examined its inner surface and top. Finding nothing of consequence, she leaned over the stone parapet to view its outer face. "Hello!"

"What do you see?" Lestrade asked at once.

"The answer," Joanna said, and stepped back to give us a clearer view. Driven into the top, outer surface of the parapet was a thick metal spike, from which extended a long rope that reached down to the garden.

"Which explains the powdery grit on the head of the hammer," I thought aloud.

"Precisely, John," Joanna agreed. "The metal spike was driven in with the hammer and a sturdy rope tied around it, which gave Dunn his escape route. The heavily leafed willow tree camouflaged his descent into the garden. This lieutenant of ours is very clever indeed, for he had earlier planned this last route of escape, in case others were not available."

Lestrade turned quickly to a sergeant. "We had an officer stationed in the rear garden, did we not?"

"Yes, sir," the sergeant said. "I called down to him from the roof and he had seen nothing unusual. All was quiet after Mr. Ainsworth crashed through the window, except for a dog nearby that was barking at the disturbance."

"I suspect the dog was not barking at the disturbance, but at a disturber," Joanna discerned. "When you examine the area around the base of the willow tree, you will in all likelihood find broken plants and shrubbery that Dunn stepped on while running for his life."

"And so he is gone," Lestrade said sourly.

"I am afraid he has given us the slip," Joanna concurred.

"I shall order an all-points warning immediately," Lestrade asserted.

"A good idea, Inspector, but one unlikely to bear fruit," Joanna said. "A clever planner such as Dunn will disappear into thin air."

We returned to the foyer where Ainsworth, still wrapped in a blanket, was now seated and shivering against the late morning chill. The scrapes and cuts on his face and arms, which had stopped bleeding, would yet require medical attention.

"No luck, eh?" Ainsworth asked.

"None," Joanna replied.

"As I expected," Ainsworth said, and asked around for a cigarette, which a sergeant provided, along with a light. Inhaling the smoke deeply, Ainsworth continued on, "You see, Dunn only partially untied the ropes binding me, and for obvious reasons. He wanted to delay my escape until he was prepared to take his. So I was the distraction, was I not?"

"So it would seem," Joanna said.

"But at least it kept me alive, although I am sure that was not Dunn's intended consequence," Ainsworth said. "That was no doubt the critical event in saving my life, along with someone decoding the messages I sent. Who was responsible? Marlowe?"

"No," Beaumont answered.

"Mary?"

"She neither."

"Then it must have been good old Montclair."

"You are half correct," Beaumont told him. "Montclair

was about to decipher the message that pointed to the traitor, but Dunn learned of it and murdered him."

"Bloody bastard!" Ainsworth cursed aloud.

"Of the worst order," Beaumont said. "But he too left behind a message and it was decoded by the lady who is with us and happens to be the daughter of Sherlock Holmes."

"I have read of you and your talents," Ainsworth praised. "It was you who untangled the most difficult code of the slanted lines, was it not?"

"It was."

"With of course Dr. Watson's help," Ainsworth added.

"I would be lost without my Watson," Joanna exaggerated, yet it still made my father smile. "But I should mention that I could not have deciphered your Exodus message without the assistance of Mary Ellington."

"That does not lessen my debt of gratitude," Ainsworth went on. "To you I owe my life and I would very much like to reward you and the Watsons in some small way by inviting you to join me at Simpson's-in-the-Strand for dinner, which of course will have to await my recovery."

"With pleasure," Joanna accepted. "Will your daughter be accompanying you?"

"She will indeed," Ainsworth said. "But may I inquire how you know of my daughter?"

"The maître d' at François informed us of your frequent visits," Joanna replied. "He also mentioned that she for the most part was schooled on the Continent."

"She was until her mother passed away five years ago," said Ainsworth. "I was of course delighted to arrange for her admission to the University of Manchester, from which she graduated with honors. She now attends University College London where she is pursuing a doctorate in archaeology."

"Like her father."

"Very much so, with a decided passion for Egyptian hi-eroglyphics."

I feigned an interest in their talk of hieroglyphics, all the while wondering how Joanna had discovered that Ainsworth had a daughter. But then I thought back to our visit to the French restaurant, and all the clues behind her line of reasoning came to mind. They seemed so obvious now. Ainsworth's companion at François was twenty or so years his junior, which would be the correct time frame for his daughter being conceived while he was a student studying at the University of Heidelberg. Moreover, their display of affection at the restaurant could well have been that exhibited by a loving father to his daughter, rather than one of romance. And in all likelihood the daughter was born out of wedlock, which accounted for Ainsworth keeping her existence a secret from his family. Upon the mother's death, however, Ainsworth felt an obligation to look after the girl, as any decent father would. Of course Roger Marlowe knew of the daughter and lied about dinner with Ainsworth to cover for his dear friend.

"Well then, I suspect our dinner together will be a most interesting one," Joanna was saying, "but before you leave I have a last question that I hope you will be permitted to answer."

"Let us hear it."

"You are a chess master and, from what I have read, there is a stratagem called the combination, in which one sacrifices something seemingly small in order to gain something great. It is a form of distraction. Did you employ this maneuver while being held by the Germans?"

"I did indeed," Ainsworth said, with a mischievous grin before turning to Beaumont. "With your permission, Admiral."

"Is it an event done and finished with?" Beaumont asked.

"It is."

"With no consequence were it now revealed?"

"It might well embarrass the Germans."

"Then, by all means, proceed."

"As you well know, Admiral, the British and German fleets were believed to be evenly matched, with the Royal Navy having only a slight advantage. Furthermore, several of our ships were known to be in port undergoing repairs, while others were busy protecting cargo ships coming and leaving British ports. Thus, if ever the Germans were to attack our navy and gain control of the North Sea, this would be the opportune moment. I thought I took care of this danger rather well. The message I saw stated the Germans had eighteen battleships while we had twenty. So I simply changed the number and told the Germans we had twenty-five battleships; that of course caused them to reconsider any attack plan they may have been considering."

"Good show," Beaumont said.

Joanna asked, "But what was the distraction?"

"The sacrifice of merchant ships."

"Not one of ours?" Beaumont asked anxiously.

Ainsworth shook his head. "A convoy had been spotted off the coast of Portugal who we know will shortly side with Germany in this war. I invented the story that these merchant ships were carrying raw materials and headed for England. I had hoped the Germans would dispatch a group of warships to intercept these merchant vessels, and thus diminish the size of their fleet in the North Sea. They did, but by then the convoy had mysteriously disappeared. They still may be searching for these ships."

"Well done," Beaumont lauded.

"I considered it one of my better moves," said Ainsworth, then unsteadily arose from his chair. "And now I must take my leave and go home, for my dear sister is no doubt terribly worried about me."

"Might I impose on you for one final question to satisfy my curiosity?" Joanna asked.

"Of course."

"How did you learn that Dunn was the traitor? Did you overhear the Germans speaking of him?"

"In a way I did, but they never mentioned him by name. During their conversation they boasted that Germany had knowledge of the Exodus plan prior to the outbreak of war. At that moment in history, the Admiralty Club had not yet been founded and none of the members had worked in Naval Intelligence. Thus the traitor could not be Roger, Mary, or Geoffrey, and that left Dunn, who was aware of the plan before the war and one of the few who knew it was the Admiralty Club who gave the plan the name Exodus. This of course was by no means conclusive evidence, but all this changed when I overheard the Germans debating how accurate my deciphering truly was. They decided to check my reliability by having me decode a message that they had already decoded. They chose the Exodus plan, but were uncertain which of the messages should be used. It was agreed the selection would best be made by the man who carried the communiqués back and forth to the Admiralty Club."

"Which could be none other than Lieutenant Dunn."

"Checkmate," Ainsworth said with a pleased smile.

Joanna watched Ainsworth walk away, now aided by two powerfully built sergeants. "And we are done here."

"It has been my honor to work with you," Beaumont said sincerely.

"And mine as well," Lestrade said, doffing his derby.

As Joanna strolled away, arm in arm with my father and me, she had a second thought and turned back to the admiral and inspector. "Gentlemen, there is an important lesson we should all learn from this case."

"Which is?" Lestrade asked.

"Do not attempt to match wits with a chess master," Joanna instructed. "For if you do, you will surely lose."

"But as I recall, you are not a chess master, yet it was you who deciphered Ainsworth's code and thus clearly matched his wits."

"That is because I had a chess master to guide me."

"Who, may I ask?"

"Geoffrey Montclair, who used his own blood to not only decipher the message, but lead us to the biblical tale of Passover."

"Absolutely mind-bending," Beaumont said, and shook his head in wonderment. "He performed magic by using his own blood."

"Quite."

"Clever beyond clever."

"And he was yet more ingenious, for in his very last breath Montclair employed a combination stratagem to defeat his opponent."

"How so?"

A Mona Lisa smile came to Joanna's face as we stepped toward bright sunlight. "On his return to supposedly discover the body, Dunn must have seen the bloodstained message in the typewriter. He beyond a doubt paid attention to it, but its relevance escaped him. This then was the move that distracted Dunn, so that he could be conquered by the next."

Beaumont called after us, "But the blood on the message was both distracting and the conquering move."

"And that, my dear Admiral, is the pure genius of a chess master."

Closure

Some ten months later Admiral Beaumont visited us at 221b Baker Street unannounced, bringing with him the fate of Lieutenant Richard Dunn. He accepted a glass of Madeira as we gathered around the fireplace and waited for the thunder and lightning outside to abate.

"First, we were correct in believing the German actress played an important role in turning Dunn," Beaumont began. "Our best intelligence has confirmed he married her secretly during his stay as a naval attaché at our embassy in Berlin. His wife and young son have a home in Bremerhaven that he had managed to visit on his diplomatic trips to France, presumably traveling through neutral The Netherlands. But there was a second key factor in Dunn's becoming a turncoat. He had always desired to have command of a warship and his dossier is filled with requests that he be allowed to do so. However, we did not feel he possessed the seamanship qualities necessary for such a promotion, and thus his requests were denied. He must have become quite embittered and disappointed by this decision, and eagerly leaped at the opportunity to eventually command a German warship. We believe this offer was made in nineteen fourteen, just before the war started. That was when Dunn turned and became a highly valued German agent. His position within the Admiralty Club was an absolute godsend to the enemy, which continued until the day he was uncovered. After Dunn escaped and fled to Germany, he was no doubt greeted with open arms."

"Was he, being a foreigner, actually given such an important station?" Joanna asked.

"He was," Beaumont replied. "He was promoted to lieutenant commander and assigned to a destroyer that had several decisive victories, for which he would shortly be elevated to the rank of captain. However, on his last voyage he had the misfortune to encounter one of the Royal Navy's most powerful warships. A fierce battle ensued and Dunn's ship was sunk, with all hands lost."

"Good riddance," I murmured under my breath.

"So Dunn and his traitorous acts now sit at the bottom of the sea," my father concluded. "Which unfortunately spares him from a well-deserved hanging."

"Quite true," Beaumont said. "But I think you would find it most fitting to learn more about the British warship that sent Dunn to his watery grave. It is His Majesty's newest and most powerful battleship, and carries the proud name *Revenge*."

Poetic justice, everyone sitting in the room thought at once. Poetic justice indeed!

Acknowledgments

Special thanks to Peter Wolverton and Jennifer Donovan, splendid editors, who make my novels ever so much better.